George Bruce Malleson

Loudon

A sketch of the military life of Gideon Ernest, Freiherr von Loudon, sometime

generalissimo of the Austrian forces

George Bruce Malleson

Loudon
A sketch of the military life of Gideon Ernest, Freiherr von Loudon, sometime generalissimo of the Austrian forces

ISBN/EAN: 9783337394561

Printed in Europe, USA, Canada, Australia, Japan

Cover: Foto ©Raphael Reischuk / pixelio.de

More available books at **www.hansebooks.com**

LOUDON:

A SKETCH OF THE MILITARY LIFE OF

GIDEON ERNEST, FREIHERR VON LOUDON,

SOMETIME GENERALISSIMO OF THE
AUSTRIAN FORCES.

BY

COLONEL G. B. MALLESON, C.S.I.,

AUTHOR OF "THE DECISIVE BATTLES OF INDIA," ETC.

LONDON: CHAPMAN AND HALL,

(LIMITED.)

1884.

CONTENTS.

vi   *CONTENTS.*

CHAPTER VII.

CHAPTER VIII.

CHAPTER IX.

CHAPTER X.

CHAPTER XI.

CHAPTER XII.

CHAPTER XIII.

MAPS.

ERRATA.

Page 58, line 19, *for* "confident to" *read* "confident in.'
Page 122, line 32, *for* "Pischwitz" *read* "Pischkowitz."
Page 149, line 14, *for* "15,000" *read* "50,000."
Page 174, line 7, *for* "a counterwork" *read* "a counterguard."
Page 176, line 8, *for* "Kaldwell" *read* "Caldwell."
Page 181, line 19, *for* "85" *read* "83."
Page 206, line 30, *for* "having" *read* "leaving."
Page 206, last line, *for* "those" *read* "his."
Page 212, line 31, *for* "selected" *read* "selecting."
Page 236, line 4, *for* "than" *read* "when."

LOUDON.

CHAPTER I.

INTRODUCTORY.

CHARLES VI., Emperor of Germany, died on the 20th October, 1740, leaving no male heir, and before he had taken the precaution to have the husband of his daughter, Francis of Lorraine, Grand Duke of Tuscany, crowned King of the Romans. To secure his vast dominions to that daughter, Charles had obtained from every state of importance in Europe a guarantee of the Pragmatic Sanction, an instrument which broke the entail established by his elder brother Joseph, and settled the right of succession, in default of male issue, first on his own daughters in the order of their birth, then on the daughters of Joseph, and, after them, on the Queen of Portugal and the other daughters of his father, the Emperor Leopold. On his death, then, his eldest daughter, Maria Theresa, succeeded, under the title of Queen of Hungary and Bohemia, to all the dominions of the house of Habsburg, and she entertained the hope that the Electoral College

B

would shortly confer the dignity of emperor upon her husband, Francis of Lorraine.

But events were very soon to prove the wisdom of the counsel addressed by Prince Eugene to Charles VI., when, noticing the ardour with which the emperor pursued the idea of obtaining from Europe guarantees for the due execution of the Pragmatic Sanction, he told him that the only guarantee worth having was an army of 200,000 men and a full treasury. Charles VI., obstinate and self-willed, was not the man to listen to advice, even when that advice came from Prince Eugene. Throughout his life he neglected the substance and pursued the shadow. Maria Theresa, far from finding, on her accession, an army of 200,000 men and a full treasury to support her title, realised to her dismay that the army, exclusive of the troops in Italy and the Low Countries, did not amount to 36,000 men; that the treasury contained only 100,000 florins, and that even these were claimed by the Empress Dowager as her personal property!

The majority of the guarantors of the Pragmatic Sanction very soon convinced the Queen of Hungary how lightly they regarded the engagements wrung from them by her father, how fully they appreciated the helplessness of her position. Charles Albert, Elector of Bavaria, at once asserted his claims to the kingdom of Bohemia and the Grand Duchy of Austria, on the ground that the will of Ferdinand I. had devised those territories to his daughters and their descendants on the failure of the male line, and that he was the lineal descendant from Anne, eldest daughter of that prince. Philip II., King of Spain and the Indies, as pretended representative of the extinct Spanish line of the Habsburgs, from which he was descended on the mother's side, demanded the cession of the Spanish-Austrian hereditary lands in Italy as well as Milan, Mantua, Parma, and Piacenza. Emanuel III., King of Sardinia, and Augustus III., Elector of Saxony and King of Poland, who had married daughters of the Emperor Joseph, put forth less extravagant demands. But the most formidable claimant was Frederic II., King of Prussia. This prince had succeeded his father but five months previously, to find ready to his hand the army and the treasury which were wanting to Maria Theresa. Seeing in the actual state of affairs a great opportunity, such as might never occur again, Frederic revived a claim once preferred by his ancestors, but expressly renounced by them in 1688, and again in 1694, to the Silesian duchies of Liegnitz, Glogau, Brieg, and Jägerndorf.

Nor was the action of the two great western powers at this crisis calculated to reassure Maria Theresa. France, guided by Cardinal Fleury, vouchsafed no public answer to the notification of the queen's accession. The tone of the private communications from her foreign office, coldly polite, signified an intention to hold aloof until the claims of the Elector of Bavaria should have been disposed of, and, in the meanwhile, to use her influence to oppose the election of the Duke of Lorraine to the imperial dignity. England, whilst acknowledging the queen, had accompanied the recognition by an exhortation to distrust the designs of France, and by a proposal that Austria should join her in an alliance against the House of Bourbon. The relations of Maria Theresa with the other powers of Germany were too uncertain to allow her to think of a war of aggression. But still hopeful with respect to France she received with coldness the proposals of the only guarantor of the Pragmatic Sanction who sincerely desired to uphold the conditions of that settlement.

The feeling of suspense and uncertainty which the conduct of the several powers of Europe had aroused at the Court of Vienna was not of long duration. Frederic II. of Prussia was the first to prove the worthlessness of treaties which cannot be maintained by force of arms. Amusing the Court of Vienna for a few weeks with protestations of his readiness to serve the House of Austria, he assembled a considerable body of troops in the vicinity of Berlin ; then, throwing off the mask, he despatched Count Gotter to Vienna to formulate his proposals. Gotter was instructed to place the services of Frederic and his army at the disposal of the queen, to defend her against all her enemies, on condition that she would cede to him the two Silesias, Lower Silesia because Frederic claimed it as a right, Upper Silesia as a compensation for the costs of the war. The Court of Vienna having been informed that Frederic, not waiting for a reply to his demands, had actually entered Silesia, refused to negotiate until his troops should be withdrawn from that province. Gotter was, in consequence, dismissed, and war ensued.

Frederic had indeed entered Silesia (16th December, 1740). His progress through that province, unopposed by an Austrian army, was a series of triumphs. On the 3rd January, Breslau opened her gates to him. The strong fortresses of Glogau, Neisse, and Brieg held out, however, and the Court of Vienna hoped that they would continue their resistance until it should be able to despatch an army against the invader. But Glogau was stormed early in the spring, and Frederic was about to undertake the siege of Neisse, when he was surprised by the march of an Austrian army on his line of communications with Brandenburg. He had nothing for it then but to fight.

The battle which followed (10th April, 1741) called from

the village near to which it was fought, the battle of Moll-witz, was decisive of the fate of Silesia. After a contest which lasted five hours, and of which all the earlier phases were in favour of the Austrians, the steadiness and superior armament of the Prussian infantry gained the day.

But Mollwitz did more than gain Silesia for Prussia. It served as the signal to rouse continental Europe against the daughter of Charles VI. Had Frederic been beaten on the 10th April, it is more than probable that the provisions of the Pragmatic Sanction would have been carried out without dispute. It was his victory which decided the course of events, which gave courage to Charles Albert of Bavaria, and which put an end to the hesitations of the Court of Versailles. When Louis XV. had been informed that Frederic of Prussia had invaded Silesia he exclaimed, "The man is mad." Five weeks after the battle of Mollwitz, May 18th, 1741, France and Spain signed a treaty with Bavaria for the dismemberment of the Austrian dominions. To this treaty the Elector Palatine, the Electors of Cologne and of Saxony, and the Kings of Prussia, of Sicily and of Sardinia adhered.

The operations of the allies were rapid. Charles Albert, supported by a French army, emerged from Bavaria by way of Passau, and following the course of the Danube, took Linz, 14th August, and pressing on to St. Polten, summoned Vienna to surrender.

Under these difficult circumstances, Maria Theresa, threatened by continental Europe, and whose only ally, England, contented herself with sending her fitful supplies of money and an unlimited quantity of advice, appealed to her Hungarian people. The noble and generous reply, and the spirit evoked by that pathetic appeal, gave to the lion-hearted queen the moral support necessary to her.

Two other circumstances tended about the same time to strengthen her cause. The Franco-Bavarian army, renouncing its design upon Vienna, turned off to Bohemia, whilst, under her instructions, one of her generals, Count Neipperg, concluded (October 1742) a secret convention with Frederic, whereby in consideration of the permanent cession of Lower Silesia with Glatz and Neisse before the end of the year, the latter, who had obtained all he wanted, and who had no desire to see a prince of the Bavarian house occupy a strong position in Southern Germany supported by a French army, agreed to remain inactive.

Maria Theresa made excellent use of the respite thus obtained. Withdrawing her Silesian army into Moravia, she joined it to another army in that province under the command of her brother-in-law, Charles of Lorraine, and despatched both into Bohemia to resist the Franco-Bavarian invasion. The Austrians were too late indeed to save Prague, but they were able to shut up their enemies in that city. Meanwhile a third Austrian army, led by Count Khevenhüller, and preceded by a crowd of Pandours, had re-taken Linz, Scharding, and Passau, and, penetrating into Bavaria, had occupied Munich on the very day, 12th February, on which Charles Albert of Bavaria, chosen by the Electoral College Emperor of Germany a month previously, was crowned by the name and title of Charles VII.

In his despair the new emperor appealed to Frederic, and Frederic, breaking the convention of the previous October, renewed hostilities, took Glatz, and after a visit to Dresden to rouse into action the Elector of Saxony, and another to Prague to concert measures with the French commander, Marshal de Broglie, advanced into Bohemia.

Here, however, his difficulties commenced. His allies

could render him no help, and whilst one Austrian army
threatened his communications, another, under Prince
Charles of Lorraine, advanced from Moravia to meet him.
It had been in the power of a really capable commander
to crush at once and for ever at this conjuncture the
pretensions of Frederic. He himself felt all the dangers
of his position, and it was an intense relief to him when,
on the morning of the 17th May, the army of Prince
Charles attacked him as he lay encamped on the plain
between the villages of Cäslar and Chotusice (Chotusitz).

The battle which followed, well contested, especially by
the infantry on both sides, resulted in leaving Frederic
master of the field. But his losses had been very severe,
his cavalry had been almost destroyed, and although he
had gained all the honours of the day, had taken 1,200
prisoners, and captured eighteen guns, the retreating
Austrians had done almost as much ; for they too, retiring
in good order, had carried off with them a thousand
prisoners, fourteen standards, and two pairs of colours.

The battle of Chotusitz, whilst it convinced Frederic
that his interests would best be served by making such a
treaty with the Queen of Hungary as would secure the
two Silesias, satisfied the Court of Vienna that to concentrate all the forces of the monarchy against the
Franco-Bavarians it was necessary to come to some
understanding with its most persistent enemy. With
a heavy heart, then, Maria Theresa, agreed (28th July,
1742) to cede to Frederic Upper and Lower Silesia and the
County of Glatz—with the exception of the principalities,
Teschen, Troppau, and Jägerndorf. Very soon afterwards
(11th September) she concluded peace, and, the year
following, a treaty of offensive and defensive alliance, with
Saxony. About the same time she gained Sardinia by the

cession to her of a few unimportant districts in the Milanese; and she concluded an alliance likewise with England and Holland.

Relieved from the presence of the King of Prussia, the Austrian armies, led by Prince Charles of Lorraine and Prince Lobkovic, marched against the French, defeated Marshal de Broglie at Frauenberg, drove him from Braunau, and compelled him to take refuge behind the walls of Prague. That city had become the last refuge of the Franco-Bavarian invaders.

It did not protect them long. Provisions within the city began to fail. The commander-in-chief of the French army, Marshal Bellisle, feeling that the toils were closing around him, offered to evacuate Prague and to quit the dominions of the Queen of Hungary, on the condition of retaining his arms, artillery, and baggage. The Court of Versailles made at the same time the most urgent overtures for peace. But the pride of Maria Theresa had been wounded. She believed her enemy to be in her power. Provisions were failing him, the winter was one of the severest ever known; an attempt made by a relieving army led by Marshal de Maillebois to force the passes had failed, and Prague was blockaded by an army of 18,000 men. Escape seemed impossible. Yet the French general, forming his army of 11,000 foot and 3,000 horse into a single column, providing it with twelve days' provisions, and taking with him thirty pieces of cannon, sallied out on the night of the 16th December, and succeeded in making one of the most daring retreats on record. He gained Eger without leaving the smallest trophy to the enemy, and was joined there a few days later by the six thousand men he had left in the city, and who, after his departure, had been allowed to march out with all the honours of war!

The practical result was not the less favourable to the Austrian arms. Maria Theresa was crowned Queen of Bohemia at Prague, and received the oath of allegiance at Munich. A few weeks later, 27th June, 1743, George II. of England defeated the French army at Dettingen.

These successes greatly augmented her pretensions. She concluded in September of the same year an alliance with England and Sardinia, and, still embittered against France and the Emperor, announced her intention of recovering Alsace and Lorraine, and of annulling the election of Charles VII. with the view of replacing him by her husband.

These successes roused Frederic of Prussia once again to action. Under the veil of hostility against France and the emperor, he detected the fixed purpose of Maria Theresa to recover Silesia. The only means he had of saving his conquest was a prompt alliance with the threatened powers. The announced intentions of Maria Theresa with respect to the Emperor Charles VII. furnished him with an excuse for intervention to protect the rights of the emperor. To resist then the pretensions of the Queen of Hungary he summoned the German princes to a meeting at Frankfort. The Elector Palatine and the Elector of Hesse Cassel alone responded to his call. With these, and with Sweden, he made then a treaty of alliance, called the Union of Frankfort, the object of which was to resist the Austrian pretensions by force of arms.

Frederic then turned to France. With her he was more successful. He concluded an alliance based upon a combined plan of operations which should at the same time relieve France from the threatened invasion and turn the blow meditated by Austria against herself. It was agreed that before the Austrian armies could overrun Alsace Frederic should invade Bohemia. This invasion would necessitate the prompt recall of the Austrians from the upper Rhine. The French undertook to follow the recalled army so vigorously that it would have no leisure to interfere with Frederic, who, but slightly opposed, would thus have Austria at his mercy.

The treaty with France was dated the 5th of June 1744. Little more than two months later (9th of August) Frederic published a manifesto in which he declared he had taken up arms solely to restore to the German empire its liberty, to the Emperor his dignity, and to Europe its repose. Immediately afterwards he entered Bohemia at the head of his army.

In the war which followed, known as the second Silesian war, there appeared for the first time serving in the Austrian ranks a Livonian gentleman of Scottish origin, who subsequently became the most formidable antagonist of the invader. As his name will occur more than once in the history of the campaign, it is fit that before entering upon its record I should make the reader acquainted with the early antecedents of Gideon Loudon.

CHAPTER II.

THE ancestors of Gideon Loudon, belonging to a branch of the noble house of Loudoun, had quitted Ayrshire in the fourteenth century, and, emigrating to Livonia, had become the possessors of two considerable landed properties in that province. One of these was registered under the family name, spelt variously as Laudon, Laudohn, and Loudon; the other under the name it had previously borne, of Tootzen. To these properties were subsequently added others which became in later years the portion of the younger branch of the family. Time did not deal very favourably with the elder branch. The policy of Charles XI. of Sweden and the wars of Charles XII. made great havoc with their resources, and when Gideon Loudon was born Tootzen was the only estate remaining to his branch of the family.

At that place Gideon was born in the year 1716. His father, Gerhard (Gerard) Otto, a lieutenant colonel in the Swedish army, had married a daughter of the noble family of the Bornemund, and of this marriage Gideon Loudon was the first child. As such he was naturally intended to be a soldier, and to fit him for that career his father instructed

him at an early age in drawing, in mathematics, and in
geography. He did not then become proficient in any of
these studies but he learned sufficient to make him wish to
acquire more, and we shall see how in his maturer years
he applied himself to that purpose.

The province of which he was a native had been ceded
to Russia in 1721. When therefore Loudon arrived at an
age to enter upon his career he took service in the Russian
army as a cadet. He was then (1731) in his sixteenth
year. Like other noblemen of the time he began at the
lowest grade. The year after his entrance into the army
an opportunity of being under fire presented itself. The
election for the succession to the Crown of Poland had
resulted in the double choice of Frederic Augustus of
Saxony and Stanislaus Leczinski. The Russians, who took
the side of the former, sent an army into the country to
uphold his claims.

Stanislaus, upon this, fled to Dantzig. The Russians pursued him and laid siege to that city. Loudon's regiment
formed part of their army, and it is recorded that during
the siege that followed, and especially during the storming
of the Stolzenberg, which cost the lives of many officers, he
gave marked proofs of courage and conduct. His health,
delicate in his youth, suffered much from fatigue and
exposure, and he was laid up for some time after the conquest
of the place with an illness of a dangerous character. The
year following, Russian troops set foot for the first time on
German soil. They came not, indeed, as enemies, but as
allies of the German empire against the French. They did
nothing more, however, than march from the Volga to the
Rhine, for on their arrival at the latter river preliminaries
of peace between the contending powers had been agreed
upon. The Empress Anna was the less unwilling to recall

them, because the check given by the Ottoman Porte to her designs regarding the Crimea had caused her to declare war against the Turks. The Russian troops then marched from the Rhine to the seat of war with all haste. On arriving there the Turks and Tartars retreated before them, forcing them to traverse, in their pursuit, steppes still burning and to suffer from a want of water almost unbearable. Loudon, who served with the army in its march from the Volga to the Rhine and thence to the Dnieper, was wont to attribute the chest-complaint which troubled him all his life to this terrible march.

The Russian army found itself, on approaching the Crimea, under the command of Marshal Münnich. That general stormed the lines of Perekop in May, 1736, then besieged and took Oczakow, and laid waste the Crimea. For his services in this campaign, Loudon was promoted to the rank of sub-lieutenant, a sufficient proof that he had done his duty. At the close of 1738 he visited his home at Tootzen, on short leave, returned thence to the army early in the following year, was present at the battle of Hawuczane, the overrunning of Moldavia, the occupation of Jassy, and the siege and capture of Choczim. He was promoted during the campaign to the full rank of lieutenant. Peace between Russia and the Porte having been signed in the autumn of 1739 Loudon accompanied his regiment to Astrakan. Whilst he was quartered there the death of the Emperor Charles VI. kindled the war of the Austrian succession. For a time Loudon hoped that Russia would take part in that war, but when she remained steadfastly quiescent he took the earliest opportunity to quit her service, and proceeded direct to St. Petersburg, in the hope of obtaining letters of introduction to some influential persons either at Berlin or Vienna. Frequenting there the salons of Count von Löwenwolde, a Livonian like himself and seneschal to the court, he became intimate with his secretary, an Alsatian named Hochstetten, who had friendly relations with more than one influential family in the capital of Austria. With this man he talked over his prospects, and eagerly clutched at an offer made him by his friend to furnish him with letters which would introduce him into good society in Vienna. But just as he was about to set out he learned that the war between Austria and Prussia had been terminated by the peace of Breslau, (June 11, 1742). Still anxious for employment, and learning that the English and Dutch were sending out ships to defend their possessions in the East Indies, he resolved to offer his services to one of those powers. Wishing, however, to take leave of his uncle on his mother's side, who filled a high office at the Swedish court, he proceeded by sea to Stockholm. The tossing which he experienced on this occasion convinced him that he could not stand the long voyage to the East, and, after his arrival at his uncle's, he would appear to have considered the proposal then made to him to enter the Swedish service. The reflection that Sweden was a declining power, and that Prussia had just begun to carve her way to the front rank, induced him to reject the idea. He returned then to Tootzen, and after a last farewell to his father, set out, with thirty ducats in his pocket, for Berlin to seek there an audience and a commission from the great Frederic.

Arrived at the Prussian capital Loudon preferred his request to the king. Frederic did not absolutely refuse it, but caused him to be informed that he might remain there and wait till a vacancy should occur. For six months he waited, presuming once during that period to remind the king of his promise. Frederic exhorted him to have patience, but when, just before the term had expired, the Governor of Berlin, of whom Loudon had made a friend, pressed the king earnestly on his behalf, Frederic gave him no encouragement to persevere, declaring that the heavy eyebrows and the thin lean body of the applicant were alike distasteful to him. The governor, however, did not accept this rebuff as final, and advised Loudon to demand a personal interview, and to press respectfully but firmly for a decisive answer.

The audience was applied for and granted. In the light of subsequent events, and in the presence of the fact that the petitioner for employment became the most formidable opponent of the king who refused it—that, not many years later, the king meeting him at a royal banquet at which the petitioner, then a general, had modestly chosen a place at the further end of the table on the side opposite to that on which he himself sat, exclaimed, beckoning to him to seat himself near him : "Come here, Marshal Loudon, I would rather see you by me than opposite to me," the interview is worthy of permanent record. At it Loudon represented to the king that he had had experience of war, that he had come to Berlin to have the honour of serving under the greatest soldier of the day, that he had waited six months, had long since exhausted all his resources, and been reduced to earn bare livelihood as a copying clerk ; that he would count the time well spent if the king would graciously bestow upon him the commission of captain in a cavalry regiment. Frederic heard him to the end, then replied : "I must indeed have many squadrons at my disposal if I could give one to every foreign officer who comes to Berlin," and dismissed him.

Loudon, baffled at Berlin, proceeded to Vienna. He took with him knowledge which could not but be useful to him were he fortunate enough to obtain service in the Austrian army. He had, in fact, employed his time at the Prussian capital to the best advantage, had thoroughly mastered Frederic's military system, and especially the reforms he had introduced into his artillery. Fortified with the letters of introduction he received from the Austrian ambassador, Count von Rosenberg, he could present himself at the Viennese court as a person who was worth receiving.

He reached Vienna in the spring of 1744. The recommendations which Count Rosenberg had forwarded on his behalf inspired Maria Theresa with a desire to see Loudon, and she gave directions that he should attend her at Schönbrunn. Whilst awaiting his turn in the antechamber Loudon was accosted by a stranger, who, in a friendly manner, inquired as to the business which had brought him there. Loudon entered freely into conversation with the man, related with great frankness the history of his past career, and expressed his hopes for the future. The stranger thereupon told him that if he would only speak as frankly and freely to the Queen of Hungary as he had to him his request would certainly be granted. He then quitted him. Summoned a few minutes later to the presence room, Loudon beheld his unknown friend standing by the side of Maria Theresa. He at once recognised that he had been speaking to her husband the Duke of Lorraine. It need scarcely be added that the request was granted. Loudon left the royal presence captain in the Austrian army.

Chance took Loudon that same evening to the theatre, and there he met unexpectedly the famous Francis, Baron Trenck, then a Lieut.-Colonel commanding the Sclavonian Free corps, known as the Pandours. Trenck had made Loudon's acquaintance in Russia, and appreciating his

value, called him into his box, and offered him the choice
of command of one of two companies of his regiment, the
first of which was in the Upper Palatinate, the second in
Bavaria. Loudon chose the latter and started the next
morning to join his command. This happened in April,
1744.

CHAPTER III.

THE Company of Pandours of which Loudon assumed command in Bavaria formed a fraction of the van-guard of the army which Prince Charles of Lorraine was about to lead into Alsace. That army consisted of 46,000 infantry and 22,000 cavalry. The van-guard, of which Trenck's Free corps was a component part, was commanded by Field-Marshal Nadasdy.

With a view to deceive the French and Bavarians who were guarding the Rhine near Mayence Prince Charles detached a corps under General Bärenklau to occupy their attention in that direction. Nadasdy and Trenck, then, at the head of 9,000 Hussars and Pandours, crossed the Rhine (30th of June) near Philipsburg, surprised three Bavarian regiments stationed there, and drove them from their camp, killing and taking prisoners 532 of their number. It is stated in the Austrian records that Trenck was the first man, and Loudon the second, to touch the soil on the left bank of the Rhine. This success secured for the rest of the Austrian army an unmolested passage of the river (1st to the 3rd of July).

The very same day, 3rd of July, Nadasdy, always with

Trenck's Free corps in the van, marched against and took possession of Lauterburg, on the 5th of Weissenburg, and on the 11th of Hagenau. The French Commander, Marshal de Coigny, after an abortive attempt to recover Weissenburg, fell back behind the Moder, and leaving Alsace to the Austrians, prepared to defend Lorraine. So acutely was the position felt at Versailles that the King of France himself set out to take the command of the army, and issued orders that no important operations were to be undertaken until his arrival. Meanwhile reinforcements from all parts of France were sent into Lorraine.

The place in Alsace which had been most fiercely assailed by the advancing and retreating armies was the castle of Elsass-Zabern, called by the French Saverne. Taken by Trenck, Loudon leading the storming party, and occupied by Nadasdy, it had been evacuated by the latter on the approach of a greatly-superior force under the Duc d'Harcourt, and had then been retaken by Nadasdy, reinforced by Bärenklau's corps. As Nadasdy advanced from this place, however, he was attacked in the night by the French and momentarily driven back. The French on this occasion took some prisoners. Amongst these was Loudon, who, fighting in the very front, had been struck by a musket ball in the right breast. The ball itself passed through the upper part of the body, but the wound was aggravated by the fact that the bullet had driven into the cavity one of the metal buttons of his dollman. It was perhaps fortunate for Loudon that he was captured, for at the moment there was no surgeon with the Austrian advance, whereas, taken prisoner, he was placed under the care of a French surgeon possessing alike humanity and skill. His cure was tedious and painful. At last, however, the surgeon was able to extract the button, and the wound then gradually healed.

Long before this had occurred Loudon was again with his own people. The Pandours, advancing a few days after their defeat, had recaptured the village in which their captain lay wounded, and with him the surgeon who was attending him. Loudon was sent to the rear of the army to await there his complete recovery. Before that happened circumstances occurred to make a complete change in the military calculations.

We have already noted why it was that Frederic II. regarded with great apprehension the success of the French in Alsace, and the measures which he had taken to baffle the designs of the Queen of Hungary. Taking advantage of the declared intention of Maria Theresa to invalidate the election of Charles VII. he had posed as the upholder of the dignity of the German empire, had enlisted on his side the Palatinate and Hesse Cassel, had made an alliance with France, and had arranged with that power a plan of operations which, if carried out as he had planned them, could not fail to succeed.

He waited then till Austria had completely entangled herself in Alsace and was about to invade Lorraine; till the reinforcements despatched by the Court of Versailles to Marshal de Coigny—30,000 men under de Noailles—had actually reached him; till Louis, on his way to join the army, had reached Metz. Then he issued the famous declaration to which I have referred, and invaded Bohemia! (August, 1744).

Information of this act of hostility reached the head quarters of the Austrian army on the 21st August. The position was very critical: an enemy of superior force in front of them, a broad and unbridged river behind them, severing them from the fatherland invaded by another enemy. Prince Charles was not a great captain himself, but, in the person of Count Traun, he had at his side a general second to none of that period, and who was yet destined to become, according to the admission of the pupil, the best instructor of Frederic in the art of war. But not even the advice of Traun, had it been on all occasions followed, would have saved the Austrian army at this crisis, had the French displayed even ordinary vigour. Frederic's calculations had been perfect, provided every man performed the part allotted to him. But just at the critical moment sickness stepped in and struck down his principal confederate, Louis XV., when on the very eve of setting out from Metz (8th to the 15th of August). This *contretemps* spoiled one part of his plan. The French commanders had received positive instructions not to fight till Louis should arrive to take command—and now Louis was detained by sickness at Metz. The Austrian commander was able, then, to re-cross the Rhine unmolested. He effected this operation on the 24th of August, destroyed the boats and pontoons he had used, and marching eastward with a haste rare in those days entered Bohemia on the 24th of September. In the course of less than three months the skilful manœuvres of Count Traun, who directed the operations of the army, forced the King of Prussia to renounce the conquests he had made, to sacrifice his heavy artillery, and to evacuate Bohemia.

One month later, January 20th, 1745, the ostensible reasons for the war disappeared. Charles VII., Emperor of Germany died. The election of Francis of Lorraine, the Queen of Hungary's husband, was certain. Frederic could no longer declare that he was waging war to restore to Germany its liberty and to the Emperor his dignity. The events which followed immediately upon the death of Charles VII. diminished still further the grounds upon which he had based his hostile position. Hesse Cassel and the Elector Palatine withdrew at once from the Union of Frankfort; on the 22nd of April, Max Joseph of Bavaria, successor of the late Emperor in that electorate, signed at Füssen a treaty of peace with the Queen of Hungary; and on the 28th of May following Saxony entered, at Warsaw, into an alliance, defensive and offensive, with the same sovereign. The preponderance had thus reverted to the House of Austria. Frederic stood alone in Germany against that power. There were not wanting symptoms, moreover, that he might have Russia on his hands at the same time. Under these circumstances he was willing to revert once again to the conditions of the Peace of Breslau. But Maria Theresa had signed that Peace under the pressure of hard necessity. She could not be expected, victorious, to confirm a cession she had made under direct compulsion—to confirm it, too, just after her enemy, unsatisfied with that cession, had thwarted her plans upon France. No—rather would she reduce this disturber of the peace of Germany to the position from which his grandfather ought never to have emerged—the position of an Elector of Brandenburg. For his part Frederic declined to renounce his plunder—and the war continued.

Loudon, meanwhile, had recovered from his wound, had joined his corps of Pandours, now transformed into a regular Hungarian regiment, quartered in Upper Silesia, and forming part of the army commanded in that province by Prince Esterhazy. In the month of May he was present at a successful attack made by that prince upon a column of 9,000 Prussians despatched from Neisse to take Jägerndorf and who had actually penetrated into that place. They were driven back with loss. During the same month, however, an event occurred which brought him more prominently into notice.

On the 20th of May a Prussian ensign, deserting from Kosel, informed Prince Esterhazy that General von Saldner, commanding in that place, had just died, and gave him such information as decided him to attempt the place by a *coup-de-main*. The enterprise he entrusted to an officer upon whose intelligence and activity he could depend, Colonel Buccow. Buccow took with him a regiment of Pandours, a Hungarian infantry regiment, and some cavalry, sending on in front Lieutenant-Colonel d'Olne and Loudon, with the advance guard of Pandours. D'Olne came within sight of the place on the 25th of May and despatched Loudon to make a thorough examination of the fortress and country. Loudon returned and pointed out to d'Olne how, with the small party at his disposal, the place might be surprised and taken. D'Olne, however, was not sufficiently adventurous to make the attempt without orders, but sent on Loudon to Buccow for the necessary authorisation. This Buccow at once gave and sent a reinforcement from the Hungarian regiment. The column of attack, composed of 200 men, was then formed, and the command of it given to Loudon. At two o'clock on the morning of the 26th of May, he crept, accompanied by eleven volunteers, at the head of his small column, to the edge of the outer ditch of the fortress, upwards of fifty feet in width and full of water. Nothing dismayed by this obstacle the twelve volunteers crossed it, and scaling the wall, gained the rampart just as the discharge of two muskets by the garrison told them they had been discovered. Loudon, the first to reach the parapet, came all at once on a battery of five guns. One of these he promptly turned against the enemy;—waited till more of his men should reach him and then sent a portion of them to assail the Prussians, now collecting in force, in flank, whilst

he attacked them in front. The fact that the fortifications were unfinished doubtless considerably aided him, for,
in a few minutes, he compelled the garrison to evacuate
them and to retreat into the town. Not long, however, was
this a refuge for them, for d'Olne and St. Ivary coming
up forced the gates and compelled their surrender. They
consisted of nineteen officers and four hundred men. The
victors captured likewise twenty-seven guns, of which ten
were twelve-pounders, a hundred munition waggons fully
laden and a well-stocked magazine. They gained these
advantages at the cost of ten men killed and twenty-two
wounded. The loss of the garrison was nearly treble that
amount, and included the Colonel commanding and the
second in command.

This was the first occasion on which an opportunity had
been given to Loudon to show his capacity in command.
His conduct attracted the attention of his comrades and
of his superiors, and gave him the reputation of a man
who could be depended upon in an emergency. But no one
yet discerned in the shy and studious foreigner attached to
the corps of Trenck, a corps always in the front, always
engaged, generally with advantage, with the enemy's outposts, a man who, in the great crisis of Austria's fortunes,
would lead her armies. Such a future never presented
itself then to the mind of Loudon. Gifted with a character
thoroughly practical he was content, in his position as one
of the advanced guard of the enemy, to observe, to carry
out orders, to show himself always on the alert, to watch
for opportunities. It was a capital school for a rising
warrior.

After the capture of Kosel, Loudon's regiment was
attached to the corps of Nadasdy, who then, as in the Alsace-
Lorraine campaign, commanded the advance of the army

under the command of Prince Charles of Lorraine. That prince, with Count Traun at his elbow, had, we have seen, forced Frederic, by a series of masterly manœuvres, to evacuate Bohemia, and, joined by the Saxons, had entered Silesia. But Prince Charles had no longer Traun at his elbow. With a fatuity which has often guided its councils, the Court of Vienna had rewarded that able soldier by bestowing upon him the Government of Transylvania. Left to his own resources Prince Charles was no match for the King of Prussia. He allowed himself to be surprised and beaten on the 4th June, at Hohenfriedburg, and forced to retreat into the Bohemian mountains. Three months later, however, strongly reinforced and spurred on by the Court of Vienna to act, Prince Charles, marching with great secrecy, took up a position, which, if he could have maintained it, would have cut off Frederic, then lying at Standenz, from Silesia. The plan, whilst being carried out, was betrayed by a deserter to Frederic, and Frederic, though he knew not precisely from which side an attack would come, prepared himself to meet one from any quarter. Still, he was to a certain extent surprised when, early on the morning of the 30th of September, he beheld the hills on the right of his camp occupied by the enemy.

The chances were all in favour of the Austrians. They numbered thirty thousand to Frederic's eighteen thousand ; they occupied a commanding position : they were acting on a preconcerted plan, and, to make assurance doubly sure, their general had ordered Nadasdy to march on Liebenthal, four miles to the south-east of the Prussian camp, with instructions that on receiving a certain order, he should fall upon it from the rear.

But never was the want of a firm and commanding will more apparent than in the Austrian camp on this eventful day. Had Prince Charles only acted with vigour he had Frederic in his toils. But through the want of that impressive will everything went wrong. He himself committed the first fault. Having the advantage of position of attack, to a certain extent of surprise, he halted and allowed the Prussians to form and to attack him. Again, the order to attack reached Nadasdy too late, and although, on receiving it, Nadasdy did capture the Prussian camp—and with it the King of Prussia's almost empty treasure-chest and his baggage—it was because there were few to defend it, and his action had no effect on the battle, which had been already won by Frederic. The advantages of numbers, of position, of surprise, were thus neutralised by a want of daring and concert. It was often the fortune of Frederic to be opposed to generals of the stamp of Prince Charles !

The victory of Soor—as the battle was called from the village occupied by the Austrians before the battle—permitted Frederic to withdraw his army into Silesia and to place it in winter quarters about Rohnstock and Hohenfriedberg. He then started for Berlin, believing that military operations had ceased for the season. In this instance, however, he did not take into calculation the determination of the Empress-Queen—for by the election of her husband to the Imperial dignity (13th of September) Maria Theresa had now assumed that title—to use to the utmost the advantages which superiority in men, in money, and in material had placed in her hands. She was resolved to carry the war into Brandenburg.

How the designs of Maria Theresa were foiled by the victories of the Prussians over her armies at Hennersdorf, (27th of November) and Kesselsdorf (15th of December), and how ten days after the last named battle the war was concluded by the peace of Dresden, by which, whilst Austria ceded Silesia and the country of Glatz, Frederic acknowledged Francis I. as Emperor of Germany, and how, rather less than three years later, England, Holland, France, Spain and Austria signed the Peace of Aix-la-Chapelle, (30th of April, 18th of October, 7th of November, 1748), are matters with which the historian of London's life has no concern. For, almost immediately after the battle of Soor Loudon quitted the Austrian service.

It happened in this manner: Loudon was under the immediate orders of Francis, Baron von Trenck. Trenck was a born plunderer, hard, cold, unfeeling, totally without mercy, and preferring pillage to war. It has been urged against him that his desire to plunder the camp of the King of Prussia was the real cause of the late arrival of Nadasdy on the battle-field of Soor. His harshness, his insolence, his cruelty, his indifference to military order, grated particularly on Loudon, whose character was exactly opposite. He bore with him long, but, after Soor, he felt he could not serve under a man who would not hesitate to sacrifice the public good for his private advantage. He resigned therefore his post and proceeded to Vienna.

Loudon was still at Vienna when the peace of Dresden was signed. As that peace shut out from him all prospect of military employment he had resolved to try his fortunes in another country, when he received an order to stay where he was, in order to appear as a witness against Trenck, just placed under arrest for malversation and other misdemeanours. Trenck, during the trial, endeavoured to implicate Loudon, but the latter had been careful enough to preserve all the orders he had received, and these documents proved that in every instance he had obeyed orders. Whilst, therefore, Trenck was sentenced to pay a fine of 120,000 florins to his accusers, the men whom he had plundered, and eventually, to imprisonment for life in the castle of Spielburg, Loudon left the court with an unspotted and even enhanced reputation.

His means at this time were very scanty. There lived in the last decade of the last century men who remembered well how he used to come every evening to take a glass of cheap wine in a garden in the Alser suburb. His leisure moments he used to devote to a study of geography, of mathematics, with a view to qualify himself more perfectly for his profession. But every day spent in Vienna diminished his resources, and he had begun to despair of the future, when a friend, who had considerable court influence, and who had formed the highest opinion of him, the well-known musician Salviatti, succeeded in obtaining for him a captain's commission in a regiment of Croats. Salviatti's kindness did not end there, for he lent him a hundred ducats to enable him to join. Loudon's regiment was at Bunic on the Croatian frontier. On his way thither he stopped at Bösing, about eleven miles from Pressburg, to present a letter of introduction he had received from Salviatti to Madame von Haagen, a widow lady who lived on her property in that neighbourhood. Well received by Madame von Haagen Loudon stayed some time at Bösing, and soon after married the second daughter, Clara. Pretty, well-educated and clever, Clara von Haagen was just the wife for a man of quiet energy, anxious to improve himself, and determined to attain a definite end. She entered into all his hopes and aspirations, and during a long married life she proved his best, his truest, his most trusted friend. The fortune she brought with her, whilst not large, was yet a sensible addition to a captain's pay. She bore him two sons, both of whom died in their infancy.

Ten years were spent by Loudon on the Croatian frontier, principally at Bunic. He spent his leisure time in pursuing his studies of history, geography, and geometry. He provided himself for that purpose with the best maps he could procure. It is related of him that the better to study a very large map which he had procured, he had removed the furniture from the centre of the room and placed the map on the floor. He repeated this process so long and so often that one day his wife, not quite understanding his pertinacity, exclaimed with a slight tinge of asperity : " What pleasure can you possibly find in always studying that big map?" "Leave me alone, my dear," replied Loudon, "the knowledge I am now acquiring will be useful to me when I become Field-Marshal"!

In other respects there was little to call for the display of the special qualities which characterised him. Though much discontent, the consequence of the introduction of new regulations, prevailed generally in Croatia, and developed a little later into a regular outbreak of the Croatian soldiers, Loudon put down the disorder in his own company with a very strong hand. Assembling the non-commissioned officers, and appealing to their loyalty, he arrested and brought to sharp trial the mutineers. So vigorous was his action that in four-and-twenty hours order was restored, never again to be disturbed. In the other districts the disturbances were more prolonged, but the result was the same.

Meanwhile Loudon's promotion had been going on. In 1750 he was promoted to be Major, and in three years later to the rank of second Lieutenant-Colonel. He was serving in that rank when the Seven years' war broke out.

CHAPTER IV.

MARIA THERESA had never forgiven Frederic the seizure of Silesia. For ten long years she brooded over the loss. Every thought of her mind was directed during that period to devise a plan for the punishment of the evil-doer and the recovery of the stolen country. Before even the treaty of Aix-la-Chapelle had been signed, she had striven hard to win over Russia to her views. The highly-gifted Sovereign who reigned over that country, the Czarina Elizabeth, daughter of Peter the Great, would not have been inclined, in any case, to view with complacency the growth on her western frontier of a military kingdom, strong enough to bar to her the road to the rest of Europe. Under the actual circumstances she had strong personal reasons for determining to seize the earliest occasion to stifle the growth of Prussia. Her private life had not been and was not so pure as to defy criticism, and Frederic, who possessed to a high degree the power of satire, and who, like all men specially endowed, could not refrain from the exercise of that dangerous talent, had given vent publicly to sarcasms which could not fail to reach the ears of the Czarina. Elizabeth, then, hated Frederic with a hatred which his destruction alone could satiate. The policy she had inherited from her father coincided in this respect with her strong personal feelings.

Sure then of the support of Russia, Maria Theresa then had to consider how it might be possible to gain France. The alliance of France would mean the hostility of England, but she had felt herself on many occasions during the previous war so hampered by the advice, and so little benefited by the active assistance, of the latter, that she did not hesitate between the two. In this view she was supported by her chancellor, Count von Kaunitz, a statesman of rare ability and foresight. As the policy of this illustrious man influenced the House of Austria during the period upon which we are now entering, a short description of him will be necessary.

Anton Wengel von Kaunitz was born in Vienna in 1711, the fifth and youngest son of a family of nineteen children. He was originally intended for the Church, but the death of his four elder brothers on the field of battle changed his career, and he was sent successively to the universities of Vienna, Leipzig, and Leyden, to prepare him for diplomatic service. Subsequently, with the same purpose in view, he visited North Germany, Italy, France, and England. On his return to Vienna in 1735 he was nominated by the Emperor, Charles VI., an Aulic councillor, and a little later was sent as second Imperial commissary to the diet of Ratisbon. The death of the Emperor withdrew him from this mission, but the following year, 1741, he was nominated by Maria Theresa ambassador to the Holy See, and was sent thence, in 1742, as Minister Plenipotentiary to Turin, to consolidate a defensive alliance between Sardinia and Austria. The ability he displayed on this occasion very favourably impressed his sovereign; she sent him to represent her at the court of her brother-in-law,

Charles of Lorraine, then Governor of the Low Countries; and when, shortly afterwards, Prince Charles was compelled, by the death of his wife, to absent himself, she confided to him the administration, *ad interim*, of those provinces. On the return of Prince Charles, he resumed his office of Minister Plenipotentiary, and was with him at the time of the French occupation of Brussels. Subsequently he represented Austria at the congress of Aix-la-Chapelle, and signed on behalf of his country the Peace which bears the name of that town.

On his return from Aix-la-Chapelle, Kaunitz resumed his seat in the Aulic Council. He was present as one of its members when Maria Theresa summoned it to deliberate on the imperial policy to be pursued now that peace reigned throughout Europe. She found opinions divided. Her husband, the Emperor Francis, declared himself in favour of pursuing the traditional policy of the empire—the policy of a cordial understanding with England and Holland—and recommended the renunciation of all thought of Silesia, and the conciliation of Prussia. Kaunitz opposed this view. In a state paper, remarkable for its logical argument, he laid down that the rise of the electorate of Brandenburg had materially affected the position of Austria; that whereas, before that rise, the latter had two hereditary enemies, France and the Sultan, she now had three; that Austria would never be safe till she had recovered Silesia; but that, to make that recovery certain, it was necessary that she should form a European confederacy to crush her rival; and of that confederacy France should be a component part.

These views, which expressed in well-argued sentences the thoughts of Maria Theresa, were adopted then as the secret policy of Austria, and Kaunitz was despatched to

Paris to endeavour to win over the French Court. The conversion of a hereditary enemy to the position of an active friend would have been an almost impossible task even for a man whose diplomatic and statesmanlike ability, and whose influence over the politics of the age gained for him at a later day the sobriquet, " the coachman of Europe ; " of whom Voltaire records that " he was as active in the cabinet as the King of Prussia was in the field ; " had he not been powerfully aided by Frederic himself. The malicious spirit which had made of the Czarina Elizabeth an implacable enemy had not spared the reigning mistress of Louis XV. It had been possible for Frederic to bind Madame de Pompadour to his interests, for, at the outset, she had a keen admiration for him. But no political consideration, no personal friendship, could restrain the love of satire which reigned supreme in the breast of the King of Prussia, and which he exercised at the expense often of his best friends. Some of his sayings, reported to Madame de Pompadour and to Louis XV., had changed their feelings into bitter hatred, and had predisposed them therefore to listen to the advances of Kaunitz.

That great statesman remained two years in France carefully preparing the bases of an alliance which, at the proper time, was to be concluded. Maria Theresa then recalled him, to assume, as Chancellor of the Empire, supreme direction of her affairs. " She expected his arrival," wrote the English minister to Dresden who had been despatched thence to Vienna on a secret mission, " with the same impatience as Henry VIII. looked for the return of Cranmer when he was tired of Wolsey." His arrival affixed the seal to the negotiations which were still pending Practically, Russia and France were secured. It remained only to gain Saxony.

D

Kaunitz proceeded then to win over that Power. He found the Saxon minister, Count Brühl, sympathetic but timid. Brühl was unwilling to strike until Russia should be actually on the move. He felt that if Frederic were to deal the first blow his own country would have to parry it. With the view of preventing this he urged patience on the Court of Vienna on the one side, whilst, on the other, he used every argument at St. Petersburg to induce Russia to assail the common enemy. The result would probably have corresponded to his wishes had Brühl used common precaution. The depositary of the secrets of two great Powers, upon whose common action depended the fate of a third, it became him to see that the correspondence did not fall into the hands of any but those of whose loyalty he was absolutely sure. This was the more essential as he knew from experience that the king he was plotting against was a man absolutely without scruple. But Brühl took no precautions. It resulted from this that before the pear was ripe Frederic obtained cognisance of the whole plan.

It happened in this way. Towards the end of 1752 a Saxon who had been employed in the public offices in Dresden, and also was about to emigrate into Prussia, gave the Prussian General, Winterfeldt, a hint that a confederacy was being formed against his master, of which Dresden was the centre. Winterfeldt informed Frederic. Frederic, naturally suspicious of the designs of Austria, at once directed his minister at the Saxon Court, Count Malzahn, to find out some instrument who should penetrate into the secret archives of its foreign office, and acquaint him with the true nature of the confederacy. Malzahn succeeded in buying a clerk, named Menzel, of a very respectable family, who had been employed for seventeen years in the secret archives of the cabinet. As Menzel had not himself access to the keys which closed the presses containing the most private documents, he was furnished with one set from Berlin, and when these would not answer, he returned them indicating the alterations necessary. These having been made and the new keys sent him, he began his treacherous and inglorious work. He continued it till the war began.

Frederic obtained additional confirmatory evidence of the plans of the confederates from the second secretary to the Austrian Embassy at Berlin, Maximilian Weingarten. This young man had fallen in love with the daughter of the Governor of Charlottenburg, a friend of General Winterfeldt. The latter, already on the look-out for some means to penetrate the secrets of the Austrian Embassy, persuaded the girl to use her influence with her lover for that purpose. Weingarten was weak enough and base enough to comply.

Frederic had thus all the information he wanted. He held the secrets of Russia and Saxony through Menzel, those of Austria through Max. Weingarten. He was very much perplexed. It had become evident in 1755 that war between France and England was impending. The whole Continent would be drawn into it. England, true to her traditional policy, would endeavour to obtain the assistance of the German Empire, represented by the House of Austria. The claims of the latter upon Silesia would certainly be renewed. To what quarter, then, could he look for an ally? The correspondence showed him that Russia had committed herself; but Austria was not quite sure of France. There was yet time then to gain the alliance of that Power. Full of this hope Frederic turned to France.

But his sarcasms had done their work at Versailles. There Madame de Pompadour reigned still supreme, and Madame de Pompadour never forgave. Even on this

D 2

occasion Frederic committed the mistake of addressing himself to others rather than to her. He soon found that he had no hope of France. His ambassador at Versailles informed him that far from responding to his overtures, the Court was meditating a closer alliance with Austria. At the same time he received information that that Power was concentrating large bodies of troops on the frontier of Silesia.

The crisis was indeed at hand. In the spring of 1756, the Czarina had proposed to Austria an immediate attack upon Prussia, with a view to the partitioning of that kingdom. Austria was to recover Silesia and the country of Glatz ; Russia was to receive Courland and other fractions of Polish territory, whilst Poland was to be indemnified by the acquisition of East Prussia. But Maria Theresa was not, at that date, quite sure of France. A little later in that year, May 1st, 1756, however, she signed with that power a defensive treaty—known as the Treaty of Versailles. But it was clear, even then, to Kaunitz, that France would not support his sovereign in an attack upon Prussia, and the Russian offer was, for the moment, declined. Kaunitz, however, still pressed his skilful negotiations for an offensive alliance. Every week added to the probability of his success. The relations between France and England were becoming more and more strained, and France showed a growing tendency to connect herself more closely with Austria. The hopes of Kaunitz were still further stimulated by the declaration of war, on the 9th of June, between France and England.

Frederic, meanwhile, had allied himself with the latter Power. It is possible—well aware though he was, as a consummate soldier, of the advantages which belong to an attacking army—that he would have hesitated to

commit any act likely to decide the still wavering Court of
Versailles to declare openly for his enemies, but that, just
after the declaration of war just referred to, he received
from St. Petersburg letters, purporting to come "in the
strictest confidence from a trustworthy source," but which,
he had no doubt, were written by the Grand Duke Peter,
the heir to the throne of Russia, and his intense admirer,
warning him that active measures against him were deferred
in consequence of the unready state of the Russian army,
but that he certainly would be attacked the following
spring. This information decided Frederic. He would
not, indeed, attack Russia, but he would dash upon Saxony
and Austria before they were ready, upset their calculations and possibly decide the war in a single campaign.
Before, acting, however, Frederic, in deference to the
wishes of England, addressed, through his ambassador at
Vienna, Count Klinggräff, a demand to the Empress
Queen, as to whether her armies, assembled on the frontiers
of Moravia and Bohemia, had been formed for the purpose
of attacking Prussia. Maria Theresa receiving Klinggräff
in a private audience (July 26th) answered him that she had
deemed it necessary in the existing crisis to take measures
for the security of herself and her allies tending to the
prejudice of no one. Frederic, disappointed with the nature
of this reply, transmitted at once orders to Klinggräff to
ask for a less oracular response—a response containing
an assurance that Austria would not attack him that year or
the next. To this demand, transmitted this time in writing,
(18th of August) Maria Theresa replied (21st of August)
that "the treaty she had made with Russia was purely
defensive ; that she had concluded no offensive alliance ;
and although the critical state of Europe had compelled
her to arm, she had no intention to violate the Treaty of

Dresden, but would not bind herself by any promise to refrain from acting as circumstances might require." Frederic received this reply on the night of the 25th of August. On the 28th he set out, at the head of his army, to invade Saxony.

In this manner began the Seven Years' War.

CHAPTER V.

WHEN the war broke out, Loudon was still quartered in Croatia. Most eager was he to be employed in it. He made application then to be included amongst those officers who were ordered from that province. But General Petazzi, who commanded there, and who during the earlier part of his service in the province, had covered him with praises which had excited the jealousy of his comrades, had, in the later months, conceived a bitter dislike to him, and abruptly refused his request. Enraged at the refusal and at the bitter and scornful terms in which it was conveyed,[1] Loudon quitted Bunic without leave and hastened to Vienna. Such a step was not to be tolerated even in those days of comparatively free service, and the military authorities were about to send Loudon back to his frontier station with a curt refusal, when a circumstance occurred to fix his destiny.

The successful inroad of Frederic into Saxony—to be presently more particularly noted—had convinced the military advisers of the Empress-Queen of the advantages which would accrue from despatching to the army

_____
[1] The words used by General Petazzi were that Loudon neither was fit for war, nor did he possess the means wherewith to equip himself.

contributed by the minor states of Germany, then about to be formed, a regiment of Croats, always to be employed in the front, and to be commanded by a man who should be distinguished for intelligence and, in the largest sense of the term, military knowledge. Maria Theresa then ordered the formation of such a corps, eight hundred strong, and commissioned Kaunitz to seek out an officer possessing the necessary qualities.

It happened that there was at Vienna at the time, living in intimate relations with Kaunitz, the same Hochstetten who had known Loudon in Russia, and who, fifteen years previously, had been the indirect cause of his entering the Austrian service. With him Loudon had, during his short visit to Vienna, renewed relations. He had given him details of his long frontier training, of the discipline to which he had submitted; had acquainted him with his disappointments, his hopes, his despair. When then Hochstetten learned the commission given by the Empress-Queen to Kaunitz, he hastened to that statesman and recommended Loudon as a man specially marked out for the command in question. Hochstetten pressed the matter with so much earnestness that Kaunitz at once sent for Loudon.

The messenger found Loudon lodging in the attic of a tailor's shop in the Ungargasse. He proceeded at once to Kaunitz, and held with him a long conversation. Upon the keen-witted Austrian statesman the demeanour, calm, quiet, and self-possessed, of Loudon, made an impression absolutely the reverse of that which the same demeanour had produced on Frederic. In a very brief period, Kaunitz recognised a self-contained man, a man of iron nerve, of great precision of thought, a man who could not only conceive great ideas, but who could carry them out. He had, he felt, before him the very man of whom he was in quest. On the spot, then, he gave him the independent command of a battalion of Croats, and the commission to lead that battalion with all speed to join the imperial army in Bohemia under the command of Field-Marshal Count Browne, with him to remain till the federation army should be formed. Loudon joined the Field-Marshal at Budin, in September, 1756.

Before that date the position of the contending parties had been defined. We have seen how Frederic had set out from Berlin on the 28th of August to invade Saxony. His plan had been to take the Saxons by surprise, and to compel them either to disarm, or to make common cause with him; then to invade Bohemia, and in combination with a second army under Schwerin, marching from Glatz, to strike such a blow at the Austrians as would give him the entire command of that country before winter should set in. Before referring to the events which followed his attempt to execute that plan, I propose to describe, as briefly as possible, the resources at the disposal of the contending parties.

Frederic, well aware that the seizure of Silesia had not been forgiven, and that he would yet have to fight for his prey, had employed the ten years' peace in increasing and in improving his army. The revenues, amounting to four million thalers, of the conquered Silesia gave him money; the permission to recruit his army in any part of Germany gave him men for this purpose. When the war broke out he possessed an army consisting, independent of the troops in garrison, of 130,000 men. Of the component parts of this army it could be affirmed that the infantry surpassed, alike in quickness of manœuvre and in correctness of shooting, the rest of the infantry of Europe; whilst the cavalry, consisting of 10,000 cuirassiers, 12,500 dragoons, and 10,500 hussars, and trained by such men as Ziethen, Budenbrock, Gessler, and Seidlitz, had a similar pre-eminence. On the other hand the artillery had been less attended to. In the first and second Silesian wars Frederic had possessed so great a superiority in this arm that he had made the mistake of concentrating all his attention upon the other two. It remains to be added that during the ten years adverted to Frederic had held yearly exercises of his army on the plains round Spandau, so contriving them that no foreign officers should be present ; that he had himself taught his generals, had impressed the necessity of diligent attention upon the more subordinate officers, and had maintained the strictest discipline.

Nor during the same period had the Austrian army been neglected. On the death of Count Khevenhüller in 1744, the practical administration of it had been conferred, under Prince Wenzel von Lichtenstein, upon Count Daun. This general, whose name will often recur, had noticed that the victories of Gustavus Adolphus in the Thirty Years' War, and of Frederic in the two Silesian wars, had been gained principally by their superior number of guns and by the skill of their gunners. Upon his representations, then, the greatest attention had been paid to increasing the number of guns and gunners, to improve their equipment, and to practise them in all manner of manœuvres, principally in those which had a defensive object. Great success had attended the endeavours of the Austrian leaders, and it is not too much to say that when the war broke out in 1756 their artillery was the finest and the best served in Europe. Unfortunately Daun had taken part in wars which had been essentially of a defensive character. He could not grasp the necessity of infusing into the army the daring and dashing spirit which is required in aggressive warfare.

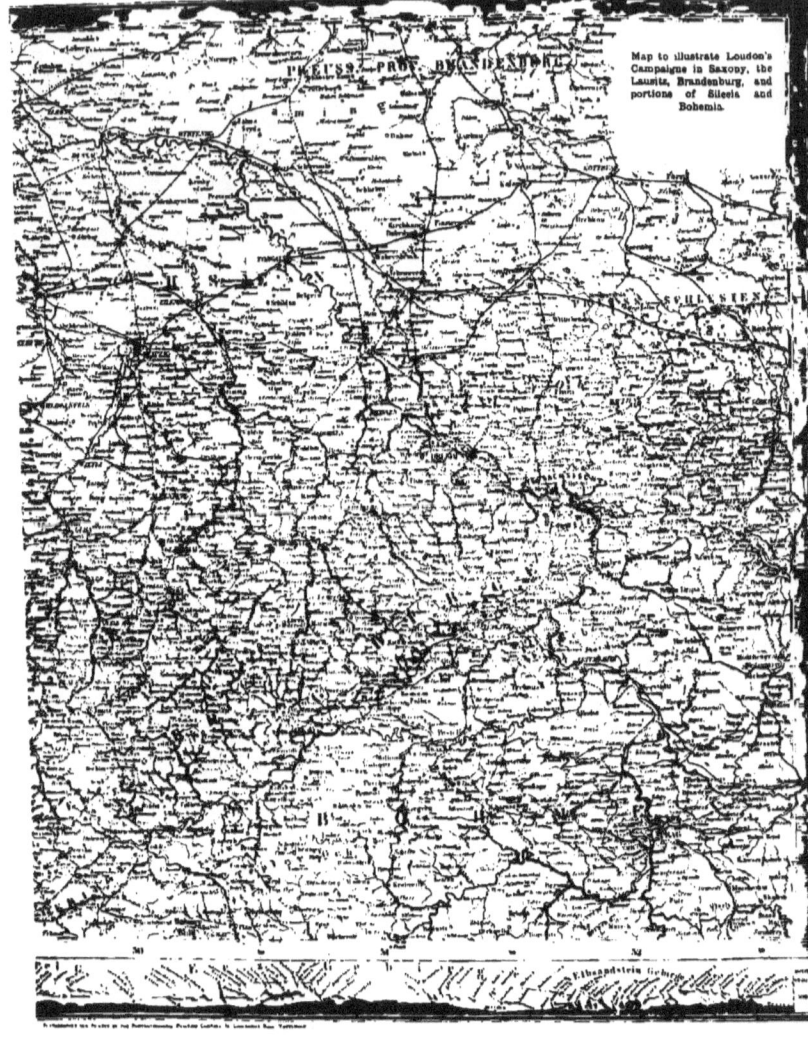

Map to illustrate Loudon's
Campaigns in Saxony, the
Lausitz, Brandenburg, and
portions of Silesia and
Bohemia.

He neither possessed nor did he understand that spirit himself. His principle of warfare may be described in one sentence—to resist attack to the utmost; to risk nothing; and only to assail an enemy when success was absolutely certain. The character of an army depends very much upon the character of the man to whom its training is intrusted. When we reflect then, that whilst Frederic was instructing his generals and his troops in offensive movements at Spandau, Daun was exercising the Austrians in defensive warfare in Moravia, we shall cease to feel surprised at the earlier results of the campaign. It remains to be added that when Frederic burst into Saxony in August, 1756, the cadres of the Austrian infantry had not been filled up; the cavalry were waiting the yearly remounts; the commissariat arrangements, the field-hospitals, and the pontoon-trains were all incomplete.

The Saxon army was in a still less forward state. The Court of Dresden, unaware that its secrets had been betrayed, had made certain that the war would break out only when Russia was ready to act, and it knew that Russia would not be ready till the following spring. Its troops then had not even been called out when Frederic marched from Berlin on the 28th of August. It was only when it received tidings of that march and its destination that summonses were issued to the several regiments to concentrate—not on Dresden, to reach which time failed them—but at Pirna and Königstein, on the south bank of the Elbe, in the hilly country then known as the Misnian Highlands (Meissnische Hochland).

Frederic had timed well his irruption. Saxony lay at his feet defenceless. He crossed its border on the 29th, at the head of 65,000 men, in three columns, took possession of Leipsig the same evening, and, pressing forward, occupied

Dresden on the 9th of September. The next day he set out for Pirna.

Meanwhile the Saxon army had collected in the Pirna country. It numbered only 17,000 men, but the position it occupied left little to be desired. Its right rested on Pirna, its left on the fortress of that name, rising upwards of eight hundred feet above the river. The ground covering these two places, eleven miles apart, was extremely difficult for an offensive army. "It is torn and tumbled into stone labyrinths, chasms, and winding rock-walls, as few regions are." Frederic did not at all like the look of it when he saw it that 10th of September. When, however, the information reached him that the Saxons had but a fortnight's provisions he was comforted. If he could not drive them out by force, he could at least starve them. But first he tried negotiation : when that had failed, when he found that the Saxons still held out, and that an Austrian army was marching on the Elbe to relieve them, he left 40,000 men to continue the blockade, and at the head of 25,000, entered Bohemia on the 28th of September to baffle the plans of the Austrian general.

Meanwhile the Austrian Government had been doing everything that was possible to supply the deficiencies in their frontier armies. Of these they had two ; one commanded by Count Browne, whose head-quarters were at Prague, and designed to co-operate with the Saxons ; the other and smaller under Piccolomini in the Königshof-Kolin region, intended on the first outbreak of hostilities to invade the county of Glatz. Hostilities having been precipitated by Frederic, the latter corps, in far too backward a state to dream of invasion, had to think how it might defend the passes against the Prussian general, Marshal Schwerin, who, at the head of 40,000 men, was preparing to debouch from that country. It was otherwise with Browne. Of Irish extraction, Ulysses Browne had risen from the lowest grade of officer to the rank of field-marshal. He was a very capable general, active, daring, possessed of great resolution, and not unworthy even to look Frederic in the face. In the prime of life, being then only fifty-four, Browne, on receiving information that Frederic had crossed the Saxon frontier, had thrown all his energies into the task of supplying the many deficiencies in his army. Under the inspiring influences which a real workman at the head of affairs always imparts, he rapidly succeeded. The cadres were filled up, the commissariat arrangements were made, field hospitals were formed, the remounts came in, and, last of all, the pontoon-train reached his camp. Before Frederic had succeeded in starving the Saxons out of Pirna, Browne had organised his army sufficiently to strike a blow for their relief.

Not only was Browne anxious to strike that blow, but the orders from Vienna left him no option but to attempt it. It can easily be conceived how keenly Maria Theresa had felt the anticipation by Frederic of her most cherished plans. Whilst she was hoping with the aid of France, of Russia, and of the Empire to crush him, he, still at peace with France, with Russia, and with the Empire—for the Empire had not yet declared war—had by the occupation of Saxony, neutralised the most precious link of the confederation, and invaded her territories, regarding them not as territories of the Empress, but as dominions of the Queen of Hungary. It was in that position alone that she was once more pitted against her bitter enemy. How her proud spirit chafed against this destruction of all her plans, may, I repeat, be easily conceived. But the disappointment only made her the more determined. Her orders to Browne breathed no uncertain sound. He was to relieve the Saxons, then seek out Frederic wherever he might be found, and smite him hip and thigh.

The task was a difficult one. Browne, on the outbreak of hostilities, had moved to Budin on the little river Eger, and had concentrated his army at that place. The Eger joins the Elbe a little above the town of Leitmeritz on the right bank of that river. It was easy for Browne to reach that point—where at that time no fortress existed—but if he were to push along the left bank he could not fail to come upon the Prussian army in a hilly and difficult country, its position chosen by its famous king. Browne's only chance then of relieving the Saxons, was to push on from the junction to Lobositz on the left bank, to cross to Leitmeritz on the right, and to march thence by the quickest possible route to Schandau and Lilienstein just opposite to the Saxon camp. When Browne should have gained that position he would find no difficulty in effecting a junction with the Saxon army. So determined was the Austrian commander to carry out this plan that he despatched letters to the Saxon camp announcing his intention to arrive at Schandau on or before the 11th of October.

The reader will not have failed to observe that the success of Browne's operations depended entirely upon his ability to effect the passage of the Elbe at Lobositz before the Prussians should reach that place. Frederic was as well aware of this as was Browne, and it was to anticipate him that, leaving 40,000 men to blockade the Pirna camp, he marched (28th of September), with 25,000 men to Lobositz. On the following day, when within ten miles of that place, he beheld the Austrian army encamped on the hills surrounding that town.

But one day earlier, and Browne could have crossed the

Elbe. To cross it now he must first beat the Prussian army. The Prussian king, for his part, thought that no time must be lost in attacking Browne. The battle then which followed, was fierce and well-contested. Loudon's Pandours were in the very front of the Austrian army occupying the Lobosch hill, between Lobositz and Sutowitz. That hill was the key of the position. Had it been occupied in force, Browne's position would have been impregnable. He had sent there, however, the previous evening, only that one regiment of Croats, and though, when the battle had joined and he recognised that Frederic had detected its value and was resolved to have it, he sent regiment after regiment to regain it—for Loudon's Croats had been speedily overwhelmed and driven from it, he failed and lost the battle.

Not, however, very easily. The Austrians fought splendidly : they inflicted upon the Prussians a loss greater than that which they themselves suffered. Frederic, by his marvellous *coup d'œil*, had recognised the decisive point of the position ; by skilful management of his troops had gained it, and had thus thrown back the Austrians from the Elbe. But he did nothing more. Browne brought off his army with great skill. He lost indeed three guns, but he was able, had he wished it, to present an unbroken front to his enemy the next day. The battle, notwithstanding, was a clear victory for Frederic. Browne had wished to cross to the right bank of the Elbe, and Frederic had forced him for the moment to renounce the idea. The next day Browne fell back on Budin.

On Loudon the day's experience could not have been thrown away. He and his Croats had occupied the key of the position. He had had to see that key wrenched from him by Frederic, and the battle lost in consequence. The fact was of sufficient importance to impress itself very deeply on the mind of a thoughtful soldier. To such a man it was a schooling never to be forgotten, and Loudon never did forget the lesson. He learned it too, not less from the point of view of defence, than from that of attack. To seek out, to fall furiously upon, the weak point of an enemy was, in the years that were immediately to follow, his striking characteristic.

But Browne, though baffled by Frederic at Lobositz, by no means renounced his plan of relieving the beleagured Saxons. Having despatched another message to their general, Field-Marshal Rutowski, to inform him that he would still be with them on the 11th, and requiring him to be prepared to evacuate his camp, and cross, opposite to Lilienstein, to the right bank of the Elbe, he set out at the head of 8,000 men, of whom one fourth, the Croatian levies, under Loudon, formed the advance, made a flank march to the point, close to Melnik, where the Moldau joins the Elbe, crossed there the latter river, and hastened round by forced marches by way of Böh-misch—Leipa, Rumburg, and Schluckenau to Lichtenhein, a village some seven miles from Schandau. It was a bold, daring, and very venturesome undertaking, worthy in that respect of Frederic himself, for he was liable to be attacked by double the number of the enemy, and he could not afford to stay on the right bank a moment longer than was necessary to effect his purpose.

The success of the plan depended, first, on its being carried out without hindrance from the enemy; secondly, on the punctuality of the Saxons.

Browne did his part well. He threw dust into the eyes of Frederic, crossed the Elbe at Melnik, and, marching with all speed, reached Lichtenhein punctually on the evening of the 11th, and encamped in the woods near the village. But there were no signs of the Saxons. Rutowski had received the warning late on the 7th, but not having got his pontoons in readiness, attempted on the night of the 8th to cross by means of tow ropes. This attempt, and another made the following night, were baffled by the fire from the Prussian batteries, which put the towing peasants to flight. On the 10th and 11th Rutowski, by great exertions, managed to fix the pontoons, and on the 12th the bridge was made ready for crossing. That night Rutowski endeavoured to lead his army across; but when the day broke only the vanguard had reached the right bank. Meanwhile the Prussians entering their intrenched camp came thundering on their rear. By the evening of the 14th their whole army, 14,000 in number, had straggled across. But Browne, alas! had not been able to wait for them. Surrounded by enemies, and with his retreat at any moment likely to be cut off, he had held his position for two days; then, hearing nothing of or from the Saxons, and believing they had failed, he had been forced to retrace his steps. The delays of Rutowski in placing the pontoons in position ruined a well-planned scheme. The Saxons, beset by the Prussians, were compelled, on the 16th, to surrender, and to enter the service of the conqueror.

Browne started on his return march at nine o'clock on the morning of the 14th. That night he reached the village of Kamnitz, and there information reached him that Frederic was throwing a bridge over the Elbe near Tetschen. Considering it probable that Frederic's object was to cut him off from his base, Browne despatched London with 500 Croats and some Hussars in the direction of that place, with discretionary orders, to reconnoitre. On reaching the vicinity of Tetschen, London ascertained

E

that though that place was occupied by a small detachment of the enemy, there was no thought in that place of interfering with the Austrian army. But the opportunity of-giving the small garrison a slap in the face was too tempting to be neglected. He dashed then into the town, cut down two squadrons of Hussars who opposed him, and carried off upwards of a hundred of their horses to the camp at Kamnitz. This was the last blow struck during the campaign. The Prussian army, evacuating Bohemia, went into winter quarters about Zwickau and Chemnitz on the one side, and Zittau and Görlitz, both on the river Neisse, on the other; the Austrians on the Bohemian frontier, facing Saxony and the Lausitz. Loudon, placed under the orders of General Lacy, the son of an Irishman who had migrated to Austria after the fall of the Stewarts, was stationed at Grottau, one of the villages in the cordon.

It is a proof of the active and energetic temperament of Loudon that even whilst the army was lying inactive in its winter quarters he was always planning some mode of inflicting loss on the enemy. Having noticed, for instance, that their troops stationed at various points on the Neisse were very careless in their military duties, he asked and obtained leave from his general to give them a New Year's greeting. On the night of the 31st of December, then, he set out at the head of six companies of Croats and two squadrons of Hussars, and making his way through the deep snow which covered the ground, surprised and cut up the Prussian posts at Marienthal, Ostritz, Laiba, and Radmeritz, carrying off all their arms and baggage, and thirty-four prisoners. His own loss amounted only to two men. But this was not sufficient for him. On the 19th of February he was appointed to lead the vanguard of a force composed of 4,000 men, and designed by Generals Macguire

and Löwenstein to surprise the important town of Hirsch-
feld, likewise in the Lausitz. Again had the assailants
to traverse ground covered deeply with snow. Marching in
the night they crossed the Neisse at five o'clock in the
morning, and fell upon the town. The Prussians, however, were prepared. Loudon, to whom had been assigned
the most difficult part of the enterprise—the carrying of
the redoubt which covered the town—led six hundred men
to the assault. Simultaneously Prince Charles of Lichtenstein attacked the place by the bridge, and Major Noyau
by the suburbs. Not only did the assailants carry the
place, but thirsting for further triumphs, proceeded further
and carried the post of Hersdorf. For his conduct on this
and other occasions Loudon was promoted to the rank
of full Colonel.

Meanwhile the war passion was gaining the other powers
of Europe. At an imperial diet held at Ratisbon on the
10th of January, 1757, it had been resolved to raise an
army of the confederated German States to punish Frederic
for his, as it was styled, unprovoked attack upon Saxony.
On the 2nd of February following, the Empress-Queen
concluded a new treaty with the Czarina, whereby, in
consideration of the payment by the former of a million
of roubles annually, the Czarina bound herself to compel
Frederic to yield Silesia and the country of Glatz to Austria,
to carry out the other stipulations she had formerly
proposed respecting Courland and East Prussia, and to
carry on the war until this programme had been entirely
fulfilled. Finally, after much negotiation, an offensive
and defensive treaty was signed at Versailles, May the 1st,
between Austria and France, having for its object the
partition of Prussia for the benefit of Austria, Saxony,
the Elector Palatine, and Sweden, France to be recompensed

by the cession of a large portion of the Netherlands.
The two contracting parties bound themselves not to make
peace until all the conditions of the treaty should have
been executed, and France undertook to pay Austria yearly
twelve million of florins during the continuance of the
war. Regarding the other powers of Europe, it may be
mentioned as a proof of the skilful diplomacy of Kaunitz
that whilst Sweden joined the allies, Spain, Holland,
and Denmark were persuaded to remain neutral ; England
alone espoused the cause of Frederic, and England then
carried with her Hanover.

Powerful as was the confederacy, enormous as was
the preponderance in men and in money against him,
Frederic retained alike his courage, his coolness, and his
nerve. Russia had declared against him, but months must
yet elapse before Russia could strike a blow. France, in
the early months of 1757, was about to join, but she had
not actually joined his enemies. Envisaging the situation
in the passionless manner which was habitual to him,
Frederic came to the conclusion that a decisive blow, struck
suddenly and effectually at the heart of his deadliest and
most persistent enemy, might yet save the situation, might
enable him, if Fortune went with him too, entirely to
master it, to dictate even terms of peace. He resolved
then, the very moment the recurring spring should render
the passes of Bohemia feasible, to pour his armies into that
country, strike down his opponents, and possibly roll up
the Austrian monarchy before her potent allies in the
present and the future could render to her the smallest aid.

With Frederic, action always followed deliberation. On
the 18th of April then, the passes having been reported
practicable, he entered Bohemia in three columns, one led
by Marshal Schwerin, from Silesia, with orders to make

straight for Prague; the second under the Prince of Bevern from the Lausitz; and the third, under the King himself, from Saxony. The three columns numbered 107,000 men, of whom 32,000 were cavalry.

To meet this invasion the Austrian army was thus posted. Serbelloni with 30,000 men occupied Königgrätz; Königsegg, under whom served London, with 16,000, Reichenberg; Ahremberg, with 24,000, Eger and Pilsen; and Browne himself, with 39,000, Budin; forming a total of 109,000 men. Unfortunately the command-in-chief did not now rest with Count Browne. Count Neipperg, then vice-president of the Aulic Council, was, though the most unsuccessful of generals, the most successful of courtiers. Anxious at once to indulge the jealous dislike which he had of Browne, and to pay his court to the Emperor, he had influence enough to have Prince Charles of Lorraine, whose incapacity was notorious, placed over the head of the general whose exploits in the previous year, though not crowned with success, had marked him out as the leader who, of all the existing Austrian generals, was the most likely to give Frederic trouble.

The Prussian invasion burst like an avalanche upon Bohemia. The corps of Königsegg, and especially the vanguard of that corps commanded by London, was the first to fall back before it. Posted with his light troops in front of Reichenberg on the right bank of the Neisse, London fell back rapidly on the main body, which then, led by Königsegg, retreated in the direction of Prague. In front of that city it linked itself to the corps of Browne, who had fallen back from Budin on the approach of Frederic. The two united corps amounted, with 6,000 men brought by Prince Charles, who now assumed command, to 61,000 men. With these the Austrian general took an advantageous

position to the east of the city. His left wing, formed of
Königsegg's corps, rested on the Ziskaberg close to the city,
his right formed at a right angle to the centre on the
little village of Sterbohol, the centre occupied the low hills
between the two points covered with intrenchments, and
forming an angle with the right, at the village of Kyge.

Meanwhile, Frederic and Schwerin marching with all
speed from their starting points, and driving the enemy
before them, had met on the morning of the 6th at the
village of Prossik, between two and three miles from
Prague. Schwerin, who arrived at the place of meeting one
day after the appointed time—his men tired after a long
night march—pleaded earnestly for twenty-four hours' rest
before making the attack. But Frederic had the strongest
reasons for immediate action. Information had reached
him on his march that a second Austrian army, led by
Count Daun, was hastening from Moravia. Frederic had
then no experience of Daun. But that general had a great
reputation, and Frederic could not fail to feel that if he
were as daring in practice as he was able in theory, he had
a great opportunity of upsetting all his plans. A single
day, even, might make all the difference between success
and defeat. Frederic then overruled Schwerin's objections
and pushed on.

The very reason which induced Frederic to hasten his
movements operated to cause Prince Charles to regard
them with equanimity. His position was so strong that
he believed it to be unassailable. If Frederic were to
attack him he would, he felt certain, dash himself to pieces
against those bristling heights, and then Daun would be on
his rear, his own victorious army on his front. What more
could any one desire ? The war would be finished at one blow.

That such would be the result was certain, if only

Prince Charles could hold his position. He had no doubts upon that point. On the other hand, Frederic was confident of success, and he was a man who very rarely made a mistake in his calculations. That day—the 6th May —was to decide whether his anticipations were better founded than those of the Austrian general.

The attack began about eleven o'clock. The Austrian right, where Browne commanded, was covered by a swamp, leading to the village of Sterbohol. The Prussians, in endeavouring to make their way across this, were exposed to a tremendous musketry fire, and after repeated attacks they were repulsed. In the first of these fell Winterfeldt, severely wounded; in the third or fourth Marshall Schwerin was killed. The death of the veteran, in his seventy-third year, added fury to the assailants, which was increased when Frederic himself came up to support them. Still the Austrians fought splendidly, Browne at their head, encouraging them, showing himself as cool and clear-headed and as energetic as when he crossed the Elbe to relieve the Saxons.

For a long time it seemed as though his splendid conduct would triumph even over the desperate resolution of Frederic. Again were the Prussians driven back. Just at the critical moment, however, a cannon-ball carried off the leg of the Austrian leader and he was carried mortally wounded into Prague. Before he quitted the field of battle he implored the generals about him to be content with the repulse, and not to follow up the enemy. His advice unhappily was not heeded. The Austrians dashed forward in pursuit of the enemy and pushed on so far that they left an opening between them and their supports, of which Frederic availed himself. After a desperate fight of five hours the Prussians carried Sterbohol!

Meanwhile the Austrian left had remained unassailed. The Prussians had concentrated all their efforts on the decisive point—and that point was Sterbohol. The carrying of Sterbohol gave them the right of the Austrian position. Wheeling them to their right they rolled up the centre already shaken by an attack of General Mannstein, and assailed the Austrian left in flank, whilst a fresh body of troops attacked it in front. Nor was this all. Whilst the fight for Sterbohol had been going on, the cavalry of the two armies had engaged. Twice driven back after desperate hand to hand encounters, the Prussian cavalry had succeeded on the third occasion in forcing the enemy to quit the field, and they now came, flushed with victory, to attack on the third side the still complete Austrian left wing. Fortunately for that wing, the fourth side, resting on Prague, was open to them. Unable to make head againt the entire Prussian army and unwilling to expose his troops to a useless slaughter, Königsegg, in the absence of Prince Charles who had been attacked by a spasm of the heart and been forced to quit the field, fell back into the city with the 32,000 men who had rallied round him. Of the remainder, 13,000, the survivors of the right wing, marched to Kollin and joined Daun; 16,000 were killed or wounded. The Prussian loss was even greater, amounting, according to the Prussian general, Warnery, who was present at the battle and contributed greatly to its success, to 18,000.

Frederic, eager to seize the fruits of his victory, at once summoned Prague to surrender. But the dying Browne, undaunted still in his last agonies, and who had insisted upon being carried to the Council which had been summoned to answer the king's proposition, exclaimed with all the energy still remaining to him: "Does the King of.

Prussia take us all for w——s? My advice is that you
should sally out and drive away Keith." Keith occupied a
position facing the Kleinseite separated by the Moldau from
the rest of the Prussian army. For such an attack to
succeed, it was necessary that it should be led by a real
soldier. After many days of deliberation and when the
Prussians had strengthened their position, Prince Charles
detached a body of 5,000 men, of whom Loudon's Croats
formed the vanguard, to carry out the plan (May 24th).
But the expedition was doomed to failure before it
started; the men were provided with no means of scaling
the walls which covered the enemy's position, and though
Loudon, as usual, forced his way to the front, he found
himself then not only unsupported, but even exposed to
the fire of the Grenadiers who should have followed him.
It was only after desperate fighting that he was able to
force his way back with the loss of a hundred men. Still
Loudon's action showed what a capable leader might do.
On the night following the failure he was detached to
drive the enemy from the vineyard they occupied on the
Laurenzenberg. Not only did he completely succeed but
he held the post, and made from it almost nightly sallies,
till the memorable day, the 18th of June, which saw
shattered all the plans of the besiegers.

Meanwhile all that bombs, grenades, and red-hot shot
could effect upon the devoted city was done by the
Prussians. Every day made Frederic more sensible of the
difficulty of the task before him. The army in Prague
consisted, including the garrison, of 45,000. The inhabitants numbered then somewhat under a hundred thousand.
To reduce these by famine was impossible; to take the
city by storm was impossible. The holding out of Prague
rendered the victory before its walls useless. Unless he

could take it, and take it quickly, its consequences would be fatal to him, for they detained him in this trap, whilst every day brought the cautious Daun nearer to his line of retreat. To reduce the city, then, Frederic considered every means justifiable. He poured red-hot shot on the palaces, the churches, the private houses, declaring that the circumstances justified his action. But it was to no purpose. The city still held out.

At last his own position became untenable. Daun, his army increasing at every march, advanced, slowly and stealthily, to within twenty-five miles of Prague. To keep him at bay, Frederic, who had by this time divined the cautious temperament of his enemy, detached the Prince of Bevern with 20,000 men to watch his movements. Daun fell back indeed before Bevern but he fell back on his reinforcements, until, when he reached Kollin, his army numbered 54,000 men. Then Bevern appealed anxiously to the king for support. Frederic responded by marching with 14,000 men to reinforce him. Then, confident to his fortune, and feeling that a victory over Daun would ensure the surrender of Prague, he attacked that general at Kollin (18th June)—but was defeated with a loss of, according to Warnery, 14,000 men and forty-three guns.

But the loss of the men and the guns was as nothing compared with the collapse of all his plans. Kollin shattered all the hopes which had inspired the invasion of Bohemia and the attack upon Prince Charles. It forced the King of Prussia to raise the siege of Prague, it let loose upon him the army beleagured in that city, and it compelled him to evacuate Bohemia. That Kollin was not made fatal to him was due solely to the extreme caution—the prudence akin to folly—of Leopold, Count Daun!

CHAPTER VI.

COMMANDER OF A CORPS.

Loudon had greatly distinguished himself at Prague. He had added to his reputation as a daring officer on the very day of Frederic's retreat by leading the vanguard of an Austrian corps which fell upon the rear of the Prussian army, and took as prisoners five officers and 379 men, besides capturing a gun. The qualities he had displayed had been of that character which win the confidence of a commander. It was felt that he was a man who could be trusted; who, if left unfettered, would dare all that might be dared, without imperilling the main army. Prince Charles, then, took the opportunity of the raising of the siege to confer upon him a small command. His little corps consisted of four companies of Austrian Grenadiers, 2,000 Croats, and 600 Hussars. With these he formed, as before, the extreme vanguard of the army, commissioned to follow the retreating Prussians.

In this comparatively independent command Loudon gave new proofs of capacity and of daring. On the 23rd he smote the Prussians as they were falling back on Welwarn, capturing a hundred and sixty prisoners and a pontoon-train. Two days later he attacked a detachment 2,000 strong near Schishitz, and after a combat of two hours duration, nearly destroyed it, taking 261 prisoners, of whom fifteen were officers. Three days later (28th of June) the army marched from Prague, Nadasdy commanding the advanced division, Loudon with his flying corps being in front of Nadasdy. Again did his daring spirit seek out opportunities. That very day he attacked a Prussian convoy between Lobositz and Welmina, cut to pieces the escort, excepting eleven officers and 146 men who surrendered, and captured a hundred laden wagons. Discovering then that the Prussians intended to halt the next day between Lobositz and Leitmeritz, Loudon sent information to head-quarters, and pushing on above Milischau took up a strong position at Kulm. Hence he designed an attempt upon Aussig, but discovering that his plan had been betrayed by a peasant, he sent a detachment to Tetschen to destroy fifteen Prussian transports lying there. Seeing that the Prussians still maintained their position at Lobositz, he sent a despatch to Prince Charles urging upon him the prompt occupation of Budin, as a manœuvre which would not only compel the enemy to retire but would place them in considerable danger.

But Prince Charles, or rather Count Daun—who, by his victory at Kollin, had now become the master-spirit of the Austrian armies,—shrank from a measure which might, they feared, bring Frederick to bay. They believed that they had him. The Reich's-army, the French, the Russians, were closing in all round him. Why, they argued, should they affront the lion already within their toils? They allowed Frederic, therefore, to remain four weeks, unmolested, at Leitmeritz. This time Loudon employed in harassing the Prussians in every possible manner. He was very successful, captured a large convoy of supplies commanded by the General Mannstein to whom Frederic attributed his defeat at Kollin; inflicted losses on the enemy at Wagenburg, at Paskopol, and at Giesshübel. The retiring armies led respectively by the King and Prince of Prussia suffered enormous losses. When the latter reached Bautzen it numbered less than three-fifths of the men whom three months before Frederic had so proudly led across the Bohemian frontier.

Meanwhile the attitude of the Reich's-army and of the French had become threatening. They were advancing rapidly on Saxony. The Duke of Saxe-Hildburghausen, who commanded the Reich's-army, had asked to be reinforced by some light troops, and Loudon was selected for the command. At the head of 4,000 Croats, two regiments of Grenadiers, and two of Hussars, he set out towards the end of July, by way of Erfurt and Gotha for Altenberg. Arrived at the seat of war he again distinguished himself in his usual manner. His most notable exploit was the surprise and defeat of the Prussian general Itzenplitz at Gottleuben (8th of August), and the destruction of the Prussian magazines in the circle of Meissen. On the 26th of this month he was promoted to the rank of Major-General. A pension of fifteen hundred gulden had, on the recommendation of Prince Charles, been bestowed upon him after the raising of the siege of Prague. The very same day on which Loudon received his promotion, Seidlitz tried to surprise the generals of the united Reichs' and French army at Gotha. Made with the skill and daring which characterised all the movements of that famous cavalry leader, the attempt would have succeeded but for Loudon, who, a silent listener at the table at which all the generals were seated, guests of the Duchess of the little principality, gathered from a remark made by the latter that treason was intended. He rose, then, unnoticed, quitted the room, and

hastened to his men, whom he had carefully posted in the
park in front of the town. He had reached them only a few
minutes when the Prussians were upon him. A little later
Seidlitz entered the town from another quarter. The
musketry fire of Loudon's troops had however given the
alarm, and before the Prussian leader could reach the
banqueting-room the birds had flown in the full belief that
the King of Prussia himself was the fowler. Loudon not
only repulsed the attacking party, but, re-entering the
town, thanked the Duchess for the remark with which she
had reminded him that he had been too long absent from
his post. The prisoners he had taken, 137 in number, he
lodged in her castle.

In spite of the gaiety manifested on the Prussian side by
such attempts as that made by Seidlitz, Frederic felt that
it would require a great effort to save himself from ruin.
The capture of Berlin by a flying corps of 15,000 men under
General Haddick (16th of October), and the march thence
of that general, after levying a contribution, to complete the
cordon of his enemies, induced him to concentrate his
army at Leipsig. As the united French and Reich's-army
pressed after him, marching carelessly and led disgracefully,
Frederic, who had carefully watched their every movement
fell upon them and totally defeated them at Rossbach
(5th of November) Loudon, though not engaged in this
battle, was sufficiently near the field to be able to rally to
himself many of the fugitives. He then, in obedience to
orders, fell back by way of Naumburg and Altenburg to
Komotau, followed all the way by a superior force under
Marshal Keith. So skilfully, however, did Loudon manœuvre,
that he baffled Keith's efforts to engage him at an advantage.
The King of Prussia speaking of this retreat in after
years, did not hesitate to compare it with that of Xenophon.

Meanwhile the Austrians had been making good way in the Lausitz and in Silesia. In the former province Nadasdy had beaten the Prussian army under Winterfeldt at Holzberg (7th of September). In Silesia the Austrian general, Janus, had beaten the Prussians under Kreutz at Landshut (24th of August); Prince Charles had taken Schweidnitz (11th of November); had defeated Bevern—who was taken prisoner—at Breslau (22nd of November); had captured that city on the 25th. Liegnitz also had been taken. Thus Silesia had been recovered for Austria.

The King of Prussia, rejoicing over his great victory at Rossbach, was now marching to reconquer that province. His approach caused a considerable flutter in the Austrian councils. Daun was all for caution, but the recent victories in Silesia had caused previous defeats and Daun's own victory at Kollin to be forgotten, and Prince Charles, who was but a poor kind of general, talked, and, for some time acted, as though Frederic were marching to his destruction. Resolving to ensure that destruction, he took up an extremely strong position, extending from Nypern almost to the Schweidnitz water, covered in front by the villages of Leuthen and Sagschütz, directly at right angles to the road by which the Prussians must advance. Too confident in his strong position, the Austrian leader left, with a very insufficient guard, a high hill called the Scheuberg, close to the village of Borne, immediately in front of his right centre. Frederic's eagle eye at once detected this mistake. He at once seized the Scheuberg, from its summit took stock of the position of the Austrian army, and formed his plan of attack. How he carried it out the next day (5th of December); how he made his famous oblique attack on the Austrian left, and after a hard fought battle rolled up their army, and gained one of the most decisive and brilliant victories the world has ever known, forms no part of the life of Loudon. Whilst Leuthen was being fought, Loudon was still engaged in guarding with an inferior force the Bohemian passes. But its results were momentous to all concerned. On the 21st Frederic recovered Breslau, a week later Liegnitz, and before the end of the year he had won back all Silesia except Schweidnitz. The Austrian army meanwhile made a most disastrous retreat into Bohemia, its losses by desertion alone being very considerable. To compensate for these misfortunes, however, it had to thank the result of Leuthen for one great benefit—the removal of Prince Charles of Lorraine from the command of the army. He was succeeded by Count Daun.

CHAPTER VII.

NOTWITHSTANDING her losses at Leuthen, the year 1758 opened full of hope for Austria. During the winter her armies had been placed on a most efficient footing : Daun had taken up a strong position at Königgrätz, and it was certain that the Russian army, to whose movements in 1757 I shall presently refer, would make its presence seriously felt in the hereditary dominions of the King of Prussia.

One of the first acts of Daun after his arrival at Königgrätz was to summon Loudon to his side. No two men could be more opposite in character than Daun and Loudon. The former, carrying caution to a point where it becomes weakness, was totally unfitted for aggressive warfare. Slow, hesitating, and suspicious, he understood nothing of the value of time in war. Even though he might gain a victory his nature would not allow him to push it home. Loudon, on the contrary, acted ever on the principle, so dear to a true soldier, that boldness is prudence. Whenever he saw a chance of success he seized it. With all this he was never rash. If Fortune extended to him her favours it was because he never presumed too

F

greatly on her kindness. He had that quick glance which showed him whether a certain end was attainable. In that case he used every effort and employed every resource to gain it. But he never dashed himself against the impossible. He was a careful, wary, daring soldier, always on the look out, always keeping his troops well in hand, always ready for attack or defence.

It was probably less even on account of the reputation which Loudon had gained during 1757 than of the conviction which Daun, not yet jealous of his fame, could not but feel that he would supply qualities in which he himself was wanting that the summons was sent to Loudon to join the main Austrian army at Königgrätz.

Hardly had Loudon joined when he was detached at the head of a *corps d'armée* to cover the march of General Buccow with a convoy of provisions and military stores for the fortress of Schweidnitz then besieged by the Prussians. The Prussian general, Fouquet, however, with an army at Braunau, barred the entrance into Silesia. Loudon was not strong enough to attack Fouquet, but he used every means in his power to induce him to break up from his position. On the 8th of April he smote Le Noble, a freelance in the Prussian service, at Hallstadt, taking forty-six prisoners; on the 12th he not only repulsed an attack made upon his position, but drove the enemy with great loss from the intrenchments behind which they had posted themselves at Dietersbach. He could not, however, penetrate into Silesia. Schweidnitz, in consequence, surrendered to the King of Prussia on the 16th of April.

Once more possessor of Silesia Frederic resolved to substitute another means of striking at the heart of the Austrian monarchy for that which had been baffled at Prague and Kollin. He would not touch Bohemia, carefully guarded by Daun, but risking the exposing of his flank to that too cautious general, would endeavour to penetrate to Vienna by way of Moravia. As soon, then, as he had seen to the necessities of Schweidnitz he ordered Keith and Fouquet to march on Neisse whilst he him-self directed his steps with all speed in the direction of Olmütz. Loudon was the first of the Austrian leaders to penetrate this plan. He sent timely intimation to Daun, who, summoning his trusted lieutenant to com-mand the leading corps of his army, broke up his camp at Königgrätz and marched, by way of Skalitz and Chotzen to Leutomischl. On the same day, the 5th of May, the van of the army under Loudon was at Hohenstadt, about twenty-three miles from Olmütz.

The position taken up by Loudon gave him so many opportunities of annoying the Prussian army, and of cutting off its communications, that Frederic, still on his march to Olmütz, resolved before undertaking the siege of that place to drive him from it. On the 22nd of May he moved against him with ten battalions of infantry, two regiments of hussars, and fifteen squadrons of dragoons. But Loudon, whose troops numbered considerably fewer, had no inten-tion to accept a battle in the open. As the king advanced, then, he fell back upon a position he had selected in the hilly regions behind Könitz. Here he was unassailable. This Frederic recognised on reconnoitring the position, so he fell back again, and marched to Olmütz, the siege of which he began on the 27th of May. During the calendar month which followed, whilst Frederic was pressing the operations before Olmütz, Loudon employed day and night in harassing the Prussian troops, in cutting off their supplies, falling upon their foraging parties. He be-came the terror of the Prussian outposts. No movement

escaped his glance, no detachment could leave the camp
without the certainty that it would be assailed. Daun had
during this period moved with the main army to Predlitz,
within supporting distance of his ever-active lieutenant.

The defence, meanwhile, was exhausting all the resources
of Frederic. He had already fired 58,000 cannon balls and
6,000 shells at the fortress, and munitions of war began to
fail him. Food, too, began to run short, and the activity
of Loudon prevented him from living, as he had lived in
previous campaigns, on the country occupied by his armies.
His situation before Olmütz was beginning to bear a strong
resemblance to the situation before Prague of the preceding
year. Now as then a great fortress defied him; now as
then a powerful army was on his flank threatening his
communications. There was just one point of difference,
and that point was not in his favour. In 1757 there was
no active commander in the field ready to dare all that
should be dared. No long time elapsed before this point
of difference made itself manifest.

Towards the middle of June Frederic was reduced to such
extremities that he sent pressing instructions to Silesia to
prepare at Troppau a convoy of four thousand wagons;
to load them there with money, meal, uniforms, munitions,
and every sort of necessaries, and to despatch them with all
speed, under a proper escort, to his camp. The officer
indicated to command the escort, which consisted of 9,000
men, was Colonel Mosel, a resolute and capable officer.
He set out from Troppau on the 25th of June.

Daun had received timely intimation of the intended
despatch of this convoy, and had resolved to employ his
most trusted lieutenant to intercept and to destroy it. He
accordingly sent for Loudon, placed under his immediate
orders 8,000 men, and directed him to proceed to a good

position on the Hof road, whilst General Sziskowitz should proceed in the direction of Alt-Liebe, to watch the convoy and to support and lend a hand to London. As soon as the two detachments had set out Daun himself began a series of manœuvres and evolutions, as though he would attack Frederic, which forced the latter to keep his army in hand.

On the 27th, London, who had set out the previous evening, reached Sternberg, and took up a position on the heights there, whence he could observe movements alike from the besieging camp and of the convoy. He wrote thence the same evening to Daun, informing him of his intention to march the following day to Giebau, a village on the road to be traversed by the convoy, and requested that orders might be sent to General St. Ignon, who was at Beerau, and to Sziskowitz, to be ready to fall on the enemy the moment he should attack them. Daun transmitted orders accordingly.

The next day London marched from Sternberg, and occupied the heights above Giebau, commanding the defile between Bautsch and Alt-Liebe, which the convoy would have to traverse. He posted his Hungarians and Croats in the woods, the cavalry in the plain.

He had just completed his dispositions when the head of the convoy appeared in sight. London had no news of St. Ignon or of Sziskowitz, but he could not wait for them, but launched his troops at the enemy. A most desperate battle then ensued. The Prussians fought with the greatest courage; they made barricades of their wagons—and when London was repulsed they assumed the offensive. Five times was the attack renewed, five times was it repelled. No St. Ignon, no Sziskowitz, came up to support the gallant assailant. At the end of five hours London, having suffered considerable loss (361 officers and men), was compelled to fall back on Bären. Just as he was falling back information reached him that Sziskowitz had just arrived at Altstadt, the position indicated to him.

But if the Austrian attack was repulsed the injury already inflicted on the Prussians was very severe. At the first shot, the peasants driving the wagons had become terrified. Along that line of 4,000 carts the greatest confusion then set in. Many unharnessed the horses and mounting them galloped away ; others tried to make their way back to Troppau. The convoy was too much engaged in resisting the Austrians to pay sufficient attention to the drivers.

Night had set in when the attack ceased. The Prussians employed the earlier hours of darkness in restoring order in the convoy, in endeavouring—for the most part a vain endeavour—to bring back the drivers, and in despatching messages to the besieging army. Loudon employed his time in effecting a junction with Sziskowitz, at Alt-Liebe, and in disposing his troops for a renewed attack on the morrow, to be made by Loudon from the right, by Sziskowitz from the left of the road.

But before the morrow came, the Prussian general Ziethen entered Colonel Mosel's camp at the head of 5,000 men. His presence effected wonders. He sent out his cavalry in search of the fugitives. Many of them were brought back, but so great was the confusion that the whole of the night, of the next day, and of the night following were needed to restore order.

At length on the morning of the 30th of June, the convoy once again moved forward. Its escort, consisting now of 14,000 men, was a little army, and was commanded by one of the most renowned generals of Prussia. Loudon, whose troops united with those of Sziskowitz numbered only 15,000, allowed the wagons to be dragged slowly on until they had begun to emerge from the defile of Domstädtl. But when 120 of them escorted by 4,000 men had left that defile behind them, the two Austrian generals, actuated by one impulse, let loose their men.

Then was the battle of the 28th renewed. Ziethen endeavoured, as had been done on that day, to form a barricade with the wagons, behind which the infantry might intrench themselves whilst the cavalry charged the invaders. But assailed as he was now on three sides he found the means quite insufficient to ward off the attack. For a moment, indeed, the splendid Prussian cavalry obtained some slight advantage, but increasing hostile numbers on the decisive point forced even them to retire. A charge of the Austrian infantry completed the attack which had been so well begun. The barricade was stormed, its defenders were scattered, the majority of them fled through the defile. Many were killed and wounded; half as many were taken prisoners. Ziethen himself, cut off from the defile, fled with the bulk of the cavalry to Troppau. The fight had been desperate but the victory was decisive.

Of the 4,000 wagons which started from Troppau, 200 reached the King of Prussia's camp; more than 1,000 were burnt for want of horses to drag them; 1,200 were captured by the Austrians; the remainder were destroyed by the Prussians. The fierce nature of the conflict may be gathered from the fact that the Prussians lost 2,500 in killed and wounded, more than 1,500 prisoners, and 14 guns. The Austrians' loss amounted to 1,000 killed and wounded.

But the real result of Loudon's splendid attack was, not the destruction of the convoy, not the loss inflicted on the

enemy, these were mere details :—it was the raising of the
siege of Olmütz. That event took place the day following
the combat. A little more than three weeks later, 15th of
July, Loudon was promoted to the rank of Field-Marshal
Lieutenant.

The raising of the siege of Olmütz gave Count Daun an
opportunity. His position on the right flank of the
retiring army, with his left wing stretching towards the
Silesian frontier, made him in reality far closer to
Frederic's line of retreat on that province than was
Frederic himself. Hence he believed that Frederic would
either fall back on the Lausitz, or, with a view to choose
his own line, would in the first instance attack him.
Frederic, who had thoroughly divined Daun's character,
encouraged this idea, induced Daun, under the belief that
he would be attacked, to strengthen his position and call
in his wings and his flying parties, and then, by a magic
stroke of genius, permissible only when dealing with a man
endowed with bastard prudence, but in that case most
commendable, wheeling to the left and exposing his flank,
marched under his very nose through Bohemia, by way of
Zwittau and Leutomischl. He was safe from a flank attack
before Daun had had time to recover from his surprise.

Nor even then did Daun, still over-cautious, move himself. He sent, however, his most trusted generals, London,
Buccow, Sziskowitz, St. Ignon, Janus, and Lanius, to
follow up his redoubtable foe, to harass his retreat, fall on
his foraging parties, and cut off his supplies. Well, indeed,
was he served. The Austrian leaders made the retreat of
Frederic almost as disastrous as had been that of Prince
Charles after Leuthen. They attacked his rear-guard on
every possible occasion, occupied vantage-posts by which
he must march, fell on his baggage, and if they inflicted

upon him no important defeat, yet caused the loss to him of a large number of men, twice plundered his wagons, twice forced him to abandon guns, and compelled him more than once to change his route.

In these operations Loudon's daring was specially conspicuous. So sensible was the king of his dangerous activity, that he made a serious attempt to crush him. Frederic was at Königgrätz, Daun behind him at a respectful distance, when Loudon deemed the moment opportune to alarm the king about his communications with Glatz. He thrust his corps, then, in the country between that country and the Prussian camp, and sending out parties of Croats annoyed them on three sides. He himself took up a position at Opotschno. On the morning of the 17th, Frederic himself marched against this place, when Loudon was still lying there, on the one side, whilst he sent orders to Fouquet to attack him on the other. Loudon's Croats were speedily driven in by Fouquet, but once within the place they re-formed and occupied the attention of the enemy, whilst Loudon, who had only 4,500 men with him, fell back through the forest to Sadol. He posted his Hungarian infantry and some guns here and kept Frederic at bay till his Croats rejoined him. He then marched unmolested on Giesshübel.

Frederic's position in Bohemia was becoming by this time very difficult. Though his own position at Königgrätz was strong, yet Daun was in an unassailable position—at Chlum close to him; the Austrian party-leaders were all about him, and, meanwhile, the Russian army was slowly advancing into his hereditary dominions. The situation was not unlike the situation of the preceding year, when after Prague and Kollin he had been disturbed by the advance of the Reich's army and the French. This time, indeed, he had suffered no Kollin, but the successful defence of Olmütz had destroyed the plan of the campaign, his retreat through Bohemia had been disastrous, and he could no longer remain in that kingdom to watch the advance of another enemy from the north. If he could only inflict upon that enemy a Rossbach blow—then all must go well. He would at least attempt it.

It was, indeed, the advance of the Russians into Branden·burg that induced Frederic, in the beginning of August, to quit Bohemia. In 1757 the Russians, led by Aprazin, had invaded East Prussia, had defeated the Prussian army at Gross-Jägersdorf (30th of August). The hereditary dominions of the king were actually in the clutch of the Russian general, when, hearing of the illness of the Czarina, and knowing that her death would produce a complete change of politics with regard to Prussia, he had abandoned his position and his conquests and returned home. The Czarina, however, had recovered, had disgraced Aprazin, and nominated Fermor to succeed him. Fermor had entered Brandenburg in July of the following year, and it was the information that he was threatening Berlin which decided Frederic to quit Bohemia and give him such a welcome as would make him repent his inroad.

Frederic carried out this design with his habitual skill and daring. Evacuating Bohemia, he made over the command of his Silesian army to his cousin, the Margrave Charles, under whom served Fouquet, and set out (11th of August), with fourteen battalions and thirty-eight squadrons to march by way of Liegnitz to Frankfort on the Oder.

Another opportunity was thus offered to Daun. He had some 60,000 men under his orders on the Bohemian frontier. The Prussians, divided into two corps, one under Prince Charles to defend Silesia, the other under Marshal Keith in the Lausitz, numbered somewhat over 40,000. They had no Frederic at their head to neutralize the superiority of the enemy. The reader can well imagine how a great general, flushed as was Daun with his practical success up to that moment, would have used the golden moments which Frederic's absence had placed at the Austrian general's disposal.

To concentrate the greatest number of troops on the decisive point is the whole art of war. The truth of this action would appear to have glimmered through the brain of Daun when, on learning the departure of Frederic, he marched into the Lausitz, with the intention, in conjunction with the Reich's army, of recovering Saxony. But all at once he deviated from the great principle. Loudon, who had as usual preceded the main army, received suddenly instructions to march northwards and to endeavour to effect a junction with the Russians.

Marching with all speed across Saxony by way of Bautzen, Görlitz, and Lauban, Loudon reached Muska on the 23rd of August. On the following day he captured Peiz—a fortress, small indeed in size, but important for the numerous munitions of war it contained. Leaving 500 men to guard that place he pressed on, the next day, towards Brandenburg. It was on that very day, 25th of August, that Frederic fought a hardly-contested battle with the Russians at Zorndorf, a battle which was terminated only by night, was in itself indecisive, but which, on the third day, 27th of August, brought to the king, by his daring persistence in remaining on the ground, all the fruits of a victory.

Loudon first heard of this result on the 3rd of September. It ruined the project of union with the Russians. He himself, approaching the homelands of Brandenburg, had been regarded by Frederic as a formidable enemy, and his old antagonist, Ziethen, had been sent to bar the way to the province.* The victory of Zorndorf decided his movements, and those of his general-in-chief. On the 5th he received a despatch from Daun directing him to interpose his corps between the main Austrian army and that of Frederic, then marching on Saxony, to allow the former to fall back on the Lausitz, and possibly on Bohemia. The apparition of Frederic had driven to the winds all Daun's feeble schemes of offensive warfare.

The conduct of Loudon in carrying out his orders is especially worthy of study.

The position of the three armies was as follows: Daun was with the main Austrian army marching on Meissen; Frederic was striding towards that point from the Oder; Loudon, with a small *corps-d'armée*, was between the two in the Prussian circle of Frankfort on the Oder. His orders were to cover Daun's army, to give his commander-in-chief time to take up a position near his communications, and to inflict on the king as much damage as possible.

As Daun fell hurriedly back towards the Lausitz, and Frederic speeded towards Dresden, Loudon, watching eagerly the movements of the latter, fell back as he advanced by way of Königsbrück and Otterndorf to Radeberg. In this place he posted his left wing, having his right at Seifersdorf, a position so harassing to Frederic that he detached (10th of September) General Putkammer to keep him in check whilst he himself should push after Daun. But Loudon had no intention of being blockaded. He waited indeed till he knew that Daun had taken up a strong position at Stolpen commanding the Silesian road and barring the king's entrance by the direct road into that province. Keeping then 8,000 men in Radeberg, Loudon moved with the remainder to the country about the Lauscha and Langenbrück, covering Bautzen, and making it very difficult for Frederic to gain by a circuitous route the position to which Daun's army barred the natural way.

For a month Loudon baffled the designs of the king. Could Frederic get to Bautzen he cared not for Daun's position at Stolpen. And it was Loudon who prevented him from getting to Bautzen. Loudon then must be forced to give way.

To accomplish this object, then, Frederic, on the 16th, despatched General Retzow, by way of Willensdorf, against Loudon's left flank, the Prince of Bevern against his right, whilst he himself, crossing the Fischbach, should assail him in the rear. But Loudon, pitted now for the first time in independent command against Frederic, proved himself no unworthy opponent of that great general. If his prudence was daring, it was that daring which strikes only when to strike brings success within the range of possibility, and which reserves its force for a future effort when to strike would ensure decisive victory. Keeping a careful look-out Loudon penetrated the designs of the king, and feeling that he was not strong enough to risk an encounter, resolved to fall back, retaining as he did so the command of the road which Frederic sought to wrench from him. His dispositions for this purpose were most masterly. Posting his artillery and four regiments of infantry on the heights of Arnsdorf, he covered his right flank with his dragoons, his left with his hussars. A wood, which the road from Dresden to Fischbach traversed beyond that town, he occupied with his Croats, supported by two regiments of dragoons. He had taken up these positions when the Prussians came in sight. Making an attack, which Loudon soon recognised to be a false attack, on his right wing, they suddenly threw themselves on the wood before Fischbach. The Croats, however, successfully resisted them until Loudon had seen his baggage and *matériel* well to the rear. He then drew them back on to his main body and displayed his army, its wings well covered, in the most splendid order, well in hand, ready for offensive or defensive attack. As the Prussians still pushed forward, Loudon retired slowly, repulsing every attack, till he reached a position on the right front of Daun's army, known as the Kapellenberg. Here he halted, still covering Bautzen, and having had the glory of baffling Frederic in their first encounter.

From this vantage ground, which faced the Prussian camp, Loudon noted about a week later certain symptoms of a movement on the part of the king. Confident that the aim of all Frederic's movements was to force an entrance into Silesia, Loudon divined that he was about to attempt a turning movement by way of Bischofswerda. On the night of the 25th then, quitting very silently his camp on the Kapellenberg, leaving the sentries at their posts, Loudon marched to that town and occupied the heights of Giessmandorf in front of it. He had not only divined correctly but he had baffled the vigilance of the Prussians. The next morning, their vanguard, led by Retzow, began to ascend in careless order the heights on which Loudon's corps rested. Rudely were they surprised at the welcome given them by that ever vigilant leader. Thrice did they come to the attack, but each time were they driven back with increasing loss. At last they gave up the enterprise. Frederic contented himself with occupying Ramenau and Arnsdorf.

But Frederic did not like to be baffled. The very next day he and the Prince of Würtemberg reconnoitred

London's position. He felt that he must have it; that it was necessary to him; and that at any cost he must carry it. He resolved then to assail him with as little delay as possible, as at Fischbach, on three sides. Loudon was not in a position with his small force to resist the attack of the whole Prussian army. Could he have relied upon Daun to attack the king in flank whilst the king assailed him in front he would have maintained himself. But this was the very last manœuvre, he knew well, to which his cautious commander-in-chief would commit himself. Certain then that he would be attacked on the 29th, he evacuated the heights on the early morning of that day and fell back on Nieder-Potzka, where he still formed the right of Daun's army.

For nearly four weeks had Loudon barred the way to Bautzen; for nearly four weeks had he baffled the endeavours of Frederic to reach Silesia. But the retreat from the heights of Giessmansdorf had left the way open, and Frederic hastened to pour his troops along it. On the 30th Retzow occupied Bautzen. He was followed a few days later by Frederic. As the entrance of the Prussian army into the Lausitz and Silesia was now assured, Daun, anxious for his communications with Zittau, broke up his camp at Stolpen and marching cautiously into the Lausitz took up a position on the wooded heights overlooking the little village of Hochkirch. Drawing here to himself Loudon, who had as usual covered the march of the main army, and had had daily skirmishes with the Prussians, he waited, whilst strengthening his position, the approach of Frederic.

CHAPTER VIII.

DAUN, not satisfied with occupying Hochkirch, and possibly recollecting the lesson taught at Leuthen, had seized Stromberg—a high and completely detached hill which commanded the country all round—and placed on it his right wing, whilst in the villages and hamlets immediately in front of these heights he had posted his Croats and other light troops. Still further to secure the position he had caused the little village of Glossen, behind the Löbau rivulet, to be occupied by four companies of grenadiers.

His army was thus ordered. Generals Sziskowitz and Brune occupied the summit of Stromberg with eight battalions of grenadiers. At its foot, facing the village of Hochkirch, were twelve battalions of infantry and all the cavalry of the right wing. Immediately to the left of these twelve battalions, and behind the village of Sornzig, was placed a battery of heavy guns supported by a battalion of grenadiers and two regiments of infantry. Daun himself commanded on the woody heights above Hochkirch, and Loudon the vanguard of the army.

Daun had already occupied and partially strengthened

this commanding position, when on the morning of the
15th of October Frederic came in sight of it. A short examination of it convinced him that the army which held
Stromberg had the command of the country around, and he
found grievous fault with Retzow, who commanded his
advance, for not having seized that hill before the Austrians had occupied it in force. It was too late then to
think of driving them from it. Too proud, however, to turn
his back upon the Austrians, Frederic, in a spirit of
bravado, and in spite of the remonstrances of some of his
most trusted officers, encamped about the village of Hochkirch within cannon-shot of the enemy. Here he en-
trenched himself, and occupied the little hilly eminences
in front of it with fifteen pieces of cannon. His right he
placed on a hillock, covered with brushwood, to the right
of the village ; his left extended beyond Rodewitz. This
place Frederic made his head-quarters. A little brook with
very steep banks covered his front. A portion of his army,
however, encamped on the other side of this brook in order
to maintain touch with Retzow's corps which occupied an
intrenched camp at Weissenberg on the extreme left.

In taking up a position under the very nose of an
enemy who outnumbered him in the proportion of three to
one, Frederic counted on the well known caution of his
adversary. That Daun—the general who was wont to
cover even the steepest hills with intrenchments, who had
never brought himself to the point of risking an attack—
that Daun should assail him—Frederic—was impossible !
It could not be ! Had Daun been alone with subordinates
of his own cautious character the argument might have
been good. But Frederic had committed the mistake of
forgetting that there were other generals besides Daun
with the Austrian army, and that one of these, the principal

G

indeed of them, for he was second in command, was the active, enterprising, quick-visioned Loudon !

This general held with his corps the country about Rachlau ; his advanced posts almost within musket-shot of the Prussians, and separated from them only by a ditch. Loudon contrived that every day between these advanced posts there should be continual skirmishes, begun by the Austrians. At last these came to be regarded as a matter of course. Daun meanwhile pursued his old system of throwing up intrenchments, thus more and more fixing Frederic in the conviction that he was perfectly safe from assault from that quarter.

Circumstances, however, were rapidly undermining the cautious scruples of the Austrian commander-in-chief. It happened that one day Loudon came upon a peasant trudging towards the Prussian camp with a basket of eggs on his arm. To an offer made to him by Loudon to buy the eggs the peasant replied that they were bespoken. The demeanour of the man exciting suspicions, Loudon had him brought into his camp, then, opening the eggs, he found that they were merely shells, inside of which were papers giving accurate intimation of Daun's secret intentions written by some one closely attached to his person.

It happened that, the very same day, Daun, suddenly entering his tent, had discovered his private secretary writing a paper, which, on observing the presence of his general, he tried to conceal. Daun, snatching it from him, read in it, to his astonishment, a complete description of his intended movements. Loudon's discovery came to confirm an idea which had begun to form itself in the mind of Daun that it might be possible to "hoist the engineer with his own petard." He therefore promised the private secretary his life on the condition that he should continue the treasonable correspondence, but should supply only such information as should be given him by himself. The wretched man consented. From that time forth Frederic received daily assurances that Daun was more than ever resolved not to attack him.

At that very time, yielding to the strong arguments of Loudon and of Lacy, Daun was making his preparations for a sudden burst upon the camp of his too confident enemy. He had fixed five o'clock on the morning of the 14th of October for the execution of his project, which was to assail the Prussian army simultaneously on four points. Whilst Daun himself, leading three columns through the forest of Hochkirch and posting himself between the villages of Waischke and Sornzig, should fall upon the Prussian right, Loudon, strengthened by four battalions and fifteen squadrons, and joined during the night by nearly all the remaining cavalry of the left wing, should advance beyond Soritz to Steindörfl and take the Prussian army in rear. The positions held the previous day by the Austrians were still to be occupied.

This programme was carried out with the greatest order and precision. Whilst the sentries paced their rounds, the watch-fires burned, and the axes of the wood-cutters re-sounded in the Austrian camp, the several Austrian columns marched silently and quietly, unmarked by the Prussians, to take up the positions selected by their leaders.

It was yet dark when the Austrians reached the ground. Suddenly the village clock of Hochkirch struck five. As soon as the last stroke had sounded, the signal, a musketry volley from the Austrian advanced posts near Rachlau, was given. As both armies were by this time accustomed to the daily and nightly skirmishes which took place about that village, the signal, whilst it set in motion the Austrian army, made no impression upon the Prussians. But suddenly the Austrians under Daun dashed upon the outlying pickets, and overpowering them, fell upon the Prussian camp. Then it was that Frederic and his troops took the alarm. Turning out, half dressed, without order, each man snatching his weapon and rushing to the front, the Prussian soldiers showed themselves that morning worthy of their renown. If they could not win the day, they were resolved that the Austrians should pay dearly for victory. The surprise, the disorder, the preponderance of the enemy, made defence difficult. After the first musket shots had been fired it became a hand to hand encounter, and here the circumstances I have enumerated gave all the advantage to the Austrians.

Loudon, meanwhile, pressed on with great vigour over the hills about Steindörfl. His Croats, stealing up behind Hochkirch, set fire to the village, and the flames threw a ghastly and lurid light over the terrible scene. The Prussians, though in the greatest disorder, fought with all their old courage; some regiments even tried to assume the defensive. The cuirassier regiment, von Schönaich, especially distinguished itself—charging and driving back a whole line of Austrian infantry. But the famous Hungarian horse did not yield even to them in prowess. The Löwenstein dragoons in two successive charges nearly annihilated the king's guard. It may be said, indeed, that on this bloody day all the nationalities distinguished themselves. Even the Croats, unaccustomed to regular manœuvring, vied with other regiments of the attacking army in their steady valour.

But though both sides fought well, the palm of combined courage and conduct is due, by the admission even of the Austrians, to the battalion commanded by the Prussian

Major, von Lange. In the description I gave of the disposition taken up by Frederic about Hochkirch, I stated that he had occupied the little eminence in front of that village with a battery of fifteen guns. These guns were supported by the Prussian battalion just mentioned. Attacked on three sides by an overwhelming number of Austrians, von Lange was forced after very hard fighting to give way. Well acquainted with the ground, he succeeded by his coolness and skill in withdrawing his men into the churchyard, which was surrounded by a high wall, and from behind this he renewed the contest. In vain did the best troops in the Austrian army—the Grenadiers—attempt to storm the position; they were driven back with great loss. At last the time arrived when the ammunition of the defenders was exhausted; when von Lange himself was sinking from the exhaustion caused by eleven wounds, and when six Austrian regiments were advancing to the storm. "My children," said von Lange to the survivors, "we must dash through them." And they did dash through, though in that splendid struggle they lost their gallant leader.

Von Lange's defence had given to the Prussian king the time so much needed to bring his army into something like order. He had scarcely, however, succeeded in doing this, when his own so hardly-won fifteen-gun battery was turned against him. Still, in this great emergency the vision of Frederic was as clear, and his spirit as resolute, as on the peaceful parade-ground. He had done all that man could do to restore the battle. Noting at this conjuncture how Loudon was pressing his right rear, he despatched three regiments to stay his progress. In vain, however; the head of Prince Charles of Brunswick was carried off by a cannon-ball, and the Prussians, hard pressed, fell back in their turn.

The circle was now closing in around them. The burning
village, which gave its name to the battle, was already in
possession of the Austrians, when Marshal Keith, rallying
round him all the regiments he could collect, made a
desperate effort to recover it. At first he succeeded ; but
the Austrians coming up again, drove him out. In the
desperate fight Keith was killed ; and the Prussians soon
after renounced the combat at this point. An advance of
five companies of horse-grenadiers, under Lacy, to the
support of Loudon, forced the Prussians at last to loose
their grip on the hills about Waditz, and threatened their
line of retreat. A simultaneous forward movement of the
Austrian right under Buccow and Ahrenberg, left indeed
but one way of escape open to the Prussians, and that
was through the defile of Drehsa.

To conduct a beaten army through a narrow pass in a
hilly country in the presence of a victorious enemy is a
feat to task all the coolness, all the skill, of a great
commander. Yet this was the difficulty which Frederic
now had to face. The Austrians were pressing him in
front, and were gradually overlapping him on both flanks.
He at once took a great resolution. Recognising that the
battle was lost, he would save all that yet remained to him
of his army. He carried out this resolve with a coolness
and a skill worthy to be studied. Covering his movements
with the fire of the guns still in his possession, and by the
cavalry of Ziethen and Seidlitz, 9,000 strong, he formed
his infantry in two lines, and led them to the entrance of
the defile. Through this he sent his cavalry first, then his
guns, and last of all, his infantry ; his troops, as they
reached the opposite side, forming up to defend those who
followed. This plan he carried out so admirably that
though the Austrian cavalry followed him up close, they

could effect nothing against him. Frederic fell back, then, by Klein-Bautzen, and took up a new position at Doberschütz.

In this memorable battle the Prussians lost between 8,000 and 9,000 in killed and wounded—of these 2,998 were buried by the Austrians the next day—twenty-eight pairs of colours, two standards, 101 guns, their camp, their baggage, and munitions of war. The victors lost 1,432 killed and 6,525 wounded, or a total of 7,937.

Victories are of two kinds, decisive and undecisive. The battle of Hochkirch would have belonged to the former category, if, placing a little more faith in the result of a surprise with an army three times greater than that of his enemy, Daun had made a point of sending a strong division on Dehsa at the moment he assailed Hochkirch. Had he done so Hochkirch would have ended the war. As it was, he left, possibly out of over-caution, one loophole for his adversary, and of that his adversary availed himself to assume a new position—proportionally the worse only by the loss of his guns and munitions of war. Consequently Hochkirch, though a victory on the spot on which it had been fought, has no claim whatever to be classed amongst decisive battles.

It was, indeed, thanks to the extreme caution of the Austrian commander, a victory which decided nothing. It did not even injure the prestige of Frederic. The daring with which he had affronted the attack, and the conduct by which he had deprived that which ought to have been an annihilating victory of all its annihilating consequences, increased the confidence and affection of his troops. He lost nothing but his camp and his guns, for in men the enemy were nearly as much weakened as he was.

To gain a victory is one thing: but a victory gained

represents but useless loss of life unless it be followed up. No battle manifested this truth more clearly than did Hochkirch. Daun, master of the field, instead of following up his enemy and giving him no peace, of attempting even to cut off the division of Retzow, which had taken no part in the battle, withdrew that same evening to the heights he had occupied before the battle, in order that his men, he says, might have a good rest under blankets after the fatigue of the day. But he rested there for six days, and only on the seventh marched very stealthily to take up a new position between Belgern and Jenkowitz, facing Frederic at Doberschütz.

Daun rested in this camp till the 24th of the month, barring the road into Silesia, where one of his generals, Harsch, was engaged in besieging the strong fortress of Neisse. Frederic had it very much at heart to save Neisse, but to reach Görlitz, the possession of which would secure his entrance into Silesia, he must give his flank to the superior army of Daun. Were Daun to have an inkling of his designs this would be too great a risk. Frederic therefore had recourse to stratagem. He sent all his wounded, all his baggage, even his tents, into the lower Lausitz, and made as though he would follow himself. Then suddenly on the night of the 24-25th, he marched his lightly equipped army to Görlitz: Loudon was at the time confined to his tent by very severe sickness, and his place in the front of the army was ill-supplied, for the deed was done before information reached Daun.

For the moment Daun sent only some light troops to follow Frederic, but two days later, he gave Loudon, who had then recovered, the command of some 25,000 men with strict orders to follow Frederic with all his energy. The task was not very difficult, for Frederic had halted two days at Görlitz. Loudon managed then to take up a position at Liebstein, threatening the Prussian rear and left, whilst Frederic was still halted. On the 29th, Frederic resumed his march and crossed the river Neisse. But the moment Prince Henry, who commanded the Prussian rear-guard, consisting of twelve battalions of infantry and Ziethen's hussars, evacuated Görlitz, Loudon dashed through the town—his cavalry in front, the infantry following, and pursued him. Noticing that he had halted in the narrow pass close to the village of Ober Schönbrunn he made his Croats drag some light field-pieces to the summit of the hill commanding it, and whilst these opened on the Prussians, he drove the enemy from the village. In vain did the latter set fire to Ober Schönbrunn and to Pfaffen-dorf to keep their pursuer in check. He followed them up vigorously, and inflicted on them a loss of 500 men. His own amounted to 300.

As the Prussian army still advanced, Loudon was ever on their track. On the 1st of November, at the passage of the Queiss, he inflicted on the Prussian rear-guard, commanded on that day by the King in person, a loss of a hundred men without a single casualty on his own side; on the 2nd he captured seventy prisoners and some baggage wagons, at Löwenberg. The same evening he caught up the enemy's rear-guard at the village of Pilgramsdorf, not far from Goldberg, and captured 400 horses, fifteen pontoons, and 120 men, amongst them Colonel Zastrow. He continued to follow up the Prussian army as far as the town of Jauer, making, to use the very words of Frederic, "the king's whole march a continued fight."

From Jauer, Loudon marched to the vicinity of Zittau, and having secured the magazines in that town, went to take up his winter quarters on the Bohemian frontier.

Daun, meanwhile, had marched into Saxony, and Frederic, after relieving Neisse, had followed him thither.

During the winter, honours and rewards awaited Loudon. In November he received the Grand Cross of the order of Maria Theresa; and when he visited Vienna in February, the Empress-Queen bestowed upon him the title of Baron (Freiherr) of the Austrian Grand Duchy and of the Holy Roman Empire, and the grant of the estate of Klein-Betschwar in Hungary. In a private audience, Maria Theresa expressed her high appreciation of, and gratitude for, the services he had rendered.

CHAPTER IX.

THE campaign of 1758, though illustrated by the defeat of Frederic at Hochkirch, had been, as far as results were concerned, a failure for Austria. At its close, Frederic still retained Saxony and Silesia. The two most powerful allies of Austria, France and Russia, had made their power but little felt, and Frederic had been more than a match for Daun. But in the year, upon the record of which I am entering, his difficulties were to increase.

During the winter Loudon had renewed a proposition he had formerly made, that two battalions of grenadiers should be permanently attached to the Croats. These latter, he said, though animated by incontestable courage, were not accustomed to make an attack in close order; they had been taught to spread themselves out as skirmishers, and as such they were invaluable; but, if supported by a solid body of some 1,800 grenadiers their value would be quadrupled. The request was granted, and the men, who volunteered from other regiments, were incorporated in March. On the 27th of the same month, Loudon quitted Vienna to take the command of a separate command—though subject generally to Daun— at Trautenau.

The plan of the campaign, concerted between the courts of Vienna, Versailles, St. Petersburg, and Stockholm, was as follows : whilst Daun, at the head of 70,000 men, should occupy very firmly the hilly ranges bordering Silesia, he was to detach a corp of 20,000 to effect a junction with the Reich's-army at Bamberg on the one side, whilst the Duke de Broglie, firmly posted at Frankfort-on-the-Main, should stretch a hand to it on the other. In this manner, an allied army, 330,000 strong, would face Frederic. Meanwhile, to take him in reverse, a Russian army, 70,000 strong, was to march on Frankfort on the Oder, to be joined there by 30,000 Austrians under Loudon and Haddik, and whilst this army should attack the hereditary dominions of the King of Prussia, a corps of 14,000 Swedes should take possession of Stettin. It was a plan, rightly called colossal, which, if carried out with fair success, ought to prove decisive of the war.

In carrying out a plan, the details of which depend upon the complete sympathy and the punctuality of other nations much valuable time is often lost. It was, in a great measure, in consequence of this dependence, that the spring of 1759 was illustrated by no great military event. Daun's army occupied a strong position between Schurz and Jaromierz, facing Frederic, whilst Loudon, whose army corps consisted of ten battalions of regular infantry, eight companies of grenadiers, the two volunteer battalions of grenadiers previously referred to, 5,700 Croats and twenty squadrons of cavalry, or, with artillery, about 20,000 men, lay about Trautenau. A reconnaissance made by Loudon with three battalions of infantry and 500 cavalry, in the direction of Liebau, on 21st of May, had shown the king to be in force in that direction.

Whilst the Austrians were thus waiting quietly the

development of the plans agreed upon with their allies, the Russian army led by Prince Soltikoff, had been gradually assembled at Posen. On the 24th of June, Loudon broke up his camp at Trautenau, and moved on Hennersdorf, Hochstadt, and Jablunzen. On the 4th of July he was marching on Friedland (in Silesia) when orders reached him to speed as fast as possible to the front and reconnoitre the Prussian position. He at once turned back, hastened with his cavalry to Marklissa, and detaching thence General Caramelli towards Lauban and Löwenberg took himself the road by way of Friedberg to Greifenberg. Here he found the enemy in considerable force, and accordingly falling back on Friedberg, and calling to himself Caramelli, he took up a strong post of observation at Gebhardsdorf. From this position he was summoned to proceed with all haste to join the Russian army.

To effect this junction Loudon set out on the 23rd of July, marching by Görlitz and Freiwalde to Pribus. Here he was joined on the 29th by Haddik.

The task of effecting a junction with the Russian army was one which would tax all the energies and skill of a great commander, for, at Pribus, Loudon was in Prussian territory, with the main Prussian army under General Wedel, greatly superior in numbers, in front of him; another at Sagan, under Prince Eugene of Wurtemberg, on his right flank, and three Prussian armies, under Prince Henry, General Fink, and the king himself, behind him. His task was so far lightened in that Wedel, having attacked Soltikoff at Kay (23rd of July) was completely beaten, losing in killed, wounded, and prisoners, 6,000 men. But from want of cavalry, in which arm the Russian army was deficient, the victory had been a barren one for Prince Soltikoff, and there was nothing to prevent Wedel from dashing down to crush Loudon. Then again, if Prince Eugene should push forward and reach Sommerfeld, south of the Oder, and nearly midway between the Neisse and the Bober, before Loudon, then the road to the junction to the Russians would be barred, and it would be impossible to regain it without a battle.

To gain his end, to be beforehand with the Prussians, and yet to cope with any enemy. however superior in numbers, Loudon arranged that while he should march to the front with 18,000 men, Haddik with 7,000 should cover his movements. He arranged a series of signals by which each should learn, as soon as possible, when the other was attacked, and should hasten to his support. To keep the Prussians still more in the dark, Loudon posted strong detachments, covering his right flank, between Halbau and Sorau. To feel his way, and to receive the quickest information of the enemy, he distributed two regiments of hussars, and three squadrons of dragoons on his front, his left flank, and his right front. He then set out. reached Linderode on the 30th, and Sommerfeld— Frederic but one day's march behind him—on the 31st. His junction with the Russians was now assured. On the 1st of August the two Austrian generals entered Guben. There Loudon took under his orders his Croats, 5,000 strong, the whole of the cavalry, 15,000, and forty-eight guns, and procuring for them bread and forage from the town, marched the same evening to Zilchendorf on the Oder. He was now separated from the Russian army only by that river, for Soltikoff was encamped at the little village of Auer on its right bank. The complete junction was effected on the 3rd. Loudon's operations had been most masterly, extorting admiration even from his enemies. He had conducted to a successful end an operation of all others the most difficult—a flank march through an enemy's country, in the face of four hostile armies, each of which was superior in number to his own !

Haddik, meanwhile, taking over at Guben the remainder of the infantry and the baggage train, set out for Kottbus in the hope of reaching the Lausitz by way of Spremberg.

Frederic, rendered anxious by the defeat of Wedel at Kay, had left Fink with 10,000 men to defend Saxony against Daun, and directing Prince Henry to meet him at Sagan, had set out for that place with all the troops he could spare. Taking up Prince Henry's army and Prince Eugene's corps at Sagan he had reached Sommerfeld the day after Loudon had left it, and had followed on his track, hoping to smite him before he could reach Soltikoff. But as we have seen, Loudon had marched too expeditiously and had virtually effected the dreaded junction. Still determined to strike a decisive blow, Frederic marched in the direction of Frankfort, and, snatching from Haddik all his meal wagons and some hundreds of prisoners on his way, reached Beeskow on the 3rd, the very day on which Loudon, passing through Frankfort, joined the Russian army on the heights about Kunersdorf, on the right bank of the river. On this spot the two generals resolved to accept battle from Frederic.

The inundations of the river Oder on its right bank, had centuries before deepened the ruts and low flat lands which contrasted with the heights or knolls with which that bank was covered. Reclaimed by the industry of the people, the ground had been partially covered with farmhouses and small villages, and to keep the water from it, dams had been built along the river as far as Küstrin. The breadth of this recovered land near Frankfort was about 3,000 paces. The uneven nature of the ground stretching as it were in ridges, alternating in heights and hollows, and shut in at the extreme end of its breadth by forests, made it very defensible. Close to the road leading from Frankfort across the river, and almost immediately after it had crossed it, lay the Jewish burial ground. In front of this, looking northwards, at a distance of about 2,000 paces, rose heights called the Judenberg, very steep, and apparently commanding the country below them as far as Kunersdorf, a little village about two thousand paces to the eastward from it, and somewhat further from the river. These heights were strongly intrenched. Between them and Kunersdorf the ground was nearly flat, though about a thousand paces south of the village rose a considerable eminence known as the Grosser Spitzberg; further on, at a distance of some seven hundred paces, another called the Kleiner Spitzberg, the ground between the two, and stretching to the east of it by the village of Kunersdorf, being a hollow known as the Kuhgrund. From Kunersdorf to the Kuhgrund a chain of heights formed a half circle at a distance of about 1,200 paces round the village, and this chain rested on a forest which again formed a half circle round the hills known as the Mühlberge.

These hills, so called from the mills which had been built upon their summit, formed the salient point to any one advancing towards Kunersdorf from Trettin. A road likewise led to them from Reppen, but this road led through a very difficult forest, the soil of which was rugged and interspersed in many places with lakes. One of these, known as the Huhnerfliess, presented obstacles which rendered it almost impassable, for it was shut in on three sides by very steep sloping rocks.

Once these difficulties overcome, an army advancing from Reppen, would come upon the south-east face of the

Mühlberge, whilst an army from Trettin would assail their north-east face. From the Mühlberge to the river the points of defence would be the following : the Grosser Spitzberg, separated from the Mühlberge by the village of Kunersdorf and the Kuhgrund ; and the Judenberg, separated from the Grosser Spitzberg by a hollow ground. It remains to be added that on the surface between the river and the forest were occasional ponds, traversed generally by planks.

On the ground I have indicated stood the Russian army, its left—facing an enemy coming from the north—on the Judenberg ; its centre on the Grosser Spitzberg, and its right on the Mühlberge. These heights were all intrenched and the salient points between them were all occupied. Loudon and his corps were formed up in the low ground below the Judenberg. But, the day before the battle, all these dispositions had to be altered. A reconnaissance made that day by Loudon showed that the attack would come from Bischofsee and Trettin. The right then became the left, and the left the right of the Russian line, whilst Loudon himself changed his dispositions, and placed his cavalry round the Kuhgrund behind the Russian centre. The Russian army numbered 42,000 ; the Austrian 18,000 —in all 60,000. Meanwhile Frederic had reached Müllrose on the 4th, been joined there by Wedel on the 6th, approached Lebus below Frankfort on the 7th, and thence reconnoitred. Deeming the enemy too strong to be attacked with the 40,000 men he had with him, Frederic resolved to leave Saxony to its fate. He sent then pressing orders to Fink to bring with all haste 8,000 men to join him. On the 10th he met Fink at Reitwein still lower down the stream, crossed it that night, and reached Bischofsee and Trettin about one o'clock the next day. Thence that afternoon he reconnoitered the Russo-Austrian position.

II

A careful examination of that position brought conviction to the mind of Frederic that its weakest and most assailable point was the left, the Mühlberge. If he could but force the Russians from that position he had no fear regarding victory. He resolved then to traverse the forest of Reppen, to turn, by some means, the difficult Hühner-fliess, and reaching the knolls on the further side of it, to attack the Mühlberge simultaneously in flank and in rear.

Loudon, on a second reconnaissance, had fully divined the intentions of the king, and as he saw that the village of Kunersdorf would both serve to screen the Prussian movements after they should have overcome the earlier difficulties of the route, and would break the fire of the Russian guns, had recommended that it should be burnt down. For this recommendation, which was complied with, he has been unjustly reproached by a great modern writer, eager to expose any blunder in the enemies of Frederic. But war is war. An apparent humanity is not always a real humanity. The burning of Kunersdorf was necessary for the plans of the allied armies. And, even in a humanitarian point of view, it was more merciful to remove the inhabitants and burn down their houses than to allow the hovels to stand, and the men, women, and children living in them to be exposed to the fire of two hostile armies.

Frederic, whilst leading in person the main column of attack through the forest of Reppen, had directed Fink with the second column to move by the Trettin road and threaten the flank and the rear of the enemy; thus to concentrate upon himself their attention until he should make his presence known. He had simultaneously given orders to General Wunsch, whom he had left on the Oder, to penetrate into Frankfort as soon as the attack should be developed, and bar the way of retreat to the enemy.

Fink, having but a short distance to traverse, reached his allotted post at four o'clock in the morning. Frederic, the difficulties of whose march had been of the most trying character, arrived at the small knolls overlooking Kunersdorf and facing the south side of the Mühlberge, some four hours later. Some hours yet elapsed before his guns could arrive, and it was half-past eleven before he was ready for the attack. Meanwhile Fink had placed fifty-six guns in position, and had begun a very heavy fire on the Mühlberge. So heavy indeed and so continuous was this fire that it attracted all the attention of the Russians and caused them to pay little heed to Frederic, still waiting for his artillery.

But at twelve Frederic was ready. He had planted 170 guns in position on the hill known as the Kleistberg and the other small hills near it; he had concentrated on his extreme left his cavalry under Seidlitz, and he had formed for the first attack in two lines, under Generals Schenkendorf and Lindstädt, eight grenadier battalions.

At twelve the cannonade, to which the Russians promptly replied, began. The distance, however, was too great to allow it to be very effective, and after it had continued half an hour the king sent the grenadier battalions to the storm.

The Russian troops on the Mühlberge had been posted with so little knowledge of the situation, and with so great a want of foresight, that whilst they exposed themselves to an advancing enemy, they could with the greatest difficulty bring their fire to bear upon the line by which he was advancing. This mistake produced a very demoralising influence—the character of which was increased when the Prussian grenadiers, halting twice to fire, caused a considerable loss in their ranks. It resulted, then, that when the Prussian grenadiers, always pressing on, reached the intrenched position, the defenders gave way, almost without an effort. Some amongst them, however, cooler than their comrades, set fire to the fascines, and the fierce fire thus caused, effectually stopped pursuit for the time.

If the king had had his cavalry in hand, and if it had been possible to turn the abandoned Russian guns against the enemy, this first brilliant success would have decided the victory ; but the cavalry was concentrated at the other end of the line, and the abandoned field-pieces had been left without ammunition. It was only then by a fire of small arms that the advantage so far gained could be improved.

On the Russian side, meanwhile, great efforts were being made to restore the battle. The generals rallied the beaten troops behind the second line, brought guns from the right wing, and offered a new and better organised front to the enemy. At the same time Loudon brought his cavalry nearer to the threatened point, ready to seize any opportunity.

The time taken to do all this had been well utilised by the Prussians. They had strengthened themselves on the conquered ground, and had, with incredible labour, brought upon it several of their guns. These now opened their fire, and under the cover of it Frederic led in person his grena-diers to the assault. But the Russians defended their position with far greater obstinacy than they had displayed on the first occasion, and for a time flattered themselves with the hope that their resistance would compel the king to retire. Just at this moment, however, Fink, who had been working steadily from the Trettin heights, made his presence sensibly felt in their left rear. They fell back then, and in a disorder so great, that Frederic might for a moment have hoped that the decisive blow had been struck, when suddenly, as the first division of his grenadiers appeared on the ground near the Kuhgrund, Loudon, whose infantry there fronted them, charged them so furiously in their flank with his cavalry, that assailed on both sides, they broke and fled.

This was the first check. Still Frederic's second line was intact, Fink's corps was yet pressing on, and his cavalry was yet uninjured. At this crisis then, and to restore the battle, Frederic sent orders to Seidlitz to come to the front and sweep Loudon from his path. But the ground was so difficult for cavalry that to obey this order Seidlitz had to break his front under a very heavy artillery fire, and to lead his men by twos over the narrow causeway leading to the scene of action. Before they reached that ground they had lost many of their men, and they had scarcely formed before a charge from Loudon on their left flank completed their discomfiture.

Still Frederic did not despair. Pointing out to his infantry the summit of the Spitzberg, he indicated that as the point the gaining of which would decide the battle. The nature of the ground had brought his two wings in close contact, and he went from one to the other encouraging them to make this last effort, and pointing how it would be sustained by Fink, now ready to assail the heights on the other side. With great heartiness the Prussian infantry responded to their king's call ; not even they, however, could conquer the impossible. The left wing, with which Frederic was not, was, after a desperate effort, driven back. The right, with which he was, had to encounter Loudon's grenadiers and Croats posted on the further edges of the Kuhgrund, flanked by Loudon's cavalry. With great intrepidity the king descended into the Kuhgrund and endeavoured to storm its banks; but the Austrians held fast, and at this point, too, he was, after some very hard fighting, repulsed.

Nor was Fink more successful on the extreme right. To hold the ground here Soltikoff had massed his most trusted battalions, and he had alike the advantage in numbers and position. He had not much difficulty, then, in repulsing the attack.

The third and decisive stage of the battle had now been reached. In the first we have seen Frederic carrying all before him, and counting on a prompt and decisive victory. In the second, the tide turned. Loudon's splendid charge had checked the advance of the Prussians; by its success had given the Russian infantry not only time to take up new positions, but spirit to defend them; whilst he himself, using his infantry as skilfully as he had handled his cavalry, had forced Frederic to fall back.

Frederic was indeed forced back; but he had before this snatched victory when all around him had renounced hope, and, at this critical moment, he resolved to use his cavalry— which was still strong enough, had he chosen to renounce the field, to cover his retreat—to make a last bold stroke to change the fortunes of the day. If he could but sweep away those Austrians, the chances would be in his favour.

Seidlitz had been wounded in the first attack. To the Prince of Wurtemberg, then, and the dragoons, supported by General Puttkammer and the hussars, Frederic gave instructions to charge furiously the left of the Austrians, and endeavour to roll them up. But the Austrian infantry, encouraged by the presence of the leader who had won their confidence, received the successive charges of the Prussian horse with a firmness which no efforts of the hostile leaders could shake. Prince Eugene was wounded,

Puttkammer was killed, and a few minutes later the Prussian cavalry fled, broken and in disorder.

The undaunted spirit of Frederic still, however, persevered; but his troops, worn out by continuous fighting, and dispirited by ill-success, fell from his hand. In vain did he encourage them; vainly fighting on foot did he give them an example of cool and resolute courage. Slowly, at first very slowly, his men gave ground. Suddenly, however, Loudon, who had waited carefully for the opportune moment, brought up his cavalry in splendid order, and, taking the shaken Prussians on their right flank, charged with irresistible fury. In a moment the battle was decided. Panic seized the so-often-victorious army. In the direst confusion the Prussian infantry fled, followed by the victorious Austrians. In the general tumult of the pressing crowd the king himself was carried away, and—fighting, as he had been, in the front rank—was nearly taken prisoner. Recognising his danger, and seeing an officer at the head of a few hussars near him, whose head was as cool and whose courage was as tried as his own, Frederic, in the midst of the crowd which bore him with it, called out: "Prittwitz, I am lost!" "Not so, your majesty," replied the gallant Prittwitz, "as long as there is any breath in our bodies;" and, pressing his horsemen to the front, formed a ring round him, which warded off the pressure of pursued and pursuers till he had reached a place of safety.

Loudon continued to pursue the enemy until complete darkness set in. They fled in the greatest disorder, losing all their guns, many of their colours—and, what was of not less consequence, their prestige. Of the army, 48,000 strong, which the king had that morning led to the attack, but 3,000 rallied to his standards the following evening.

To the king himself the defeat caused a depression, the like of which he had never till then experienced. "Is there no bullet that will reach me?" he had exclaimed, as he recognised defeat as inevitable. "All is lost—save the royal family!" he wrote from the battle-field to his minister in Berlin. "My misfortune is that I yet live." And again, to the same: "I shall never survive the loss of my country. Adieu for ever." Yet we shall see his splendid energies reviving, especially under the view of the little advantage taken by his enemies of a victory which ought to have been decisive.

The actual losses on both sides were enormous. The Prussians lost 18,000 killed and wounded, 5,683 prisoners. 172 guns, twenty-eight pairs of colours, and two standards. The Russians lost 2,614 killed, and 10,863 wounded: the Austrians 425 killed, 1343 wounded, and 447 missing. Loudon regarded it as the bloodiest battle in which he had been engaged.

There can be no question but that to him and to his Austrians the defeat of Frederic was due. After the defeat of the Russian front line the King of Prussia had counted on victory. It was, first, Loudon's rude cavalry charge, and, secondly, the obstinate defence by his infantry of the Kuhgrund, which changed the face of affairs, and enabled the Russians to rally from their earlier defeat.

Had Loudon commanded the entire army the Prussian monarchy would not have long survived the day of Kunersdorf. As it was, he commanded only a corps of 18,000, of whom but 15,000 were available; and his instructions placed him at the disposal of the Russian commander. In vain the morning after the battle did he implore Prince Soltikoff to pursue the shattered army of the defeated king. In vain, when he found Soltikoff immovable upon

that point, did he ask permission to conduct the pursuit
with his own corps. The fact was that Soltikoff, like
Aprazin on a previous occasion, hovered between his dread
of the Czarina and his desire to conciliate the heir to the
Russian throne. To please the former he beat Frederic,
to conciliate the latter he did not follow him to destruction
after the victory. He allowed Frederic, therefore, to remain
quietly in the camp he had occupied, to cover Berlin, at
Madlitz, to accumulate there fresh guns, stores, and troops,
from Berlin, Küstrin, and Stettin ; to gather to himself
Kleist's corps from Pomerania ; and, thus, in a few days,
to increase his army to an effective corps of 20,000 men.

It was not until the 16th that Loudon, after many fruitless
efforts, induced Soltikoff to recross the Oder. They pitched
their camp that day at Lossow. The day following, Loudon
made a show of attacking the Prussian outposts, whilst
with another portion of his corps he covered the advance
of a convoy from Guben. He then seriously proposed to
Soltikoff to march direct on the King of Prussia's camp.
But the Russian general not only refused, but requested
that no such propositions might be made to him in future ;
he further threatened that in the event of Loudon, in
despite of his orders, advancing beyond Fürstenwald, he
would withdraw towards the Russian frontier. A few
days later an interview between Daun and Soltikoff took
place at Guben. Both cautious men, they arrived at a
decision not likely to compromise the armies they respectively commanded. They agreed that the Russian army
should move towards Saxony to cover, in communication
with Daun, the Reich's-army, then besieging Dresden,
alike from the king and Prince Henry ; that after Dresden
should have fallen, the two armies should march to besiege
Neisse ; that Loudon, his force increased by four battalions

of infantry and two regiments of cavalry, should remain with Soltikoff.

The march of the Russians towards Saxony was so slow and cautious as to drive Loudon nearly wild with vexation. Many splendid opportunities for overwhelming the inferior army of the Prussians were thrown away. At last, in reply to the repeated instances of Loudon, Soltikoff agreed to seize one which presented itself, of attacking Prince Henry in flank and rear. With this view he marched, on the 30th of August, to Lieberose. Frederic, who divined his plans, hastened to thwart it by marching after the Russians, and taking up (31st of August) a position at Waldau, in their rear. Encamped here, he forced the combined army of the enemy to remain halted, expecting an attack, but never attacked, from the 1st to the 15th of September.

The Reich's-army, meanwhile, had been busily engaged in Saxony; had recovered Leipsig, Wittenberg, Torgau, and, 4th of September, Dresden itself. Any other generals but Daun and Soltikoff would have now finished the war; but Fortune is kind only to those who will grasp her favours; she withdraws those favours from those whose over-caution causes them to hesitate to undertake the smallest risk.

On the 15th of September, Soltikoff, urged by Daun, with whom his most trusted general had had an interview at Bautzen, marched to Guben, Loudon covering the march. There he remained three days, awaiting the course of Frederic. The latter, who was well apprised of the secret desires of the Russian general, seized the opportunity of his marching to re-open communications with Prince Henry. In vain did Loudon urge Soltikoff to march on Glogau, as he had promised Daun. He would only crawl on slowly to Sommerfeld. Loudon was pushed on to Christianstadt (19th of September), where a reinforcement of 10,000 troops awaited him.

Soltikoff, his own army likewise strengthened, moved now towards Glogau, but so slowly, that the king, who divined his projects, had time to intervene between his army and that fortress. On the 24th Soltikoff declined a splendid opportunity for overwhelming the Prussian army, over 24,000 strong, at Klein-Wirbitz, but preferred to encamp, three times their number, within sight of them. Three days later, again, Loudon reconnoitred the Prussian position, saw that it was vulnerable on its right flank, and sent General Campitelli to Soltikoff to point out the weak spot, and to say that he, Loudon, was prepared to attack it himself if only the Russian commander-in-chief would support him with 12,000 infantry. Soltikoff refused to give him a single man.

To co-operate with such a man was, to a spirit like Loudon's, almost unendurable. It was therefore with relief that he heard the decision of Soltikoff, arrived at on the receipt of the news that the king had received a re-inforcement of 6,000 men, to re-cross the Oder. This retrograde movement took place on the nights of the 29th and 30th of September, and of the 1st of October. Loudon covered this retreat; and, when he found that Frederic on learning it had marched to Glogau, he urged upon the Russian commander the advisability of striking a blow at Breslau, left open to his attack. Soltikoff, for a moment inspired, advanced as far as Grossoften and Rützen, but, on learning here that Frederic, divining the intention, had crossed the Oder to baffle it, he renounced it, and again remained immovable. A little more than a fortnight later, in spite of the advice pressed upon him by all his generals, and of orders, twice repeated, from St. Petersburg, Soltikoff began his retreat into Poland (25th of October). Loudon remained a week longer with him vainly endeavouring to persuade him to undertake a movement which might be advantageous to the allied cause. On his failure, he separated from him, and, in obedience to orders received from Daun, set out to return into Austrian territory.

This was no easy march. Between him and Silesia lay the Prussian corps of Fouquet and Schmettau. His idea was to march through Poland along the borders of Silesia and then to seek an opening through Upper Silesia into Moravia. But the roads in Poland in the month of November were traversable with difficulty; the maps of the country were rude and imperfect; the distance was some 240 miles, and he could not but expose his flank to an enemy occupying Silesia. Yet he must reach Austrian territory. With this object he marched, after separating from Soltikoff at Jietroschin on the 2nd of November, in the direction of Cracow. He reached this ancient capital of Poland unmolested, on the 25th. The rawness of the weather, the difficulties of the country, especially that great difficulty of procuring carts, had added greatly to his sick list, and these amounted now to about one-tenth of his whole force. Receiving intelligence that Fouquet's corps was not far from Pleiss, the very place through which he intended to break into Silesia, he halted then one day at Cracow to make further arrangements. The sick referred to, who were still some marches in his rear, he despatched from Petrikow by a road not liable to hostile attack through Käsmark and Leutschau, into Hungary. He then wrote to Daun explaining his situation, announcing his intention to march on Troppau, and requesting that supplies of food might be sent to that place, as his men were suffering greatly from the privations they had endured. He then set out, 27th of November, crossed the Weichsel, and reached Vrzesiza on the 28th.

At this place the joyful intelligence reached him that five days earlier (25th of November) Daun had surrounded Fink's corps, 12,000 strong, at Maxen in Saxony, and compelled it to surrender. The same day he received from the Empress-Queen his patent of promotion to the rank of feld-zeugmeister—a rank the nearest equivalent of which in the English army is master of the ordnance, although in its working it is not precisely the same.

Continuing his march, Loudon succeeded, the first week in December, in placing his army in winter quarters, having his headquarters at Tetschen in Austrian Silesia. To insure his troops the complete rest they required, he concluded with Fouquet, the Prussian commander opposed to him, a truce till the 24th of March following. He then proceeded to Vienna, to arrange for the thorough organisation of his army for the coming campaign.

He had reason to look back with pride on his achievements during the year now ending. Placed under the orders of a man as timid and as cautious as Soltikoff, who, whilst anxious for the co-operation of the Austrians, grudged them every mouthful of food they devoured, who cared more to maintain his army intact than to risk a single man to further the objects of the ally of his sovereign, Loudon had, on the field of battle chosen by that leader, displayed a readiness, a coolness, and a courage which, more than anything else, gained the day. If Kunersdorf could not have been won but for the masses of the Russians, certainly it would have been lost but for Loudon. The battle had, in point of fact, been lost; the first and second Russian lines had been driven back in disorder,

seventy guns had been captured by the Prussians, when
Loudon stepped in—*Deus ex machinâ*—and changed the
Prussian victory into a defeat. Every Prussian writer
admits that had Loudon occupied the post of Soltikoff,
Kunersdorf would have finished the war. The Prussian king
believed at the moment that it had finished it. He could
not imagine that the combined stupidity and caution of the
Russian commander would give him another chance!

After Kunersdorf we see Loudon, curbing his own
daring spirit, endeavouring by patient remonstrance and
by cool argument, to win over his commander to decisive
action. The three months passed in this trying endeavour
must have been amongst the most bitter of his life. To
a capable man the experience of opportunity after opportunity thrown away—deliberately lost—because of the
obstinacy of his superior, must be a torture hardly
bearable. That torture Loudon had to endure. And
that he did endure it without an outburst is not the least
proof of his real greatness. Separated at last from his
unenterprising commander, it devolved upon him, in the
cold wet days of November, to conduct a retreat along
the borders of a province occupied by the enemy. During
the entire period of that march—twenty-five days—the
weather was stormy, the cold was intense; his infantry
had no shoes, his troopers had to lead their horses. Nay,
more, the people of the country, though ruled by an ally,
looked with no friendly eyes on the Austrians. Loudon
had to arrange for the supply of provisions, of forage,
of transport. Yet so well did he conduct his negotiations
that he halted but for one day; provided his men daily
with meat; marching them in order of battle, kept up
their spirits; and won the regard even of the unfriendly
Poles. The enemy on his flank but slightly molested him;

their only serious effort, made at Bieletz, on the 29th of November, the third day after Cracow had been quitted, was repulsed with loss. Well, therefore, had Loudon deserved the thanks which, on his arrival at Vienna, were bestowed upon him in the gracious manner habitual to her, by the Empress-Queen.

CHAPTER X.

LANDSHUT, GLATZ, LIEGNITZ.

Not long did Loudon remain in Vienna. Frederic having displayed an intention to employ the winter in field operations, and an apparent design to enter Bohemia, Maria Theresa commissioned the new Feldzeugmeister to proceed, 25th December, to Prague, to assume command of the troops in Bohemia, Moravia, and Silesia, and to use the means at his disposal to baffle her hereditary enemy. The rescript which gave Loudon this mission conferred upon him full powers to act according to his own discretion. Having some 30,000 men under his orders, Loudon so arranged them that Frederic, whom the campaign of 1759 had all but ruined, did not dare to disturb them. Saxony was likewise secured by the presence of the main army under Daun in and about Dresden.

As soon as he had distributed his troops, Loudon set to work to comply with the order of the Aulic Council, transmitted likewise to Daun and Lacy, to furnish it with a paper containing his views as to the manner in which the coming campaign should be conducted. The following is a summary of his memorandum on this subject.

Beginning with a comparison, in very full detail, of the

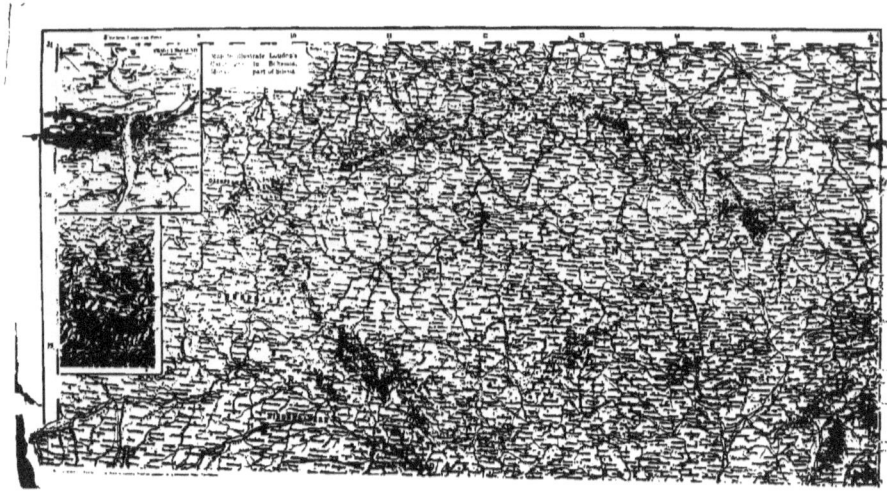

Map to illustrate Landor's Campaign in Britanio,
Illustrating part of Island.

composition, of the rival armies of Austria and Prussia, Loudon expressed his conviction that the morale of the Prussian army was no longer what it used to be. That of the Austrians, he affirmed, was, on the contrary, all that could be desired.

With respect to the Russians he declared himself totally opposed to any system of joint operations with that people; unless indeed they would attach 20,000 men to an army commanded by an Austrian general.

The campaign, he affirmed very strongly, should be an offensive campaign; it should begin early; there should be no waiting for the Russians, who would not come, he thought, unless the Austrians were to show boldness in attacking the enemy.

On the subject of the distribution of forces, he argued thus. Supposing that, as proposed, there were a total of 160,000 men; 100,000 of these would be with the main army in Saxony; 40,000 should be used to reconquer the strong places in Upper Silesia, especially Neisse; and, should the Russians place from 20,000 to 30,000 men at the disposal of the Austrian general, these should join the army in Upper Silesia and attack the enemy wherever he might be found. In this case, and if the operations in Upper Silesia were conducted with energy, the position of the main army would be greatly strengthened. The principle was never to be lost sight of that the king was to be allowed no opportunity of re-uniting with a corps which had once been separated from himself. The remaining 20,000, Loudon proposed to station at Gitschin in Bohemia, alike to guard the frontier against any sudden incursion of the enemy and to strengthen the Silesian army.

Returning again to the Russians, Loudon argued that

I

if these, to the strength of 50,000 men, should march on Frankfort-on-the-Oder, and effect there a junction with the Swedes, the king, who would risk much rather than allow his capital to fall into the hands of such an enemy, would certainly rush towards Berlin, and in his haste would place his army between two fires. Loudon held it to be far better that the Russians should be moved to act against the Prussian capital than that they should be brought into Silesia to eat up the resources of the country and hamper the movements of the Austrians. These latter, he insisted, must act energetically in Silesia, and only begin to besiege the fortresses after they had beaten the enemy in the open field.

This paper would appear to have made considerable impression on the Aulic Council, for immediately after it had been discussed Loudon was directed to transfer the command in Bohemia to Field Marshal Lieutenant Campitelli and to assume that of the troops in Upper Silesia. On his way thither he wrote, 7th March, from Prossnitz, to his friend Kaunitz to remind him that the truce concluded with Fouquet would expire in exactly a week from that date ; that he had certain intelligence that that general was massing his troops with the view of taking the initiative against the Austrians, and not, as he gave out, against the Russians ; that it was very important that he, the writer, should be in a position to anticipate him, and he therefore hoped that no delay would occur in sending him the troops placed at his disposal : he concluded by complaining that with respect to the composition of those troops, hard measure had been dealt out to him ; that of the division of 13,000 men commanded by Draskowitch, and placed under his orders, six battalions were garrison battalions who were not to be employed far from the fortress of Olmütz, and that it was very weak in cavalry: further, that there was a disposition to send him only those regiments which were weak in numbers and whose reputation had yet to be made. He appealed to Kaunitz whether a commander could effect anything great with such materials. He also solicited some mark of distinction for the generals who had served under him during the preceding campaign. To this letter he received in due course a very satisfactory reply, and an assurance that his remarks should be duly attended to.

Pursuing his journey from Prossnitz Loudon reached Jägerndorf on the 13th. As the truce was to expire the following day, he ordered his troops to turn out on the 15th, to be ready for an attempt which he contemplated to make on the town of Neustadt, just across the frontier of what is now Austrian Silesia, and to cut up the troops in its neighbourhood. On the 14th, he sent a trumpeter into that town to warn the Prussian commander, General Goltz, that the truce would expire at midnight.

Very early on the morning of the 15th Loudon set his troops in motion. They were formed in four columns. The first, consisting of the grenadier battalions called after himself, the dragoons of Löwenstein and the cuirassiers of Palffy, he led in person; the second, composed of four regiments of infantry, was commanded by General Draskowich; the third, of two regiments of hussars, by General Bethlen; and the fourth, of four battalions of infantry, one of Croats, and a hundred cuirassiers, by General Vogelsang. Loudon's plan was to attack Neustadt with the first and second columns, whilst the third should cut off the Prussians from Kosel, and the fourth should fall on Leobschütz, and, if possible, seize Ratibor.

The four columns set out at the appointed hour for their destination. Unfortunately for Loudon, however, the heavy rains had flooded the country and made the roads extremely difficult for his infantry. Leaving Draskowich to bring these on as best he could, Loudon pushed on with his horse and reached the environs of Neustadt at daybreak, just as the Prussian commander, General von Goltz, was about to march at the head of two battalions of Pomeranians, one squadron of the dragoons of Baireuth, four six-pounders and one howitzer, for Neisse. Loudon at once despatched the Löwenstein dragoons to bar the road to that place, whilst, following on the rear and flanks of the enemy, he should seize the first opportunity to attack him. The Prussian leader divining this intention, changed his plans, and took the road to Steinau. Loudon followed him nevertheless, charged him repeatedly, and though owing to the non-arrival of his infantry he could make no decided impression on the gallant Pomeranians, he killed forty of them, took forty more prisoners, and captured thirty wagons laden with meal and regimental clothes. What is more, eighty men deserted to the Austrian standard.[1] The other movements failed to cut off the Prussians from Kosel because the inundations so delayed the advance of the infantry as to give them time to retire ; but it is not the less true that the entire district from Weidenau to Neustadt and from Neustadt to Ratibor fell into the hands of the Austrians.

The failure to cut off the Pomeranians was due entirely to the non-arrival at the appointed time of the infantry, and it is a fact that, though Loudon considered that the state of the roads was difficult, he attributed the failure mainly to the want of energy displayed by Count

[1] This account, which is taken from Loudon's own letter to Kaunitz, dated 18th March, differs materially from the "Carlylean" version of the same episode.

Draskowich. This feeling was shared by the officers generally. In a letter to Kaunitz Loudon expressed his opinion that whilst Draskowich was capable of rendering good service under superior leading, he was quite unfit for the responsibilities of a detached command. He complained likewise of the little capacity displayed by two other divisional commanders, Biela and Vogelsang.

The plan of the Austrian campaign recommended by Loudon had not been adopted by the Aulic Council. Instead of allowing the Russian armies to act in Pomerania and threaten the Prussian capital, it had insisted upon their moving into Silesia. Daun, moreover, always erring on the side of caution, was most indisposed, notwithstanding the weakness of Frederic, to assume the offensive. France was less than ever willing to act vigorously; there remained only Loudon to attempt something great for the House of Austria.

The want of systematic energy on the part of the allies is the more unaccountable if we take into consideration the number of the forces on both sides. In Saxony Daun stood in and about Dresden at the head of 80,000 men opposed to half that number under the king. On the borders of Silesia Loudon had 10,000 men—shortly to be increased to 40,000—mostly raw troops, and opposing him were Goltz and Fouquet with 15,000, keeping up communications with Frederic by means of a small corps under Schmettau, posted at Görlitz. Prince Henry of Prussia at the head of 35,000 men was observing 50,000 Russians; Prince Ferdinand of Brunswick with 70,000, the French; and General Stutterheim with 5,000, the Swedes. Whilst then, Prussia could dispose, exclusive of garrisons, of 165,000 men, Austria alone had, including the troops on the Bohemian frontier, 160,000; France 100,000; the

Empire 20,000; Russia 60,000; and Sweden 10,000. Pleased naturally as the King of Prussia would be to see the Russians diverted from an attack upon his hereditary dominions towards Silesia, it became for him no less an object with him to prevent, by all means in his power, their junction with the Austrians.

After his affair with Goltz, Loudon, whose corps did not even then consist of more than 10,000 men, was directed (23rd of April) to make over his command to Draskowich pending the arrival of Campitelli, to see it march to take up a position in and about Zittau, and then to proceed himself to Vienna. He obeyed these instructions to the letter, reached the Austrian capital the 4th of May, attended an extraordinary meeting of the Council on the 6th, and then started to Dresden to arrange with Daun and Lacy regarding its conclusions. The result of the various conferences, as far as they concerned Loudon, was that he should proceed to Königgrätz, collect there troops which would increase his army to 40,000 men, then march through the county of Glatz on to Frankenstein—nearly midway between Schweidnitz and Neisse—and then act according to circumstances. But Loudon could not expect to have his troops in hand before the 24th: it was then the 14th, and his active spirit grudged every moment of the interval. He wrote then to Vienna, laid before the Council his own plan, begged that he might be allowed "free hand" in its execution, so as to act according to the circumstances of the hour, and promised to run no unnecessary risk. On the 26th of May Loudon received a reply, generally favourable to his plan, and granting him the powers he desired. When this permission was received the troops already at his disposal were well in hand. They consisted of thirty-four battalions of infantry, thirty-three companies of grenadiers, seventy-five squadrons, and forty four guns.

With such an army Loudon resolved to give the Prussians the same lesson which Frederic had so often given to his enemies—to be beforehand with them, to carry the war into their country, and to smite them a blow under which their king would reel. His plan was to penetrate into the county of Glatz, storm the fortress of that name, and if, before it could be stormed, Fouquet should attempt to relieve it, to turn upon and rend him.

With this view Loudon united his troops at Kostelitz the 29th of May, crossed the frontier the next day, and pushed on for Frankenstein. Close to this town he (30th of May) formed his camp, his right wing resting on the town itself, his left on the Grochberg. Here he remained till the 7th of June, ostensibly waiting for his transport train. Meanwhile he issued a proclamation to the inhabitants assuring them that he intended to enforce the strictest discipline among his troops, and promising to give payment for the country produce they should deliver.

But, though ostensibly waiting for his supplies, Loudon was not the less planning the intended surprise against the fortress of Glatz. He had ascertained that the garrison of that fortress was small—1,500 infantry and fifty to sixty hussars—that the commandant, Colonel d'O, was in great trouble regarding their *morale*, and that the citizens were tired of the Prussian yoke. Much depended upon concealing his plans from every one. On the 3rd of June then he caused the heights of Kleutsch and Habendorf, in the direction of Landshut, to be occupied. Fouquet, who lay at Landshut with 12,000 men, completely deceived, considered himself threatened by this movement, and, quitting Landshut, fell back by way of

Würben and Schweidnitz to Rommenau (6th of June), every step taking him further from Glatz. Loudon forth-with directed General Wolfersdorff on the one side to occupy Landshut with six battalions of infantry, five squadrons of cavalry, and twelve guns, whilst, on the other, he sent instructions to Field Marshal Lieutenant Müffling, com-manding his reserve of grenadier companies just formed in Moravia, to move up beyond Mittelwalde and take post at the village of Ebersdorf, twenty-three miles to the south of Glatz.

He himself marched on the 7th to Pischkowitz, a place which over-looked and blockaded Glatz. But entirely to secure himself against Fouquet, who, he thought, might, after effecting a junction with Prince Henry, turn round and endeavour to overwhelm him, he directed (10th of June) General Beck to follow the former with his cavalry and use every effort to attract his attention.

On the 11th he learned that the enemy intended to unite and attack him. As he could not, by any possibility, cover at the same time both Glatz and Landshut, Loudon drew back Wolfersdorff from the latter place, leaving only General Jahnus with three battalions and the Palffy hussars to observe it. He sent likewise instructions to Beck that if the enemy should advance towards Landshut he was to hover on their flanks and rear, whilst he, still blockading Glatz, held himself ready to act according as Fouquet's movements should develop themselves.

Meanwhile Fouquet, informed by spies of Loudon's movements against Glatz, had marched from Rommenau to Gröditz. Here he received, in quick succession, three letters from the king, full of rebukes for his abandonment of Landshut. The last of the three letters gave him categorical instructions to march at once by way of

Schweidnitz, drive the Austrians out of Landshut and maintain himself there. Fouquet felt that the king had issued orders without a due knowledge or proper appreciation of his position. He knew that to obey them was to march to destruction, and he told his officers as much. But he had to obey—and he obeyed.

Loudon himself was scarcely less hampered by his instructions. Neither of his official superiors, the minister of war, Count Von Neipperg—who had always been beaten in the field—nor the commander-in-chief, Count Daun—possessed one tenth part of his military foresight. Neither of them could understand why he had abandoned Landshut to secure Glatz, and they pressed upon him advice and even orders to concentrate his army at the former place. But for the strong confidence felt in him by the chancellor, Kaunitz, Loudon would have been forced to renounce his entire plan of campaign just as it was about to bear fruit. As it was, he held to it, though, to save appearances, he, still against his will, sent four battalions of infantry and a regiment of cuirassiers under General Gaisrugg to support Jahnus near Landshut.

Meanwhile Fouquet, in spite of his conviction that his proper course was to occupy a central position, watch Loudon's operations against the Silesian fortresses, and act as circumstances might demand—the course, there can be no doubt, which will commend itself to every military reader—had, in obedience to Frederic's positive orders, retraced his steps (17th of June) to Landshut. On his approach the Austrian general evacuated the town and withdrew to the heights of Reichshennersdorf, covering the Bohemian frontier. Fouquet, who had been strengthened by three battalions, then occupied the intrenched camp, extended his position as far as the heights known as the

Doctorsberg, and fortified that also. So confident, however, was he that the position was a false one,—so satisfied that Loudon, if he should turn upon him with his whole army, could overwhelm him, that he wrote the same day a pressing despatch to the king pointing out the dangers he was incurring. He received an ungracious answer directing him at all hazards to maintain his intrenched camp. On reading this reply Fouquet declared to those about him that in obeying the order he would either die in the king's service or never draw sword for him again. So intensely did he feel the false position in which he was forced! He kept his word.

Great was the surprise of Loudon to find that, after all, no junction had been effected between Prince Henry and Fouquet; that whilst the former was marching further away—towards Frankfort-on-the-Oder—the latter had returned, but slightly strengthened, to Landshut. He saw that it was with Fouquet alone, then, that he would have to deal. He recognised, then, with joy, that a great opportunity was at last offered to him—an opportunity of striking a blow which Frederic could not but feel most acutely. He resolved then to march at once on Landshut and storm the Prussian intrenchments.

The 16th of June Loudon, to carry out his plan, detached Wolfersdorff with five battalions of infantry and one regiment of cavalry to Friedland to support Gaisrugg. The next day Generals Weichs and Jaquesmain marched to Reichshennersdorf with three infantry battalions and two cavalry regiments for the same purpose. On the 18th, leaving only General Unruhe with three battalions and two regiments of cavalry to blockade Glatz, Loudon with the rest of the army quitted his camp at Pischwitz, marched the same day to Waldenburg, and on the 19th by way of

Gottesberg to the heights overlooking Schwarzwaldau. Here his advanced guard, led by General Nauendorf, came in contact with a reconnoitring party of the Prussians and drove it back with considerable loss.

On the 20th Loudon sent his infantry to occupy the heights known as the Forstberge and the Ziegenrücken—both to the east of Landshut and overlooking it—whilst he spread his cavalry from the last named eminence in a north-easterly direction to Hartmannsdorf, thus severing the Prussian communications with Schweidnitz. In order likewise to prevent the possibility of a retreat upon Schmiedberg, an important town lying due west of Landshut—he recalled Beck from his post of observation at Friedberg —still further westward—and directed him to take up a position at Hirschberg, the chief town of the district, nine miles north-west of Schmiedberg, all the roads to which it commanded.

The only way of retreat now left open to Fouquet was that by way of Bolkenheim. But even this way was morally barred to him, for the king's orders had left him no discretion. He endeavoured, indeed, by two letters, dated respectively the 19th and 21st of June, to inform Frederic of the great danger to which he was exposed and to induce him to modify his orders, but he failed. Frederic, believing the intrenched camp of Landshut to be unassailable, did not believe in the danger. His replies, however, never reached Fouquet. Before the messengers bearing them arrived at Landshut his fate had been decided.

The Prussian position at Landshut was rightly regarded by the King of Prussia as extremely strong. The town itself was situated on the right bank of the river Bober, into which, at this point, there emptied itself a mountain stream running from the south, called the Ziederbach. The slopes of the mountain range known as the Riesengebirge were well suited to constitute a strong natural defence against an enemy approaching from the south. The hills on the other sides formed likewise points of support easily connected with each other and verging on a common centre. The reader will judge from the manner, now about to be stated, in which Fouquet had disposed his troops, of the importance of the position, which in those days was regarded as the key to Silesia.

Fouquet, who had with him 11,000 men of all arms, posted them in the following manner :

On his extreme right, on the hills by the village of Johnsdorf, looking nearly south by south-west, he placed four battalions of infantry and eight guns.

To the left, on the plain below, between those hills and Hahnberg, two battalions of infantry, five squadrons of cavalry, and twelve guns.

Still further left, on the heights joining each other at Galgenberg and Gerichtsberg, on the left bank of the Ziederbach, three battalions and sixteen guns.

The above constituted the right of the position. In the centre, on the imposing hill Kirchberg and round its base, were posted one battalion of infantry, two squadrons of cavalry, and twelve guns. Immediately to their left, divided only by the stream, on the hills Burgberg and Thiemberg on the right bank of the Ziederbach, were three companies of infantry and two guns.

The left wing was distributed as follows :—

On and about the hills Buchberg and Tilgenberg were one battalion and three companies of infantry, five squadrons of cavalry, and ten guns. On and about the Doctorberg and Mummelberg, two battalions of infantry, two squadrons of cavalry, and eight guns. In Landshut itself one battalion

of infantry and sixty detached men. About Ruhbank and
Einsiedl, to the north of the town, one battalion and two
hundred and fifty cavalry. In a wood running in a south-
easterly direction from Mummelberg, 200 detached men ;
and in the advanced posts by Vogelsdorf 500 cavalry.

Of all these positions, that of the Kirchberg, in the
centre, was the most important. This is a bare sandstone
rock, commanding not only the town but the whole country
as far as the base of the chain formed by the Doctorberg,
the Mummelberg, the Buchberg, and the Tilgenberg.

Of the four hills just mentioned, all of them higher than
the Kirchberg, two, the Doctorberg and Tilgenberg, are
perfectly bare and smooth. The other two, the Mummelberg
and Buchberg, were well wooded, but the wood had on both
been cut down to a certain point, to form palisades and to
supply other requirements. Of the other hills mentioned, the
four on the right of the Kirchberg, it may be briefly stated
that whilst they are bare, they are all steep, almost pre-
cipitous, on the sides which look towards the Bober.
They are still higher than those mentioned previously.

Not only were all these hills regularly fortified ; not only
had redoubts and flèches been erected upon them, but they
had been furnished with blockhouses, palisades, drawbridges,
deep ditches—extending all along the line. The trenches
were connected likewise by regular communications. Since
the beginning of 1759, Frederic, who, as we know, regarded
the position as one of the greatest importance to hold, had
lavished all his care to render it unassailable.

According to the Austrian official muster rolls, the army
corps under the command of Loudon consisted, in the
beginning of June, of thirty-eight battalions of infantry,
twenty-three companies of grenadiers, six battalions of
Croats, three regiments of light horse, three regiments of

dragoons, six of cuirassiers, and three of hussars—a total, deducting the sick, of 34,000 men. From these 34,000 must be deducted the 5,000 left with General Unruhe for the blockade of Glatz. It follows that to attack Fouquet's 11,000 men posted in the strongly fortified position I have described Loudon had 29,000 men.

On the 22nd of June, Loudon, after a long and patient examination of the enemy's position, decided on his plan of attack, and wrote out his orders to each several general, assigning to each his exact work. His instructions are a model of clearness and precision, and prove how thoroughly he understood all the points—the strong as well as the weak—of the Prussian fortifications.

His plan was to attack simultaneously on his right four of the enemy's fortified hills, the Buchberg and Tilgenberg, the Doctorberg, the Thiemberg ; on his left, the hills above Johnsdorf and the Hahnberg. These captured, the enemy would be surrounded, and would have no choice but to surrender.

The troops detailed for the attack were to march silently to take up the positions assigned to them at nine o'clock on the evening of the 22nd. The attack itself was to be made at two o'clock in the morning ; the signal for it to be the firing of four howitzers from the summit of the Steinberg.

The night of the 22nd was ushered in by a terrible thunderstorm. So overwhelming was the deluge of rain by which it was accompanied that one of the Austrian generals, he to whom was assigned the first attack—on the Buchberg—sent to his commander to state that the rain had rendered his muskets useless for firing purposes. "Tell him," replied Loudon to the messenger, " that the rain which falls on us does not spare the Prussians ! "

As soon as the signal was fired, the storming parties, under cover of a heavy artillery fire from the heights above them, rushed forward to the attack. General Nasseli was the first to reach the Doctorberg, but he very soon had the satisfaction of hearing the sounds of assault on the Buchberg and the Thiemberg. The enemy opposed a very steadfast resistance, but, step by step, the Austrian stormers, well supported by the reserves of the first line under Baron Müflling, made their way. The difficulties of the steep ascent, the obstinacy of the Prussians strengthened by reinforcements sent by Fouquet from his right, were all overcome, and in three-quarters of an hour the Austrians stood triumphant on the summits of the three conquered hills.

When the left of their position was thus taken from them, the Prussians, still defiant, fell back on the Kirchberg, to offer thence, with the aid of the troops already on that hill, a new resistance to their still advancing foe. But they little knew how matters had progressed on their right. Whilst the three Austrian divisions had attacked the left, Wolfersdorff had assailed with scarcely less success the hills near Johnsdorf ; for though his first attack had been repulsed, his second had been completely successful. The Prussians, driven from the heights above Johnsdorf, were forced shortly after from the Hahnberg, and just as the fugitives from the Prussian left fell back on Kirchberg, those from their right sought a last refuge on the Galgenberg. These were the only two heights that now remained to them.

To attack these two heights, Loudon, whilst sending his cavalry to Vogelsdorf—to the north of the town—to prevent the possibility of any escape on that side, formed his infantry into two columns. Whilst one of these columns assailed the Kirchberg in front, the other attempted to storm it in rear. The attack was supported by the fire of a battery of twelve guns from the summit of the Riesnerberg. The first column, opposed by Fouquet in person, steadily made its way up the hill and stormed the redoubt upon it. The second, assailed on its ascent with great fury, was forced to give ground; but hearing of the capture of the redoubt it pushed forward with renewed energy, and gaining touch with the first column, all but surrounded the Prussians, and compelled them, with great unwillingness, to retreat on the Galgenberg. They did this in the most perfect order, with the greatest precision, and with still undaunted bearing—the worthiest of enemies.

Once on the Galgenberg, Fouquet recognised the impossibility of defending the heights. No thought of surrender however entered his heroic soul. It might be possible, he thought, with the small but compact body still under him, to cross the Bober and cut his way through the enemy to Schreibendorf. He made the attempt, but in vain. Scarcely had he crossed the Bober than he came upon the cavalry of Nauendorf and St. Ignon. Still determined to cut his way through, Fouquet formed his men into a square and repulsed the first attacks of the Austrian cavalry. But that cavalry held him fast till the infantry came up. The contest became then too unequal. In a short time Colonel Voigt's regiment of light horse broke through the face of the square, and furious at their previous repulses began to cut and hack on all sides. Fouquet's horse had been killed just as the face of the square was broken. Falling under the animal he received three wounds from the victorious Austrians, and would certainly have been killed but for the devotion of his servant, who, covering him with his person, exclaimed—"Are you going to kill our general!" Colonel Voigt heard the words, hastened to the spot, cleared the ground, raised the fallen Prussian general, had his own charger brought, and would have assisted Fouquet to mount it. But Fouquet, covered with blood and dust, refused the offer, exclaiming— " I would not for anything spoil those trappings by staining them with my blood." "I can assure your Excellency," replied Voigt, "that my trappings would gain immeasurably in my estimation if they were sprinkled with the blood of a hero." Voigt had his prisoner's wounds attended to as well as under the circumstances was possible, and then accompanied him to Loudon, by whom he was received with the greatest politeness.

Such was the battle of Landshut. Of the 11,000 men with whom Fouquet began the action, 1,185 lay at half-past nine o'clock dead or dying on the battle-field ; 8,315, including three generals, eleven colonels, one lieutenant-colonel, fourteen majors, a hundred and fifty lieutenants, and thirty ensigns surrendered prisoners of war; 1,500 managed to escape to Breslau. In material and trophies the Austrians captured sixty-eight guns and thirty-eight ammunition wagons, thirty-four colours, two standards, and a pair of silver kettle-drums. The loss of the Austrians in killed and wounded was naturally, considering they were the stormers, greater than that of the enemy. It amounted to 2,864, of whom 750 were killed, amongst them eighteen officers of rank. Of the wounded, 2,114, eighty-one were officers.

Great as was the victory, the moral effect of it was greater still. It was a blow sufficient to drive to despair any other man but Frederic. Silesia, that Silesia the seizure of which when Maria Theresa was helpless had caused so much bloodshed, seemed now in the grasp of victorious Austria. The defending army had disappeared —had been wiped out. This blow, too, had been dealt by the same hand which had destroyed the Prussian army at Kunersdorf. Well might Frederic exclaim when he heard of the catastrophe : " Is it only to me that such misfortunes happen ? "

Yet he had caused the catastrophe. Fouquet had only obeyed orders against which he had protested. Frederic had only his own obstinacy to blame. But, it must be added, never was he greater than when once confronted by a calamity which would have been fatal to a second-rate commander. It is impossible, however embittered one may feel against the man, not to admire the splendid genius of this warrior-king. When all the world was talking of his approaching downfall, Frederic—with the daring, which, in him, confronted by an over-cautious man like Daun, was the surest prudence—was preparing to take the initiative, and to begin by besieging Dresden !

Loudon, meanwhile, prepared with all possible expedition to take advantage of his victory. The first blow was naturally to be directed against Glatz, already beleagured. He had now, by the arrival of a division from Zittau, 50,000 men under his orders : the siege train was awaiting his orders at Olmütz. Once master of Glatz all Silesia lay before him.

Yet just as he was about to make the one spring necessary, the orders of the over-cautious Daun forced him to inactivity. Daun himself with a powerful army lay at Görlitz, a position covering Silesia, on the side of the upper Lausitz; Lacy, with a corps of 10,000 men, at Bischofswerda, watching Frederic at Gross-Dobsitz. Suddenly Frederic, secretly hatching a design upon Dresden, made as though he would force his way into Silesia and disturb Loudon. Lacy, who was to have been swept from his path, discovered betimes his danger, and fell back on Daun; Daun hastened then to Bautzen, and, alarmed by Frederic's action, transmitted orders to Loudon to defer his operations against Glatz, to leave two small corps only to observe Schweidnitz and Breslau, and to hasten with his whole force along the left bank of the Bober. Compelled then to turn from Glatz, Loudon marched in three columns in the direction indicated by Daun. The first of these columns moved on Guttenberg, the second and third on Kleppelsdorf, where Loudon had his head-quarters. Here he remained till the 8th. The day of his arrival at Kleppelsdorf Daun marched into Naumburg on the Queis. Loudon then rode over to Naumburg to consult with that commander. It was arranged between them that whilst Daun should continue to occupy the advantageous position he then held, Loudon should march by way of Wolfsberg to the vicinity of Hochkirch, and, placing his own head-quarters at Eichholz, watch there the course of events. These movements of the two Austrian generals were sufficient to baffle any attempt on Silesia. Frederic prepared then, with the fertility of a great commander, to strike the well-considered blow against Dresden. Daun first heard of this intention only when it had begun to take effect. Hastening himself to the relief of the Saxon capital, he gave permission to Loudon to resume his operations against Glatz.

Still maintaining his position at Eichholz to cover the siege operations, Loudon despatched one corps under General Caramelli to observe Breslau whilst he directed General Draskowich to press Glatz.

The town of Glatz is defended by two fortresses, the old and the new, separated from each other by the river

Neisse. The town itself lies in a hollow along the left bank of the river. On this side also, pushed forward some three thousand paces and hewn out of the rock, is a flèche connected by a covered way with the town. The old fortress commands the new one. Colonel d'O commanded in the former, Colonel Quadt in the latter. The united garrison consisted of about 2,600 men. Two hundred pieces of cannon were mounted on the works.

Before this place Draskowich, although his entire siege-train had not yet arrived, opened trenches on the night of the 20th and 21st of July. On the 23rd the heavy guns arrived, and on the same day Draskowich, who never enjoyed the complete confidence of Loudon, made over his command to General Harsch, a very vigilant and pains-taking officer. Two days later Loudon himself arrived on the spot personally to direct the storm.

At daybreak on the 26th a heavy fire opened on the doomed fortress from the Austrian batteries. One of the first effects of this fire was to cause many of the enemy's magazines to explode. The second was not less satisfactory. As Loudon, accompanied by Draskowich and his adjutant, Colonel Kray, proceeded from battery to battery, he noticed several of the enemy abandon their posts and come over to him. He then observed that the flèche of which I have spoken as having been hewn out of the rock, was either deserted or occupied by but a few men. He at once called for volunteers to storm it. Three hundred men answered to the call and climbing up found the place evacuated. The Prussians, aware now of their mistake, endeavoured to retake it, but the Austrians, supported by fresh troops, not only repulsed them but pursued them along the covered way. Here the Prussians offered a stout resistance, but they were overpowered and driven to take refuge behind the defences of the old fortress.

Loudon, seeing the discouragement of the enemy and wishing to spare further bloodshed, summoned the place to surrender. The garrison, without discontinuing their fire, refused. Upon this Loudon directed Colonel Rouvroy, who commanded the left attack, to storm. Loudon himself superintended the attack, which was entirely successful. As the Austrians advanced, a panic seized the enemy, whole companies threw away their arms, and the old fortress surrendered.

There remained yet the new fortress, which I have said was commanded by that which Loudon had just gained. About an hour later this also surrendered unconditionally. In this manner, after an attack which lasted four hours, and which cost them eleven officers and 203 men, did the Austrians storm the most important fortress in Silesia. They took 2,513 prisoners, of whom 110 were officers. They found the forts full of supplies of all sorts, including 203 guns of varying calibres and a large quantity of munitions of war.

Whilst Loudon was storming Glatz, Frederic was engaged in besieging Dresden. The better to accomplish his aim he had not hesitated to submit the city to "the torture of fire." His bombardment, though fatal to the innocent inhabitants and magnificent buildings of the Saxon capital, had no effect on the commandant—the brave and steadfast Macguire. With him, too, Daun, approaching from the northern side of the Elbe, opened communications. Frederic had already given up the enterprise as hopeless, when he learned (the 29th of July) that Glatz, a fortress capable of holding out for months, had surrendered to an assault lasting four hours. He at once raised the siege and marched with all haste towards Silesia.

Loudon was on his way to meet him. On the very day of the capture of Glatz he had despatched the vanguard of his army in the direction of Breslau. For weeks he had been in correspondence with the Russian general, Soltikoff—who at the head of 70,000 men was approaching from the north the borders of Silesia—relative to an attack upon its capital. Soltikoff, in a letter dated the 18th of July, had promised to agree to a request made by Loudon to detach 20,000 men to co-operate with him against Breslau, whilst he should cover the operation with his army. But Soltikoff whilst ever ready to promise, was always slow in performing. When Loudon had captured Glatz, Soltikoff was still some seventy miles from Breslau. Just at this moment Loudon received a letter from the Emperor Francis, husband of the Empress-Queen, urging him to try himself a sudden stroke against the Silesian capital with the view of saving it from the horrors of a Russian assault.

There were many reasons which would naturally impel Loudon to comply with this strongly expressed wish. He knew Frederic well. He was confident that the blow dealt at Glatz, following so quickly upon that struck at Landshut, would draw him to Silesia; that he would march as rapidly as Soltikoff would march slowly; that his one chance of gaining Breslau was to attempt a *coup-de-main* before Frederic could arrive, before also the garrison had recovered from the consternation caused by Landshut and Glatz. He at once then sent off the vanguard of his army towards Breslau, despatched the main body to follow it on the 28th, and set off himself the same day for Eichholz to bring up the rest of his troops; thence, leaving only a small corps under Wolfersdorff at Hochkirch, he hastened to Breslau and appeared before that town on the 1st of August.

The garrison of Breslau consisted of 6,000 men commanded by General Tauentzin. But of those 6,000 one-third were on the sick list, and the remainder had to guard, besides the fortifications, prisoners numbering as many as the entire garrison. On the approach of the Austrian vanguard Tauentzin had withdrawn his troops behind the walls, abandoning the suburbs. These Loudon found in the occupation of his Croats. He at once summoned Tanentzin to surrender.

Tauentzin not only refused, but opened forthwith a heavy fire on the suburbs, which he speedily reduced to ashes. Loudon, not wishing to retaliate on the city, wrote then with his own hand to the Prussian commander a letter in which he set forth his own overwhelming strength, the near approach of the Russians, and the impossibility that the place could offer a lengthened resistance. Tauentzin, however, was not to be cajoled. He replied that Breslau was surrounded by regular fortifications, that its defence had been intrusted to him by his king, and that even were its defences destroyed he would maintain its very last hovel. Loudon's siege train had not arrived, but he had bombs and mortars. To shake Tauentzin's resolution, he, following the very recent example of Frederic before Dresden, caused three batteries of these to be erected, and at ten o'clock of that same night (1st of August) opened fire on the city, and continued it for two hours. At the end of that time, the king's palace, the barracks at the Schweidnitz gate, the convent of the Dominicans, the entire quarter known as the Neumarkt—in all about thirty buildings—were in flames.

The next morning Loudon sent Colonel Rouvroy again

to Tauentzin to offer him the most favourable terms if he would surrender, and to warn him of the consequences of forcing him to storm the place. But the gallant Tauentzin remained unmoved and defiant.

Loudon had now to consider his position. He had failed to take the place by a *coup-de-main.* To storm it, with the fortifications intact and the ditches full of water, was impossible. The Russians, despite their promises, were still only creeping along. On the other hand Prince Henry was hastening by forced marches at the head of 30,000 men to the relief of the place. Under these circumstances Loudon resolved to accept the failure and reserve his army for a more tempting opportunity. He therefore broke up on the evening of the 4th, and, in obedience to instructions from Daun, marched to Striegau, a position whence he could maintain his touch with that general, and if necessary unite with him.

The action of the King of Prussia had rendered such a movement more than ever advisable. Frederic, we have seen, had, after a long and useless bombardment, in which he destroyed more than four hundred houses, raised the siege of Dresden on the 29th of July. Daun, who had drawn to himself Lacy's corps, and whose army exceeded the king's by two to one, had sat watching him, too cautious to attack, and, with no Loudon at his side as at Hochkirch, not daring to take advantage of the many splendid opportunities which offered themselves. Frederic, alarmed at Loudon's progress in Silesia, broke up his camp on the 29th, and marched towards that province. Daun, however, foreseeing this movement, had sent out parties on the 28th to break down all the bridges, to destroy the cross roads and forest paths by which the king could advance, whilst he himself with his main army occupied the high road, leaving Lacy to hang upon the rear of the Prussian army. Seen from a height, the three armies marching towards Silesia might have been taken for 'one, so small was the distance between them. At Bunzlau the king halted in order to facilitate the junction with Prince Henry. But between that prince and the king there still lay the army of Soltikoff. Frederic, however, hopeful still, marched to Goldberg on the 9th, to Liegnitz on the 10th. On the latter day he had but seven days' provisions left for his army. His supplies were at Schweidnitz and Breslau. Between him and those places lay the armies of Daun and Loudon.

For, it was the more completely to hem in the king that Daun had summoned Loudon to Striegau and Jauer. Loudon moving with the celerity characteristic of him had obeyed. The king at last was shut in. With one week's provisions, shut out from his supplies, the roads barred by three armies, and confident that if he fell upon one he would draw the other two upon himself, Frederic was never in greater danger. Never had the Austrians greater reason for believing that the hour of supreme triumph was at hand.

On the 10th Daun and Loudon effected a junction at Koischwitz behind the Katzbach, their armies occupying the ground stretching from Parchwitz to Goldberg, completely closing to Frederic the road into Silesia by Jauer. They occupied this position till the 14th. During these four days, they, by their position and attitude, baffled the attempts daily made by Frederic to force a way to Schweidnitz.

On the 14th Frederic had but supplies for three days. He had scarcely more than 30,000 men. The Austrians had 90,000, and it was known that 20,000 Russians, detached by Soltikoff from his army, were marching to join them. Daun, who had every day planned to attack Frederic on the morrow, had been foiled by the daily change of position made by the king. Frederic no longer, as at Hochkirch, remained in one position careless of his enemy. His object being to effect a junction with Prince Henry, who had reached Breslau, he had felt every day one or other of the positions occupied by the enemy. Baffled always by their watchfulness, he had returned to the vicinity of Liegnitz on the night of the 14th. He had occupied the same position before. Daun had reconnoitred it with the greatest care. As soon then as he heard that the king was marching on Liegnitz, he summoned Loudon and Lacy to his tent, and planned with them an attack from three sides on the king's camp, to be undertaken in the small hours of the coming morning.

The consultation between the three generals resulted in the following arrangement :—Loudon was to march that night across the Katzbach, then push on to Pfaffendorf and Rüstern, and at daybreak attack the left wing of the king's army in flank and rear : Lacy, with his corps, was to cross the same river at Rüchlitz and attack the rear of the right wing ; whilst Daun, crossing the Katzbach between Kroitsch and Hohendorf, should turn then to the right, and attack the centre and right wing of the Prussian army. A glance at the map will show how absolutely perfect was this plan—provided, first, that Frederic still occupied the position which Daun believed that he did occupy, and, secondly, that each of the three Austrian generals punctually carried out the plan assigned to him.

But Frederic, very sensible of the danger of his position, displayed on this occasion a caution which, two years before, he would have scorned. It was not the caution of Daun—

a caution which neglected the most favourable opportunities unless success were absolutely certain—but a caution the twin sister of daring, a caution which, whilst always ready to strike when opportunity should offer, would yet give the least possible chance to an enemy. Never was this quality more conspicuously displayed than on the days immediately preceding the battle whose history I am about to record.

Let the reader mark the position of Frederic. He had perhaps a few hundred men over 30,000. Between him and Breslau, where was Prince Henry, lay Daun with 40,000 men, Loudon with 30,000, and Lacy with 20,000. For several days immediately preceding the 14th of August he had tried to pierce the cordon which these three generals had formed to bar the way to him. He had failed. On the 14th, with only three days' provisions, including the supply for that day, he had returned to Liegnitz, convinced that the direct road to Breslau was not to be forced, and that it remained to him to march by way of Parchwitz on the Oder, cross that river, and march along its right bank to the Silesian capital. With this object in view he had determined, whilst the three Austrian generals were marching on his camp at Liegnitz, to quit that camp, cross the Schwarzwasser, and proceed, in the direction of Parchwitz, to the heights of Pfaffendorf and encamp there. To deceive the Austrians he directed that the sentries and pickets should be left standing at the camp he was quitting, with instructions to keep up the watch-fires and to keep on challenging every quarter of an hour. Between 9 and 10 o'clock, when darkness had set in, Frederic carried out this plan, marched in all stillness past the town of Liegnitz, to the heights known as the heights of Pfaffendorf, and encamped there.

The reader will recollect that these very heights of

Pfaffendorf formed one of the points by which Loudon's march was to be guided. He was "to cross the Katzbach, and then pushing on to Pfaffendorf and Rüstern attack the king's camp at Liegnitz at daybreak." With this view he, too, quitted his camp as soon as darkness had set in, crossed the Katzbach, and marched in the direction of the places indicated. Loudon possessed many of the military qualities which distinguished Frederic. Like that great leader he, too, combined a daring bordering on audacity with the prudence which neglects no precaution. Although he had no reason to believe that Frederic had quitted his camp at Liegnitz he marched with his troops in order of battle as though he might come at any moment upon an enemy. Knowing the immense value to an attacking party of a night surprise, and aware that the king had sent his baggage wagons northwards, he sent out no skirmishers to give warning to an enemy, but led himself the advanced party, which on this occasion consisted of his reserves, 7,000 strong. About 3 o'clock in the morning, marching in this order, Loudon came upon five squadrons of Prussian hussars posted in the village of Panthen. These fell back before his greater force, not, however, before Loudon had gathered from the villagers that a small division of infantry occupied the heights of Pfaffendorf. Believing he had come upon the troops escorting the baggage, Loudon at once pushed forward to seize those heights.

That a small division only occupied the heights immediately in front of him was, in a literal sense, strictly true. The heights of Pfaffendorf consisted of three hills, known as Wolfsberg, Hummeln, and Pfaffendorf. On the first of these was a strong battery of artillery guarded by a weak division of infantry; on the second, covered by a thick forest, the left wing of the Prussian army commanded by the king in person; on the third the right wing. With the last we have nothing to do on this occasion.

One word regarding the terrain. The ascent to the Wolfsberg was extremely difficult for an attacking enemy. Shut in by a morass on the right and by a lofty spur on the left, there was no room for an army to deploy. It was impossible to crowd in more than 5,000 men in the space between the two. On the other hand the access to it from Hummeln, the higher spur, was easy. On this height, besides the Prussian left wing, was posted the greater part of their field artillery.

The night was clear, the sky cloudless, the stars shone brightly, as Loudon, believing he had to do only with the escort of the baggage wagons, ascended the Wolfsberg. So prompt was his attack that he drove back the division, not yet recovered from its surprise, which guarded it, and captured all the guns. He was preparing to pursue his advantage when suddenly he beheld advancing to attack him the left wing of the Prussian army led by the king in person.

Frederic, indeed, rendered cautious ever since the surprise of Hochkirch, had, though not expecting an attack, placed his army in the best possible position to receive one before he lay down to take some rest. His right, on the Pfaffendorf hill proper, watched the camp of Daun, in which, though Daun had quitted it, the watch-fires were still burning and the sentries were still posted; his left, on Hummeln, faced that occupied the previous day by Loudon and in which the same mock ceremonial was being performed; the small detachment on Wolfsberg not only secured his main army against a sudden attack, but assured him likewise a very advantageous position for attack upon any enemy who might seize it. Having made these arrangements he had lain down to sleep. From this slumber he was awakened by the shrill voice of Major Hundt, who commanded the five squadrons which had been forced from the village of Pauthen, calling for the king. Frederic jumping up asked the cause of the cry. "The Austrians are within four hundred paces of us," replied Hundt, "they have driven back my vedettes and are marching on with all haste." Frederic, after sending prompt orders to the Wolfsberg to resist as long as possible, mounted his horse and ranged his order of battle.

Day was beginning to dawn when the Prussian king set his troops in motion to drive Loudon from the height he had just won. But with the coming day there rose from the marshes below a very thick fog which obscured the light of heaven. The obscurity acted very unfavourably to Loudon, who knew nothing by experience of the conformation of the ground. He saw, however, enough to convince him that he had a rude morning's work before him. He promptly then sent back orders to his two wings to join him with all haste, and to his cavalry to endeavour to make their way across the marshes and take the enemy in flank.

Meanwhile the king attacked him. Frederic had 15,000 men in hand; at the moment Loudon had but 7,000; and though as detachments from his wings came up his numbers increased, yet the nature of the ground prevented his employing them to the best advantage. He met the king's attack with great vigour, gained some advantage at the outset, and pushed half way up to Hum-meln. He laboured under this difficulty, however, that his supporting columns could not extricate themselves from the narrow way behind him in sufficient time to give him the support he required. He was thus always inferior at the decisive point of the battle to the enemy. The Prussian guns too, on the heights of Hummeln, commanding the only road by which he and his supports could advance, caused him enormous losses.

But at this conjuncture the conduct of the Austrian general commanded the admiration even of his enemies. Amid the roar of cannon he was as calm, as collected, as decided as in the council chamber or on the parade ground. He was supported, even amongst all the disadvantages of his position, by the belief that Daun was on his march against what was now the right wing of the enemy, and Lacy against his rear: If he could only hold his own till their attacks should make themselves felt, he might yet hope for victory. He made a vigorous effort to gain one. But though he was well seconded by his generals, the disadvantages of the surprise—for on this occasion London, hoping to surprise, was himself surprised—were too great, and he was forced to give ground.

Still, if the cavalry could only reach the enemy's flank! In that hope he manœuvred to support them should they come on. His cavalry indeed crossed the marshes, and riding up the slope overthrew the hussars in front of them, and were about to make a charge which might have been decisive, when the mass of the Prussian horsemen took them in flank and drove them back. After that the only hope that remained to London was to preserve his army. Of victory there was now no chance; the guns he had brought up the Wolfsberg must be sacrificed, but he had his men still in hand. He sent then pressing orders to Colonel Rouvroy to occupy with his remaining artillery the height of Binowitz. He, then, still in perfect order, and with great composure, drew back his army to that new position, and offered thence a bold front to the enemy. He had lost the field of battle, but the manner in which he had fought that battle had gained him the respect of his enemies.[1] It was then only 5 o'clock in the morning. The Austrian losses had been considerable, amounting in all to 10,806 men. Of these 1,422, including one general and thirty other officers, were killed ; 4,648, including six generals and eighty-two officers of lesser rank, were wounded ; and 4,736 were taken prisoners. They lost also sixty-eight guns, twenty-three colours and 730 horses. The Prussians counted 1,800 killed and wounded ; they lost also fifteen colours and one standard.

But, meanwhile, where was Lacy? Where was Daun? Why had not these generals fulfilled their engagements? They had, that morning, all the possibilities before them. Why had they not even attempted to seize them?

Daun, we have seen, had arranged to leave his camp, four miles south-east of Liegnitz, cross the Katzbach between Kroitsch and Hohendorf, and attack the right and left of the position supposed to be occupied, close to Liegnitz, by the Prussian army. Daun, always over-cautious, sent on his light troops to feel their way before he set his army in

---

[1] Carlyle writes :—"Loudon's behaviour, on being hurled back with his reserves in this manner, everybody says, was magnificent." Again : "Had his subordinates been all Loudons, it is said, there was once a fine chance for him." The Prussian historians unite in praising his splendid conduct. Loudon himself wrote the following modest report to Kaunitz. After describing the battle, he adds :—"I accordingly fell back, and I am bound to say, to the credit of the generals, the staff officers, the regimental commanding officers, and the soldiers, that this retirement was effected in no haste, with no loss of coolness or courage, but with the most perfect self-possession and the most complete order in the presence of a greatly superior enemy. As soon as I found that Colonel Rouvroy had posted his guns on the heights of Binowitz, I had the most perfect confidence that the further advance of the enemy was checked, and that my retreat was secure."

motion, and these returned about 1 o'clock in the morning
with the information that though the watch-fires were still
burning and the guards were all set, the Prussian camp
had been abandoned. A circumstance of this sort was just
the one to drive a man of Daun's temperament to the
extreme of perplexity. He marched indeed across the
Katzbach, convinced himself of the truth of the reports
given him by the Croats, and then pushed on slowly and
cautiously by way of Schemmilwitz, Pahlowitz, and Grosing,
feeling towards Lacy, who was between Waldau and Seedorf.
At daybreak Daun was within five miles of Loudon, on
the opposite side of the Pfaffendorf heights. Though a
hundred and forty pieces of cannon and some thirty
thousand muskets were blazing on those heights, Daun did
not, or at least said he did not, hear a sound. He still
moved with the same caution, reached Liegnitz about 5
o'clock, and emerging from it first noticed the smoke of the
firing—retreating alas! from him. He appears then dimly
to have divined that Loudon, carrying out his orders to
march on Pfaffendorf, had fallen in with the king's army
and been beaten. To make doubly certain he sent on his
cavalry to feel the enemy. The cavalry rode up the nearer
slope of the Pfaffendorf height, called the Töpperberg,
driving before them the Prussian posts. Soon, however,
they came upon the right wing of the Prussian army,
firmly posted. That was enough for Daun. He dared not
now risk the blow, but fell back, meditating, first on
Liegnitz, then slowly on the camp he had quitted a few
hours previously.

Lacy had not done more than Daun. He had been
commissioned to cross the Katzbach at Röchlitz and attack
the rear of the Prussian right wing. It would appear that
he set out at the appointed time, reached the hilly country

L

between Seedorf and Waldau, and there heard that the king had abandoned his camp at Liegnitz. Lacy was then on the direct road to Rüstern, was distant from it less than two miles, and knew that that place was one of the points on which Loudon was to have advanced. Had he only pushed on with his 15,000 men, mostly cavalry, he would have taken Frederic's army on Hummeln in rear just at the very crisis of the battle. Loudon would have done it had he been in Lacy's place. But Lacy was not equal to the occasion. Instead of his whole force, he despatched on the Rüstern road only two hussar regiments. These passed through that village and came on the rear of the enemy only to realise their own impotence and the great mistake Lacy had committed in not coming on with his whole force. After a feeble attempt on the Prussian baggage they fell back.

No defence then can be made for the conduct of those two generals. They stand condemned alike by their contemporaries and by posterity. Shallow contemporary opinion, judging from the result, attempted likewise to include, upon other grounds, Loudon in the condemnation. What right, they asked, had he to attack before Daun had set him the example? It appears to me that the answer given for Loudon by his Austrian defenders is most satisfactory. Loudon had been instructed to occupy the heights of Pfaffendorf, as their occupation would cut Frederic's line of retreat. He marched without skirmishers so as to take the enemy by surprise should he meet him. His astonishment was great when, arriving at the Pauthen, he found that those heights were occupied by the Prussians. He could not tell at the moment whether the latter were in force, or whether a detachment only of their army occupied the heights. The flight of the hussars from Pauthen would certainly give the alarm to the enemy, and it seemed to him that a retreat along a road which their guns on the height commanded, would be more dangerous than a sudden and resolute attack. He determined then, in the spirit of a daring leader, to deal his enemy a blow before he should have time to complete his formation. His first success encouraged him to persevere. The promise of support given him by Daun and Lacy fully justified his conduct. Had only one of the two come up, the battle would have been decisive of the war. It was only when he found he was left to himself, on most unfavourable ground, unable to use more than 15,000 of his infantry—the total engaged on his side that day—that he withdrew to a safe position. Of his losses in guns and of the reason for them, of the hopes that animated him, he thus wrote the same day to Kaunitz :—

" As soon as the returns reach me, I shall send a minute report regarding my losses in men and guns. A considerable number of the latter has fallen into the hands of the enemy, partly because many were dismounted and the horses were shot, partly because my reserves " (which it will be recollected, formed the front of the battle) " were driven by the overwhelming force of the enemy from the ground on which the guns were posted, before, from the nature of country they had to traverse, my wings could come to their support.

" Had," continued Loudon, " the army under the Feld-zeugmeister Lacy acted in accordance with the settled agreement, and joining touch with mine at daybreak, have attacked the enemy in rear, we should have gained a complete victory. This is the only conclusion to be drawn from the fact I have already related, that, although 1 had only 15,000 men under fire, I drove back the enemy in the first instance. It would have been very easy for the field-marshal and for Count Lacy to profit from my action."

To return. If Daun had possessed a mind to understand, the victory of Liegnitz would have been a barren victory for Frederic. He had but two days' provisions, and Daun could still have barred to him the road to Breslau. But, always over-prudent and over-cautious, Daun had only begun to think of the possibilities before him, just after Frederic had slipped past him, and had secured a junction with his brother, Prince Henry.

Loudon meanwhile had fallen back on Koischwitz; had halted there three days, and had then marched on Striegau, (18th of August). Hence he endeavoured to arrange first with Daun for a sudden attack on Schweidnitz, and then with the Russians for the siege of Breslau. The latter plan was soon rendered impossible by the retreat of Prince Soltikoff across the Oder—a retreat caused by a stratagem on the part of Frederic. The king, as great in trickery as in war, caused to fall into the hands of the Russian commander a letter to his brother Henry, in which, after describing in an exaggerated form the defeat of the Austrians, he added that he was on his way to deal similarly with the Russians. Prince Soltikoff did not wait for him.

Daun, meanwhile, had joined Loudon at Striegau. The court of Vienna was daily pressing upon him the necessity of bringing Frederic to battle and finishing the campaign by a great victory. To a large party at that court, at the head of which was the chancellor, Kaunitz, the inactivity of Daun on the day of Liegnitz had acted as a revelation, and great efforts had been made to induce the Empress-Queen to transfer the command-in-chief to Loudon. But Maria Theresa could not forget that, of all her generals, Daun had been the first to defeat Frederic, and the recollection of Kollin and Hochkirch rose to her mind whenever any one suggested his removal. Even Maria Theresa, however, keenly alive to the importance of the crisis, sanctioned the despatch of pressing instructions to Daun to attack. Daun, though he was probably aware that his credit was failing, could not nerve himself to so desperate an enterprise, and in reply to the orders he received from Vienna, constantly represented the unassailable position taken up by the king.

Frederic himself was by no means at ease. It is true he had effected a junction with Prince Henry's army, and had thus raised his army—deducting a small corps he had detached, under Goltz, to the Oder to observe Soltikoff—to 15,000 men ; he had bread, he had munitions, and he had won an important victory ; but, on the whole, he had cause for great anxiety. The Austrian armies greatly exceeded his own in number (70,000 to 50,000) ; they still, should they dare, had many possibilities in their hands ; nor, whilst they occupied a position in the very centre of Silesia could he quit that province. Glatz had already fallen, and his absence would leave Breslau and Schweidnitz at the mercy of the enemy.

It became then with Frederic an object to manœuvre in such a manner as either to sever Daun's communications with Bohemia, or so to alarm him as to force him to quit his hold on Silesia. The aim of Daun, on the other hand, was, whilst maintaining his communications with the Bohemian mountains, to keep a firm hold on Silesia, to have an eye always to the capture of Schweidnitz, and, should Frederick offer an opportunity, to deliver a battle which should be decisive. I should add that the latter was less his aim than the aim of those who instructed him at Vienna.

Towards the end of August the position of the hostile armies was as follows. Frederic—himself at the castle of Hermannsdorf—lay encamped near Breslau, watching thence the siege of Colberg by the Russians, and the movements of the Austrians in Saxony and Silesia. In the former county the affairs were little more than skirmishes; but in Silesia, the bulk of the Austrian army, under Daun, lay between Striegau and Schweidnitz; its right flank was covered by Lacy who leant on Bögen, its left by Loudon, whose right wing stretched beyond Freiberg, and whose front was covered by the Zobtenberg, on which he had posted the corps of General Brentano. The advantage of this somewhat extended position lay in the fact that it barred the road to Schweidnitz, whilst Daun, in the centre, had it in his power to reinforce, in a comparatively short space of time, either of his wings. Well might Daun believe that he was unassailable. Unassailable perhaps he was, but, nervous and cautious, opposed to a skilful leader who knew how to play upon his fears, certainly not immovable. By a series of bold marches, of masterly manœuvres, of feints, of threats of attack, Frederic succeeded during the month of September in forcing Daun, without striking a blow, to quit one strong position after another, to relinquish his hold on the Schweidnitz road, and to fall back, to preserve his communications with Bohemia, on the mountainous country about Landshut. To use the expressive term of the biographer of Loudon, Herr von Janko, the process resembled nothing so much as that of pushing a piece of heavy furniture from one end of a room to the other. It might have gone badly with Daun, if in his successive movements he had not been covered by so skilful a commander as Loudon. That commander so manœuvred that Frederic, though he pushed his heavy antagonist before him, failed to inflict upon him the smallest injury.

Once in the "Giant Mountains" Daun and Frederic took up positions close the one to the other, and both alike unassailable, Frederic hoping that now that Daun was thrust on to the very borders of Bohemia he would hasten to put his army into winter quarters, Daun on his side meditating a stroke which should repay him for many hours of anguish. For the moment he was repaid.

The court of Vienna had long been urgently pressing upon Prince Soltikoff the necessity of retracing his steps towards Silesia, and had proposed that Loudon, with 40,000 men, should co-operate with him. This proposal was not accepted, but on the other hand the Russian court agreed to send a corps of 20,000 into Brandenburg to attack Berlin provided that the Austrian commander-in-chief would detach 15,000 men, mostly cavalry, to co-operate with them. This proposal was acceded to, and Lacy's corps was indicated for the work. This, then,—how to detach Lacy's corps without exciting the suspicion of Frederic, whilst Frederic lay within sight of his camp,—was the stroke which occupied the attention of Daun in the Giant Mountains.

He succeeded, playing off against Frederic a device which Frederic was playing off on him. Frederic, not well supplied with provisions, had sent a detachment of 4,000 men to Neisse to escort a convoy from that fortress. To deceive Daun, he caused him, by the means so familiar to him, to be informed that the detached corps consisted of 15,000 men and had the mission to penetrate into Moravia, there to effect a diversion. This time Daun had good information; he was not deceived, but, affecting to be so, he detached Lacy's 15,000 men ostensibly to follow and observe the Prussian detachment. Lacy followed it at a distance; but no sooner was he well away from the eagle eye of Frederic than he turned round and hastened with all speed to join the Russian corps, commanded by Czernichef, then marching on Berlin.

Frederic, who had watched with comparative composure the march of Czernichef on Berlin, no sooner became aware of Lacy's movement than he broke up his camp in the Giant Mountains and hastened by way of Princkenau, Sagan, and Guben towards his capital. Daun thereupon marched into Saxony to join there the Reich's army. Loudon, at the head of 30,000 men, was left behind in Silesia to capture, if it were possible, one of the four great fortresses garrisoned by the Prussians.

It rested with the war department in Vienna to decide as to the special fortress he should first attack. The Empress-Queen, whose passionate desire for the recovery of Silesia was as strong as at any period of her reign, was very anxious that Neisse, a strong fortress on the river of the same name, and the conquest of which, and of Kosel, would secure the whole of the upper division of the province, should be attempted. It was calculated however that the siege of Neisse would require the employment of an army of 36,000 men and a hundred guns for six weeks. The preference was therefore given to an enterprise against Kosel.

Kosel, then a strongly fortified but small town, rises on the morasses formed by the overflowing of the Oder, between Oppeln and Ratibor, but nearer to the latter. Armed with orders to endeavour, if the enterprise should seem feasible, to take it, Loudon, detaching a corps of observation under General Wolfersdorff to observe Schweidnitz and to cover Glatz, marched by way of Striegau, Reichenbach, Frankenstein, Münsterberg, and Tültz, and on the 21st of October reached and completely invested Kosel. It unfortunately happened that heavy rains had not only swollen the morasses, but had greatly delayed the transport of his siege train, and it was not till a week later that the guns composing it arrived.

But the arrival of these guns did not solve the difficulty. The rains, which had still continued, had converted the entire country round the fortress into an impracticable morass. There was not a foot of dry land within cannon shot. Meanwhile, the Prussian king, alarmed for the result of Loudon's manœuvres, had sent General Goltz at the head of 12,000 men to observe him. He himself, once that the Russians and Lacy had quitted Berlin, had turned back towards Saxony, and was marching on Torgau. Goltz had reached Glogau on the 25th of October; from Glogau to Kosel the distance could be traversed, by making forced marches, in seven or eight days. It was impossible, declared General Count von Harsch, appointed by the court of Vienna to direct the siege operations, and General von Gribeauval, the chief engineer, even if the batteries could be made ready within that period, to conduct siege operations, under such circumstances, to a successful issue; difficult, should Goltz prove enterprising, to avoid the loss of the entire train. Loudon resolved then to content himself with making an attempt to frighten the commandant into surrender. This attempt, made by the Croats on the night of the 26th of October, having failed, he withdrew his army from before Kosel, sent his heavy artillery in part to Olmütz, in part to the nearer Freudenthal, and marched, on the 29th, to Ober-Glogau, there to act according to the opportunities offered by his Prussian antagonist.

Five days later, 3rd of November, Frederic attacked Daun

at Torgau, and after a most desperately contested battle, in which both the commanding generals were wounded, defeated him, and forced him to fall back on Dresden. The losses of the Prussian army were, however, so severe, that Frederic was in but little condition to follow up his victory. When he was in readiness Daun was unassailable. The two armies then went into winter quarters—Daun in and about Plauen, Frederic in the Freiberg-Meissen country. As for Loudon, having concluded an armistice with the Prussian general to last during the raw winter months, he placed his troops in winter quarters in the county of Glatz and the bordering Bohemian districts, and proceeded (towards the end of December) to Vienna. The gains of the Austrians, in a campaign from which so much had been hoped, had been but small, but such as they were, they were due only to Loudon. He had won back Landshut and the small tract dependent upon it ; he had reconquered the county of Glatz. The over-caution of Daun and the genius of Frederic had combined to render further results impossible

CHAPTER XI.

• MANY and long-continued were the conferences which took place during the winter in Vienna with respect to the coming campaign, which it was hoped would prove decisive. Many were the secret intrigues to change the command-in-chief. To these Loudon was a complete stranger. He possessed none of the arts of the courtier. A remarkable proof of this is to be found in the fact that whilst the names of Lacy and O'Donnel, both far inferior to Loudon, were put forward as the successor to Daun, his own name was never once mentioned. He attended, when summoned, the military conferences which took place, but he never obtruded himself.

Finally the following arrangements were arrived at :—

Daun, in command of the army of Saxony, was to use all the means in his power to detain the king in that province, whilst Loudon, in concert with 70,000 Russians, should complete the re-conquest of Silesia. To this end, and the better to enable him to co-operate with the Russian commander, Field-Marshal Boutourlin, Loudon was freed from all subordination to Daun, and intrusted with the command-in-chief of the Imperial-Royal army of Silesia.

There seemed some ground for the hope, entertained alike at Vienna and St. Petersburg, that this campaign, vigorously conducted, might close the war. To meet 180,000 Frenchmen on the side of Hanover, 90,000 Austrians, and 70,000 Russians, Frederic could with all his efforts dispose 187,000. Of these, 80,000, under Prince Ferdinand of Brunswick, were set against the French. To meet 160,000 Russians and Austrians he had then only 107,000.

These, in the early spring of 1761, were disposed in the following manner. In Silesia, General Goltz with 24,000 men occupied the country about Neisse; Prince Henry with 32,000 in the Freiberg-Meissen country faced Daun; Prince Würtemberg with 15,000 in Pomerania watched the Russians; whilst the king himself with 36,000, held himself free to join Prince Henry and crush Daun, or to join Goltz and prevent the conquest of Silesia by Loudon.

Many reasons combined to induce the king to adopt the latter course. The negotiations between the courts of Vienna and St. Petersburg had not been so secret but that their nature had oozed out. Silesia, it was clear to Frederic, left to the corps of Goltz to defend, could not be maintained. But Silesia had been the cause of the three wars he had waged against the House of Austria. Silesia, the temptress, was dearer to him for all the sacrifices he had made to keep her. In no case must Silesia be sacrificed. Counting then upon the fact that the homogeneity of his force would compensate for its slight inferiority in numbers—opposed as it would be to an army composed of the two nations, each commanded by its own general—Frederic resolved to leave Daun and Saxony to his brother, and to join Goltz in Silesia.

On the 13th of April Loudon joined his corps in the county

of Glatz. On the morning of the 19th he notified to Goltz that the truce between the two nations would expire on the 23rd. Goltz thereupon retired to the Hohenfriedberg. Loudon, who had the most positive instructions to attempt nothing till he should be joined by the Russians, and whose army then did not exceed 30,000 men, followed him and took up a position whence it could hold a hand to the Russians, at the same time that it covered the passes through which his reinforcements could join him.

This retreat of Goltz on Hohenfriedberg, and the movement after him of Loudon, induced Frederic, ignorant of the orders which for the moment tied Loudon's hands, to hasten his march into Silesia. On the 3rd of May, then, at the head of 50,000 men, he set out from the Meissen country, joined Goltz in the neighbourhood of Schweidnitz, and, after a brief survey of the state of affairs, detached that general to watch the Russians. His aim was to prevent a junction between his two enemies.

On the approach of the king, Loudon had fallen back to a position between Wernersdorf and Brannau, covering alike Bohemia and Glatz, and yet ready when his army should be strengthened to spring forward. The king, advancing towards him, occupied a position between Freiburg and Kunzendorf--a position admirably adapted for the purpose he had in view.

The end of June arrived before Loudon's army had been increased to 50,000 men. In the meanwhile he had despatched a trustworthy general, Caramelli, to the Russian camp, to hasten the movements of the Russian commander. But if Soltikoff had been slow and difficult to move, Boutourlin was still slower and still more difficult. Frederic, too, had many friends at the Russian head-quarters, and though one of these, Todtleben, convicted of being in correspondence with him, was sent off to St. Petersburg to meet a traitor's doom, the spirit that had animated him remained. So strong indeed was it that the Russian generals were resolved on no account to attack Frederic ; to fight him only in case he should attack them.

Animated as they were by this spirit, it is not surprising that their march was slow—painfully slow to the active-minded Loudon. This general made proposition after proposition to Boutourlin, at one time to render his advance absolutely safe by making such a demonstration as would force the king to remain on the defensive, at another to make a rapid march and join him, at another to entice the king towards the Russians and then to fall upon him. To all these propositions he received very polite answers, but no definite acceptance or refusal. The Russians still advanced, but so slowly and so cautiously that Goltz, who with 14,000 men was observing them, thought that, with a little additional strength, he could stop them altogether. He implored the king then to send him 6,000 additional men. Frederic sent the men, but before he could use them Goltz was carried off by a fever. Ziethen, who replaced him, contented himself with watching the advancing foe, and continued to do so till Frederic recalled him to Breslau.

In the first week of July the Russian army reached Czempin, a few miles south of Posen. Hence Boutourlin wrote to Loudon that he intended to push on vigorously by way of Militsch to Brieg. On the 11th, Loudon, who meanwhile had made arrangements to meet him on that side, received a letter from him stating that he had renounced that plan, that he intended to march along the Polish frontier in the direction of Wartemberg, and inquired whether if Loudon were to advance to the Oder

to meet him the king would still remain in the position he
then occupied. He declared also his intention of dragging
his siege train with him.

Loudon's reply is a model of clearness. After pointing
out the reasons which rendered it impossible for him entirely
to quit his position in front of the king, he promised
Boutourlin, nevertheless, to march the following morning
to Frankenstein—nearly midway between Schweidnitz and
Neisse—and thence to conduct his operations in such a
manner as to compel the king either to attack him or to
permit the junction between the two armies. He further
begged the Russian general so far to dispense with his
siege train as to despatch it to the fortress of Glatz,
where it could remain in safety till required.

The 19th of July, however, arrived, before Loudon, always
hampered by the orders from Vienna to attempt nothing
until the junction with the Russians should be effected, was
sufficiently assured of their near approach to quit his
position facing the king. On the morning of that day he
broke up his camp in the Glatz hills and pressed forward
in two columns to Frankenstein. Although he endeavoured by a demonstration of a portion of his troops,
under Generals Brentano and Luzinsky, in the direction of
Weichesdorf to conceal his real object from the king,
Frederic at once penetrated his design and resolved to
prevent him from crossing the Oder without a battle,
which, should it prove unfavourable to Loudon, could not
but produce a decisive effect on the already timid councils
of the Russians. In this view it behove Frederic above all
things to maintain his communications with Neisse. He set
out therefore from his camp at Bunzelwitz the same day,
and after a series of manœuvres, in the course of which the
hostile armies came within touch, reached Neisse and

encamped under its walls on the 23rd. But Loudon had so well employed his time that he had, so to speak, turned that position and occupied the heights of Ober-Pomsdorf overlooking the king's camp on the south-eastern side.

The following morning, Loudon, who had now 60,000 men under him, reconnoitred the king's position. He found the Prussian left occupying Glumpenau, the right Stefansdorf, both covered by the guns of the fortress, and therefore practically unassailable. But the great object, the junction with the Russians, was yet to be attained, and attained in spite of Frederic. This was a difficult task for a commander, an impossible task for any other living Austrian general but Loudon. The manner in which he carried it to a successful conclusion deserves careful study.

Encamped on the Ober-Pomsdorf heights, Loudon had arranged with Boutourlin that he should cross the Oder at Leubus. It was still in the power of the king to thrust himself between the two armies and to prevent the junction. The task before Loudon then was to give a hand to Boutourlin on the one side, whilst on the other he should by a powerful demonstration fix the attention of Frederic on a point which should not be the true point of the situation, and compel him to give to it his almost undivided attention. This was a dangerous manœuvre to attempt in the very presence of such a commander as Frederic, quick to penetrate the designs of an enemy, and always ready to take advantage of the smallest opening. Yet Loudon, by the exercise of great skill, untiring watchfulness, and supreme energy, succeeded in every point.

Between the 24th and the 28th, Loudon employed his time in strengthening the corps of General Bethlem, posted between Schellewald and Wiese, covering the magazines in Upper Silesia. The object of thus reinforcing Bethlem was to convey to Frederic the idea that London had not yet renounced the plan of effecting a junction with the Russians in that part of the province on the other side of the Neisse.

Having completed this arrangement, without any attempt at concealment, London, on the 28th, fell back with the rest of his army to the country about Frankenstein, and encamped there, his right resting on Baumgarten, his left on Buchbergen and Krachbergen. General Brentano at the same time moved with his division to the heights of Stolze, whilst Luzinsky took a position near Camenz on the Neisse.

London's object in thus taking a step backwards was to draw the attention of the king on General Bethlem, whilst he himself, left free for a moment, should effect the long desired junction.

The backward movement of London perplexed Frederic. It could not be caused, he argued, by an intention on the part of that general to march by the Nimptsch road to Strehlau and Ohlau, and hold a hand to the Russians on that side, for in making such a march London would cut himself off from the county of Glatz; it could only mean, he concluded, that London was resolved, at the risk even of a battle, to effect the junction by means of Bethlem, now so greatly strengthened, in Upper Silesia.

To hinder the success of that movement, Frederic, leaving Count Wied with one wing of his army at Oppersdorf to watch London, crossed the Neisse, and pressed forward (29th of July) to Schnellenwald with the intention of attacking Bethlem. The same day London, partly to be able to support Bethlem in case of need, partly to keep the king's attention fixed on that general whilst the Russians should make the promised passage of the Oder at Leubus,

M

crossed likewise the Neisse, and leaving Brentano on its left bank to maintain the communications with the county of Glatz, marched to Bärsdorf. The same day likewise, Draskowich, whose division formed a part of Bethlem's corps, fell back in the direction of Jügerndorf to cover the magazines in that town, endangered by the advance of the king. These movements completely mystified Frederic. On the 30th he sent Ziethen to follow up Draskowich ; whilst he himself rejoined his right wing at Oppersdorf. To that place, on the 1st of August, a reconnaissance in force made by Loudon with a view of inducing him to keep his army concentrated on that position, forced him to recall Ziethen.

Meanwhile the Russians had set themselves in motion— their general called it—in earnest. Their earnestness however, did not compass more than five miles a day. It took them twelve days to compass the distance, something short of sixty miles, between Namslau and Leubus. The tortures inflicted by this tortoise-like movement upon Loudon, willing even to expose himself to come in touch with them, but resolved to risk nothing till he was assured of their passage, may be imagined : it would be impossible to describe them.

On the 2nd of August, Frederic, still believing that the Russians would cross into Upper Silesia, fell back by the Strehlen road, and marching about thirty miles, encamped between Schönbrunn and Ober-Eck. Loudon, who had received no news of the Russians since they had quitted Namslau, drew back still further, posting his left resting on Patschkau, his right on Weisswasser, whilst he pushed on Brentano to Ober-Pomsdorf. Continuing his march the following day, Loudon recrossed the Neisse, and following Brentano, occupied that night his old position on the

Buchbergen and Krachbergen near Neisse, and pushing Brentano forward to the heights of Stolze, made as though it were his fixed intention to march, by way of Strehlen, on Ohlau.

Frederic, more than ever firmly convinced that such was his intention, summoned his generals, and announced to them his fixed intention to attack Loudon wherever he should meet him, either on the march or in camp, and directed them to conduct their movements in accordance with that design. The next day he took the road to Strehlen and reached it on the 5th. But there was no sign of Loudon, either on the road or at the place itself. Uncertain then as to the Austrian general's movements, he encamped on the heights rising above that town, sent thence a corps under General Knobloch to frighten Czernichef, who was threatening Breslau, and light bodies of observation in the direction of Nimptsch, Münsterberg and other places, to report instantly any discovery they might make of Loudon's movements. Strehlen he regarded as a central position whence he could still, at his pleasure, sally to prevent the junction between the two armies.

Loudon, meanwhile, still without any information of Boutourlin's movements, had remained till the 8th still encamped on the Buchbergen and Krachbergen heights. At midnight, on that date, certain intelligence having reached him that the Russians were in the close vicinity of Leubus, he broke up, hoping to gain a march on the king towards Schweidnitz—to which place, he felt confident, Frederic, on hearing of his movement, would direct his course—and marching thirty miles at a stretch, encamped with his main body on the heights of Bögendorf, not far from Schweidnitz. Of the advanced corps under Brentano, one portion occupied Striegau, whilst the other marched to Hohenfriedberg ; Luziusky at the same time, with a smaller corps, pushed on to Pölnisch-Weistritz, and cavalry detachments were sent to Leubus itself.   Whilst Loudon was engaged in directing these operations he sent orders to Field-Marshal Lieutenant Beck, whose corps was at Zittau, to push forward to Goldberg, and, with a view to encourage the Russians, to send a detachment to Parchwitz.

Loudon had gained his object.   He had stolen a march on the king.   Frederic heard first from the commandant of Schweidnitz of Loudon's daring flank march.   Though he followed him instantly he found him (10th of August) ready to receive him between Bögendorf 'and Hohenfriedberg. Leaving Ziethen, then, with a corps of 20,000 men at Rothschloss, he marched to Canth, twelve miles (twenty kilometres) south-west of Breslau.   Either at that place, or on the march to it, information reached him that the Russians would certainly cross the Oder at Leubus.   He felt now absolutely confident that Loudon intended to effect the junction in Lower Silesia, and that, to do so, he would promptly quit the slopes of the hills he then occupied and march on Leubus.   He was confirmed in this belief by the information which reached him the same evening—that Loudon had sent on detachments to Striegau and Jauer.   He felt then that he had him.   This conviction became so overpoweringly strong within him, that, leaving the Russians to their own devices, he marched on Jemkau and occupied the heights there with the intention of falling upon Loudon as he passed, on his way to Leubus, through Jauer.

But Loudon had no intention of marching through Jauer. Still very anxious to receive some definite information regarding the Russians, he pushed forward, on the 10th, detachments to Oels to support Brentano in case of need.

On the 11th he received a despatch from Caramelli with the glad information that one Russian corps had actually crossed the Oder at Leubus. He at once despatched General Botta to Boutourlin to obtain certain information as to the further intentions of that general. Botta found the Russian commander-in-chief in a state of doubt as to whether he would not order the re-crossing of the corps which had already crossed, and march back to Posen. It was only the positive assurance of the advantageous position occupied by Loudon and of his power now to effect a junction as soon as he should be assured that the passage had been effected, that induced Boutourlin, on the 12th, to resume his forward movement.

On the 12th the Russian main army crossed the Oder at Leubus, and, stretching beyond it, encamped at Dame. The same day their advanced posts pressed on to Liegnitz, drove out the few Prussians who occupied that place, and thus came in alignment with the Austrians. The King of Prussia, unable to attack them without exposing his flank to Loudon, took up a position the same day in the neighbourhood of Gross-Baudis, his left resting on Kostenblat. Ziethen was pushed on to Neumarkt.

The effecting of this important junction with a crawling ally, scared by every rumour, and threatening every day to fall back to his own country, in the face of a watchful, resolute and daring enemy such as Frederic, was one of the greatest military feats achieved during the seven years' war. The numbers on both sides were very nearly equal —sixty thousand to fifty-seven thousand. But it must always be borne in mind that whilst the great towns of Silesia, Schweidnitz, Breslau, and Neisse were Prussian, and furnished Frederic with supplies, Loudon had to draw his supplies from Bohemia, and to cover the Riesengebirge and the county of Glatz. He dared not, in the face of a general of ordinary talent, much less of such a general as Frederic, sever himself from the passes. The king, on the other hand, was in a position akin to that so repeatedly occupied by Napoleon in 1796— he held a central post between two armies allied to each other, and enemies to him. Napoleon triumphed because he had not a Loudon as one of his opponents. Frederic was as great a master of the art of war as Napoleon. Yet he did not dare to put in force the action which naturally suggested itself to his mind, simply because he had before him an adversary to whom he could not give a chance. Had he marched to Leubus to scare the Russians he would have been instantly placed by Loudon between two fires. He dared not attack Loudon, because, granted that the chances would have been even, a victory would have been almost as fatal as a defeat. He could only manœuvre to prevent the junction—to be in readiness to seize the smallest chance. But Loudon gave him no chance, and by a series of manœuvres, which have extorted his admiration and the admiration of military critics of all ages, baffled him.

The Austrian and Russian outposts touched each other on the 12th of August. The day following, Loudon rode over to the Russian camp to concert with Boutourlin the movements that were to follow. He returned late that night fully satisfied with the promises he had received. But he found that during his absence Frederic had not been idle. The Prussian army was even then in full movement. Loudon rested not during the night, and, reconnoitring in the early morning, discovered the main body of the hostile army resting on Weissen-Leife and Nieder-Moys—its advanced posts at Genowitz and

Metzdorf. This was a position very threatening to the Russians, as yet joined only by a thread of outlying posts to the Austrians; it was threatening likewise to the Austrians, for if Loudon were to quit his camp to give a hand to the Russians, it would give the king the passes of the Riesengebirge. Comprehending this on the instant, Loudon despatched a confidential officer to Boutourlin to explain the situation; why he could not leave his position; but begging him to press on to Jauer, giving his word of honour that if the king were to attack him on the way, he would assail him in flank and rear with his whole army. Boutourlin, frightened at the bare idea of exposing himself, returned only an evasive answer. On the 15th, however, he pushed forward and took up a position near Hünnern. The day following, after a skirmish with the Prussian cavalry, Loudon sent detachments under General Jahnus to occupy Kunzendorf, Hohen-Gursdorf, and Burkersdorf. Frederic, at the same time, took possession of the heights of Wahlstadt.

Loudon now proposed to Boutourlin to make a joint attack upon the king. If Boutourlin would take the initiative, Loudon would send him Brentano's division of 20,000 men, and the moment the battle was engaged, would himself attack Frederic in flank and rear; or he himself would take the initiative, provided the Russian general would send him 20,000 men to co-operate. But Boutourlin was as nervous and timid as a deer; he would neither attack nor aid in attacking, and he dreaded to be attacked.

Frederic, meanwhile, well acquainted with the temperament of the Russian general, was waiting calmly for the moment when Loudon, irritated by the continued refusals of his allies to march on without his aid, should in sheer disgust quit his position covering the Riesengebirge, and give him the opportunity he was longing for. This moment had almost arrived on the 17th, when, in consequence of Boutourlin's firm refusal to move on Jauer unless Loudon should make the way safe for him, the Austrian commander moved back to Tschernitz, sent Brentano to occupy the heights above Jauer, and remained there covering the crawling approach of the Russians. Seeing Loudon apparently glued to that position, Frederic, on the 19th, broke up from his camp at Wahlstadt and marched on the Pitschenberg in the Jerischau, with a view to dash in behind Loudon and cut him off from his supplies. But Loudon, whilst helping forward Boutourlin with his hands, had kept his eyes fixed on the king. He made in one day a rapid march from Tschernitz to Freiberg. As the Prussian troops approached that place they beheld the hills commanding it crowned by the Austrians.

Baffled in this attempt, and seeing the junction now accomplished, Frederic, acting on the principle adopted later by Wellington at Torres Vedras, fell back on the country between Bunzelwitz—two or three miles from Schweidnitz—and Tscheschen, and, with his head-quarters at the former village, began to dig and raise up the intrenched camp which has given its name to this portion of the campaign.

It was the first time in his life that Frederic had ever fortified his position against an enemy, and, it must be admitted, he did the work thoroughly. He made every soldier a pioneer. In an incredibly short space of time there rose up intrenchments in front, in rear, and on both flanks. The intrenchments were everywhere sixteen feet thick; they were covered by ditches twelve feet in depth and sixteen in breadth. The front on every face was covered with strong palisades, whilst the outer portions of the works were undermined. In front of the mines deep pits were prepared, and these pits were fringed along three of their four faces with *chevaux-de-frise* interlaced with each other and firmly planted in the ground. The only face not so fringed was that which communicated with the fortress of Schweidnitz. The several works were armed with 460 pieces of artillery, and 182 loaded mines were ready to be sprung at a moment's notice. On the hills and undulating ground behind the works lay the king's army, consisting of sixty-six battalions and forty-three squadrons. All its communications with the outer country were conducted through Schweidnitz.

Whilst Frederic, who looked forward to the death of the Czarina, then apparently looming in a very near future, to convert the Russians from enemies to friends, and whose object was simply to live through the intervening period, was engaged in rendering his position as unassailable as possible, Loudon was occupied by the all but heart-breaking task of persuading the Russians to move forward. At last, on the 20th, he dragged them as far as Jauer; on the 24th to Hohenfriedberg. Here he once again, in a personal interview, endeavoured to persuade Boutourlin to agree to make on the 27th a joint attack upon the king. He offered that the whole weight of the attack should devolve upon the Austrian army, provided that Czernichef's corps were placed at his disposal, and Boutourlin would promise to support the attack. Boutourlin did not absolutely reject the proposal, but declared he could not decide until he had reconnoitred the king's position. On the 26th—the two armies meanwhile having taken up a position from which an attack on the then uncompleted works would have been feasible—Boutourlin replied that he was ready to join in the attack, but not so soon as the 27th, as the

Russian army required rest and a fortnight's supply of food. He declined to fix the precise day on which he would co-operate, until he should receive certain assurances regarding the precise employment of Czernichef's corps, guarantees regarding the care of the wounded, and the fortnight's supplies referred to.

Loudon, after a careful reconnaissance, had detected what he considered a weak point in the king's position, and he had felt confident that up to the 27th a joint attack made with greatly superior forces must succeed. But after the 27th every day increased the difficulty of the enterprise. Every hour added to the strength of the Bunzelwitz intrenchment. The time he was forced to spend in humouring the Russian Bear was employed by the king in rendering any understanding Loudon might arrive at more difficult of execution. The king himself feared only the watchful activity of his Austrian enemy. "It was little to be feared," he wrote subsequently when describing the campaign, "in the daytime that any mischance should befall the Prussians ; unless, indeed, under cover of darkness, Herr Loudon should surprise a portion of the camp, in which perhaps the troops, buried in sleep, might not have time to hasten to its defence." But he took every precaution in his power to render even the watchful activity of Loudon of no effect. Every evening, as soon as twilight had set in, he caused the tents to be struck, the baggage, including his own, to be sent under the guns of Schweidnitz, and the regiments to be ranged, each in its proper position, behind the intrenchments. Throughout the night the three arms remained in battle array. The king himself generally took his post behind one of the principal batteries. Only after the sun had risen were the soldiers allowed to pile their arms and break off. Not against every Austrian general would Frederic have taken such minute precautions, but he had had experience of Loudon.

Still, more and more formidable as grew every day the works which covered the Prussian army, Loudon, who had detected, as I have said, one weak point, always unrectified in their plan, continued to press upon Boutourlin to consent to a united attack. So persistent was he that on the 29th Boutourlin convened a council of war of all his chief officers and invited Loudon to attend it. At this council the strength of the king's position, the difficulties attendant upon an attack, were discussed : the arguments of the bold and adventurous, the objections of the bastard-prudent, were heard. It is strange that whilst men individually are daring, congregations of men are almost invariably timid. Councils of war almost always decide against action. Is it that even a bold man dreads to appear rash in the eyes of his fellow-man ? I know not. But this occasion was no exception to the rule. Loudon's earnest pleas were unheeded, and a resolution against action was arrived at.

But Loudon belonged to that resolute order of men who never despair of attaining their end—who never let that aim out of their mind. Returning to his head-quarters from this sham council of war, he sat down and wrote out his order of the battle he still hoped to deliver, assigning their own task to the Russians, and to every commander of a corps or a division in his own army the part he would have to play. With this in his hand he went back the next day (1st of September) to Boutourlin, and after many persuasions wrung from him his consent to join in an attack on Frederic on the 3rd of September. But this promise was recalled the following day. It was written that the irresolute nature of the wretched man to whom the Czarina had confided her armies should thwart the combinations of the greatest of the Austrian generals. It had been better for Loudon had Boutourlin never crossed the Oder ! The reason given by the Russian commander in the presence of Count Fermor and Prince Galizin for the withdrawal of his consent was the fear that the Austrian attack would miscarry, and that then the whole fury of Frederic would be turned upon himself !

His refusal was absolute. He talked of the necessity of recrossing the Oder. The utmost he would agree to was to leave with Loudon Czernichef's corps, consisting of ten infantry regiments, two of dragoons, and one of Cossacks. On the 9th, then, Boutourlin and his Russians set out on their return journey, accompanied as far as the Oder by Field-Marshal Beck's corps.

The morrow of the retreat of Boutourlin Loudon fell back on the lines between Kunzendorf and Bögendorf, leaving his cavalry in the plain of Zirlau to watch the Prussians. He had become aware that the confinement behind the intrenchments of Bunzelwitz had caused great sickness, and that the rigorous discipline enforced had produced considerable discontent in the rank and file of the Prussian army, and he still hoped that Fortune would give him the chance so long denied.

Seventeen days after the departure of the Russians (26th of September), Frederic quitted his intrenchments. He quitted them so hurriedly and with so little warning, " under cover of a thick mist," that he left the mines still charged. He marched in the direction of Neisse, with the object, in the first place, of obtaining provisions and forage for his army ; in the second of compelling Loudon, by threatening Glatz, to quit the vicinity of Schweidnitz.

But Loudon was not duped by Frederic. Not only had he divined his intentions, but he had resolved, in return for

Bunzelwitz, to deal him a blow which would atone in part for the enforced want of enterprise of the preceding three weeks. His plan was, almost in the very presence of the king, to surprise and storm the fortress of Schweidnitz.

When Frederic, then, on the 29th, took up a position at Gross-Neisse—not far from Neisse—and made as though it was his intention to penetrate into Moravia, Loudon contented himself with detaching Brentano and Bethlem with all speed into Upper Silesia to watch him there; with the rest of his army he marched close to the uncovered fortress.

Schweidnitz, though wanting in many conditions of a fortress of the first order, was still a place of considerable strength. It lay on a well-cultivated, undulating, and nearly open plain on the left bank of the Weistritz, the centre-point of many convening roads. When Frederic first seized Silesia he had been greatly struck by the advantages offered by such a position, and had traced out a series of detached works to cover the town and to form a fortified camp for a beaten army. Although these works had not been entirely completed they were quite sufficiently advanced to fulfil the original purpose of their construction.

The town itself, which contained then about ten thousand inhabitants, was surrounded by a stone wall, strengthened at intervals by round and square towers, but possessing a very insufficient flanking fire. This wall was propped up outside by an earthen parapet, about six feet high, and this was defended by a narrow ditch which contained water only on one face. There were six gates in the wall, known as the Peter, the Köppen, the Strigauer, the Bögen, the Kroschwitzer, and the Water, gates.

But it was in the outer works traced by Frederic that the real strength of Schweidnitz consisted. Of these the most important were four star-redoubts known as the Galgen, the Jauernicker, the Garden, and the Bögen, a small fort known as the Water fort, and, close to it, the Water redoubt. These redoubts had been constructed with a scarp possessing a height of twelve feet, a parapet of about twenty-six. In front of each main work was a counterwork or bulwark, possessing a scarp wall of only ten feet, whose gorge, eighteen feet high and covered with a wall, formed the counterwork of the main ditch. The ditch of the counterguard itself ran in the form of a trough, from the foot of its scarped wall to the terreplein of the covered way. The masonry of the counterguard, it should be added, was completely covered and hidden by the crest of the glacis.

In the re-entering angles of the star-redoubts posterns led to a kind of walled caponnières, some twelve feet distant from the counterguards, and defended by strong, though at this time partly dilapidated, palisades. Earthen parapets with a sort of trellis door protected the gorges of the star-redoubts. They had no palisades. The comparatively easy entry from without into these gorges was the weak point of the defence of the redoubts, for their curtains consisted of simple parapets, the banquettes of which were protected only by palisades. The breadth of the ditches of the star-redoubts varied from eighteen to twenty-four feet. They were traversed by a simple drawbridge, whilst under the counterscarp of the gorges were casemated powder magazines, each containing about five tons, and furnished with a door leading to the main ditch, and inwardly a step communication with the fort. In the terreplein of the counterguards before the projecting parts of the star-redoubts were double steps communicating with the main ditches, protected by a crenelated wall.

The entrances into the mines lay beneath the main lines of the five corners of each star-redoubt; they branched out from eighteen to twenty-four feet beyond the crest of the glacis.

The redoubts in the centre between the five forts had open gorges, walled escarps, broad ditches, covered ways, and glacis. They were however very narrow. In their gorges were walled watch-towers and midway small posts for a guard. The ditches of these redoubts were traversed by simple drawbridges.

The water fort was a kind of crown-work. To the right of it was the water-redoubt with a parapet and walled scarp. The ditches of both works were fed by a brook and were provided with the necessary appliances for the storage of water.

To the right of the Galgen fort was likewise a narrow, detached work, and before the Jauernick gate an earthen redoubt.

It remains only to be added that in consequence of faulty construction the star-redoubts possessed no command over the counterguards; that their star-like tracing allowed no vertical enfilading of the ditches, so that the attacking party, when it had reached the bottom of these, was to a great extent protected. It must not be forgotten moreover that the heights and undulations about the place offered no inconsiderable protection to an advancing enemy.

The garrison of Schweidnitz was composed of 4,083 men, of whom eighty-three only were artillerymen, about two hundred cavalry, and the remainder infantry of the regiments Treskow, Münchow, Zastrow, and Mellin. The number of guns was two hundred and forty, but the carriages of nearly all of those on the town wall were in a deplorable condition. The commander was Major General von Zastrow, up to that time considered one of the most promising officers in the service of the King of Prussia.

Loudon designed to attack the place suddenly at 3 o'clock in the morning of the 1st of October in four columns, the first, led by Colonel Count von Wallis, directed against the Galgen redoubt; the second, under Major Link, against the Jauernicker; the third, led by Lieutenant-Colonel Kaldwell, against the Garden redoubt; the fourth, under Lieutenant Colonel de Vins, against the Bögen redoubt. A fifth party, composed of the Croats, was at the same time to mask, and at the proper time to attack, the Water fort. The first four columns were placed under the direction of General Amadei, who received instructions to assemble them, in attacking order, at Kunzendorf at 4 o'clock in the afternoon of the 30th of September. General Jahnus, who was to command the attack on the Water fort had, however, the supreme direction of the whole attack. Early in the morning of the same day a strong cordon of infantry and cavalry vedettes was to be placed round Schweidnitz to prevent all ingress into the place; four battalions were told off as supports to the attacking columns.

The instructions given to these were precise. They were to trust only to the bayonet, to storm the glacis and make an immediate dash into the covered way; to spare soldiers who at once should demand quarter, but to deal mercilessly with all who might offer resistance. The prisoners were to be made over to a reserve of four squadrons, led by the Prince of Liechtenstein, who was to follow immediately in rear of the stormers. As soon as the main works of the redoubts should be gained, one party of the stormers was to turn the guns against the town, whilst another should closely follow up the fleeing garrison with the view of entering the city with them or of cutting them off from it; the cavalry were to follow close to prevent plundering.

The storming parties numbered 7,000 men; the supports of all sorts about 8,000.

Before midday on the 30th of September General Jahnus inclosed the place, at a considerable distance from it, on all sides, with strong cordons of Croats, Hussars, and Cossacks. As the day advanced he gradually drew in the circle. till at nightfall all communication between the town and the surrounding country was completely cut off. Some suspicion of the intentions of the Austrian general would seem to have dawned on the mind of Zastrow, for he had all his garrison under arms, and saw that they occupied the positions assigned to them.

General Amadei had, meanwhile, assembled his storming columns at Kunzendorf. There Loudon inspected them, saw that they were furnished with ladders, that the reserves were handy, that nothing had been forgotten. He then addressed to them a few inspiring words, told them to be daring whilst obedient, to avoid plundering, and to win the town for their Empress-queen. He then bade them God-speed, and sent them forward on their work.

Exactly at 3 o'clock in the morning the signal was given, and the storming parties set out. But though they started at the same moment and had to traverse the same distance, the varying difficulties of the ground prevented a simultaneous arrival at their destinations. The fourth column marching on the Bögen redoubt reached the glacis of that fort a quarter of an hour before the third column reached the Garden redoubt. This, however, was followed very closely by the first and second against the Galgen and Jauernicker respectively.

The attack on the Bögen fort, made with great dash and

N

daring by de Vins, was completely successful. He was discovered by the garrison only when within a few paces of the glacis. Before the defenders could turn out he had mounted its crest; their guns had fired but thrice when his men dashed into the covered way, drove the garrison before them, and took possession of all the places of arms. Then, a portion of the stormers turning to the right attempted to storm the redoubt, whilst the remainder attacked the gorge. Scarcely had the garrison of the counterguard recognised the fact that firing was taking place in their rear, than, thinking only of their own safety, they crowded, huddling together, behind the rampart. Then, stricken by a sudden panic, they made a rush for the bridge, with the view of entering the fort. But the drawbridge was up; the disorder increased every second; the garrison then, in batches, and under cover of the darkness, endeavoured to make their way partly to the Garden redoubt, partly to the town. The Austrians, meanwhile, made a dash at the redoubt, and though twice repulsed, succeeded the third time in storming the parapet and forcing the garrison to surrender. Well had De Vins carried out his orders. It was only then half-past 3 o'clock. But scarcely had he time to congratulate his men on their success when the powder magazine in the gorge of the redoubt exploded, almost buried the redoubt itself in ruins, and killed or severely injured 400 of his men—besides many of the Prussians.

Meanwhile, Caldwell, a quarter of an hour later than his colleague, had assailed the Garden fort. Seizing the crest of the glacis with a rush, he had dashed into the covered way before a man of the garrison had sought to stop him. Driving these before him, Caldwell planted his ladders on the scarp, and leading up his men, took the place by storm.

From the moment of his attack to that of his complete success only a quarter of an hour elapsed.

Nor was Major Link less successful at the Jauernicker redoubt. Renowned in the Austrian army for his splendid daring, Link led his men to the assault with cool courage. The task before him was difficult, for the Jauernicker garrison had been thoroughly aroused by the fighting at the Bögen redoubt. Before, however, they had fired three shots at their assailants, Link had stormed the *flèche* in front of the redoubt, and had attacked the counterguard. This he gained after a fight which lasted fifteen minutes, then without a moment's delay he set his ladders against the scarp, and sending some of his men to attack the gorge, pressed on with so much vigour that in a few minutes he gained the redoubt.

The Galgen redoubt was not gained so easily. Not only were the difficulties of the approach to this fort greater, but its garrison was stronger, and its commandant, Lieutenant-Colonel von Plotho, was a man of the greatest resolution.

Well aware of the difficulties before him, Colonel Wallis, who commanded the attacking party, divided it into four columns. He led himself four companies of grenadiers and two fusilier battalions against the front face of the redoubt, whilst Count Truchses, with two companies, attacked the right, Major Patkul with his Russian grenadiers the left, and Count Dombasle with a battalion of fusiliers, the small redoubt between it and the Jauernicker fort.

Despite a well-directed fire of the enemy, Wallis pressed on to the palisades of the covered way. Here the defence was very determined, and for a moment seemed likely to succeed. But Wallis gave an example of courage which

N 2

had a wonderful effect, and with a tremendous effort the covered way was carried.

But the fusiliers led by Major O'Donnel were not so successful in their attempt to reach the crest of the glacis. Four times did they rush to the storm, four times were they repulsed. Everything depended upon the success of the fifth assault, and this, made with the energy of despair, did succeed.

There remained now to storm the redoubt. Here again the victory was nearly imperilled. An unfortunate delay occurred in placing the ladders against the scarp. All this time the fire from the parapet was unceasing and deadly. There seemed some hesitation on the part of the men. At the critical moment Wallis rushed to the spot, and reminding the men that they belonged to the regiment of Loudon and that they must conquer or die, himself mounted a ladder. In a brief space the counterguard was carried, then the redoubt itself. Similarly Captain Dombasle stormed the redoubt against which he had been directed.

The fire of these four redoubts was then directed against the town. Under its cover the Austrian grenadiers pressed forward, and scaling the wall and forcing the gates, dashed in with the élan of victory, and forced Zastrow and the remnant of the garrison to surrender at discretion. A few of the defenders, however, made their way into the Water fort which up to this time General Jahnus had contented himself with masking, but now began to attack in earnest. He was assisted in this attack by two hundred Austrian prisoners of war within the place, who, breaking loose from their bonds, let down the drawbridges. A few minutes before 7 o'clock, this, the last of the defensive works of Schweidnitz to defy them, fell into the hands of the assailants.

In this manner did Loudon gain the most important fortress of Silesia, almost in the presence of the King of Prussia. Frederic was at Münsterberg, midway between Schweidnitz and Neisse, threatening the county of Glatz. He had hoped, by his demonstration, to force Loudon to rush to the defence of that county, possibly even to take refuge in the slopes of the mountains of Bohemia. But Loudon, refusing to be intimidated by a demonstration, had used against Frederic the weapon which Frederic had so often employed against Daun, and, by one bold stroke, had deprived him of one at least of the results of the defence of Bunzelwitz!

The storming of Schweidnitz had cost the Austrians 12 officers and 270 men killed, 51 officers and 986 wounded, and 140 men missing. Their allies, the Russians, lost 51 men killed, 5 officers and 41 men wounded, or a total of 68 officers and 1,488 men. The loss of the defenders amounted to about 700 in killed; the number of fighting men who surrendered was 3,271 cavalry and infantry, and 85 artillerymen; of these 115 were officers.

The capture was of enormous importance to Austria, for it enabled an Austrian army, for the first time since the outbreak of the war, to take up its winter quarters in Silesia. Yet so punctilious and formal were the habits of the Aulic Council, that that splendid act of daring very nearly caused to Loudon the loss of his command. Unable to find fault with the act itself, the Council blamed him severely because he had undertaken it without asking their sanction! Its members proceeded even so far as to endeavour to persuade Maria Theresa to recall him, and to subject his conduct to an inquiry. It was only the calm counsels of Kaunitz, the powerful influence of the old Prince Liechtenstein, and the pleadings of the Emperor Francis, which diverted Maria Theresa from the fatal course pressed upon her. "I am sorry for Loudon," she said to her husband as he entered her cabinet, when, as he knew, she was on the point of signing the decree which would have condemned him, "for having carried out such a stroke, but I cannot save him." "What stroke?" inquired Francis, as though he were ignorant of her meaning. "Why, that about Schweidnitz" answered the Empress-queen. "In that case," replied Francis very earnestly, "you must punish me too; I am at least equally to blame; for it was with my foreknowledge, on my commission, and on my responsibility, that Loudon acted." Maria Theresa, surprised, once again perused the documents before her, then, as if by a sudden impulse, she took up the inkstand and poured its contents over the paper. Further reflection convinced her still more of the injustice of the act she had been about to perpetrate; and the following day she wrote to the greatest of her generals (10th of October) a letter, of the first paragraph of which the following is a free translation :—

"DEAR FELDZEUGMEISTER LOUDON,

　　"The heartfelt joy which you have caused me by your glorious conquest of Schweidnitz is the more vivid as I had so little cause to expect it, and impresses me every moment the more strongly when I reflect what a great advantage it is to me and to my empire, what a loss and discouragement to the enemy. Added to this, the honour of my arms and the new proof of the valour of my troops, and the fact that my pleasure has been greatly augmented by the consideration that you have found a fresh opportunity of adding so largely to the services you have already rendered to me. You may be sure that I shall never cease to bear this act in grateful remembrance."

The rest of the letter was occupied with thanks to the generals, officers, and soldiers, who had fought so well ; to the Russian general, Czernichef and his troops, and for special services rendered.

Frederic obtained the first intimation of the loss of Schweidnitz from a deserter. The bitterness of the blow was increased by the fact that it was utterly unexpected. Frederic had never even taken into account the possibility of it. So far indeed was the idea that Loudon would so dare, and so daring would succeed, that he had arranged to march still further from Schweidnitz, upon Neisse, and canton his army in its vicinity. He did in fact march to Neisse on the 3rd. But Loudon's bold stroke rendered his stay there impossible. It might invite another blow. If Schweidnitz had fallen, why should not Breslau be attempted ? To prevent such a possibility, then, Frederic decided on hastening to Strehlen, a very central position whence he could communicate with Breslau, distant only two marches, on his right ; and with Neisse, still nearer to him, on his left ; and at the same time kept a sharp lookout on Loudon. This general, meanwhile, having placed a strong garrison in Schweidnitz, had resumed his position on the heights of Kunzendorf, occupying, with the corps of Draskowich, the passes of Wartha and Silberberg, and placing Brentano at Faulenbrück, not far from Reichenbach, to watch the right side of the Zobtengebirg towards Strehlen ; and Uihazy, with the Hussars and Cossacks at Floriansdorf and Marxdorf to watch its left side and to take note of the movements of the enemy. The two armies were thus in close proximity.

Frederic was very anxious to entice Loudon from his mountain position to attack him in the plain. But there were very many excellent reasons why the Austrian general should decline to be enticed. Already had the winter set in, the snow lay nearly a foot deep on the ground, the capture of Schweidnitz had given him a position whence he could advantageously begin operations the following spring, whereas Frederic had a good retreat on Breslau, and even if he were beaten would, with such a line open to him, be scarcely in a worse position than that held by him at the moment. On the other hand, a defeat or a repulse would deprive Loudon of all the advantages his boldness had gained, and would force him back on the Bohemian passes. Under these circumstances he wisely abstained from an action which could bring him no great gain and might entail great losses. For a similar reason Frederic did not attack Loudon. He could not do so without exposing himself to be cut off from Breslau, and that was not to be thought of.

Other reasons combined to prevent Loudon from attacking the king. He had been long urged from Vienna to send troops to reinforce Daun in Saxony, and these instructions became at this time more positive and more pressing. In the third week of October, then, he despatched nine infantry and six cavalry regiments, under Field-Marshal Lieutenant Butler, on that errand. He had previously strengthened the corps which maintained his communications with that country, so that, notwithstanding the continued presence of Czernichef's corps of 16,000 men, he was at the end of November considerably weaker than the king—sufficiently strong to meet an attack in the mountains, but not strong enough to descend into the plains to make one.

In the following month both armies went into winter quarters, the Prussian army about Breslau and Brieg— Frederic himself, who had narrowly escaped being surprised in Strehlen by a body of Austrian hussars, at Breslau; the Austrian main army in the villages of Ratibor, Leobschütz, Hotzenplatz, Ziegenhals, Weidenau, and thence to Johannisberg. Here it joined the corps of Draskowich, which occupied Wartha, Frankenstein, Reichenau, Schweidnitz, and Hirschberg. This corps linked on here to the corps of General Wolfersdorff, occupying the hill ranges which united it to that of General Beck, posted in the delta between the Neisse and the Queis, with head-quarters at Görlitz. Czernichef's corps occupied the county of Glatz. Loudon's head-quarters were at Waldenburg. It deserves to be recorded here that before the Austrian army took up its winter quarters, Loudon, who had many reasons to be dissatisfied with Draskowich, recommended the Empress-queen to recall him from active service, giving as his reason that "not from badness of heart, but from weakness of nature, he was a babbler who could not be trusted with weighty affairs." Unfortunately, alike for Austria and for Draskowich, this recommendation was not followed.

All the arrangements for the winter quarters having been settled and an armistice agreed upon, Loudon proceeded to Vienna. He arrived there on the 2nd January, 1762, to meet a reception worthy of the great services he had rendered.

CHAPTER XII.

EVERYTHING in the winter of 1761-2 seemed to forebode
the early triumph of the allies. The resources of Frederic
were at their last ebb; the supplies of money to him from
England were stopped; his own revenues were quite inade-
quate; it was with the greatest difficulty that he could
raise an army sufficient to oppose to the superior force of
his enemies; he himself was despondent, fretful, at times
utterly hopeless. He spoke to but few, went no more to
parade, and ceased to play his flute. The allies on the other
hand, though their resources too had been much tried, and
though one of them, France, was utterly weary of a war
which had brought her no glory but a large accumulation
of debt, were confident that the end was now approaching,
that one supreme effort would reduce their enemy to
the status of an elector of Brandenburg. From this
impending ruin Frederic was saved by an event always
possible, certain at one time or other to occur, but the
exact period of which no one could foresee. This was the
death of the Czarina Elisabeth.

It was early in January that Frederic received secret
news from St. Petersburg that his implacable enemy was

dying. Of the certain issue of her illness there was, he was informed, no doubt whatever. The news roused him from his dejection. He directed that the fords across the Oder should be narrowly watched, and that any courier from the north should be brought at once to his head-quarters at Breslau. On the 19th of January the earnestly-longed-for courier arrived.

Elisabeth had died on the 5th of January; Peter, the admirer, the friend, almost the worshipper of Frederic, had succeeded her. Russia had not only dropped off from the coalition, but was about to unite herself with him. Frederic was equal to the occasion. A man of tact, always looking to the main chance, he caused all his Russian prisoners to be released from prison, and sent them clothed, and with minds full of gratitude to Prussia, back to St. Petersburg.

The news reached Vienna on the 20th of January. The generals who had served in the war were at once summoned by the war minister to a conference, and each was asked to give his opinion as to the course to be followed. When his turn to speak arrived, Loudon declared that it was clear to him the king would concentrate as many troops as possible in Silesia, with the view in the first instance of recovering Schweidnitz, and possibly of making a diversion in Moravia; he advised, therefore, that whilst a small corps only should be posted in the neighbourhood of Dresden and Dippoldiswalde to protect Saxony, the great bulk of the Austrian forces should be concentrated in Silesia; that magazines should be established on the Bohemian frontier at Königgrätz and Leutomischl; that whilst one flying corps of five battalions of infantry and four regiments of cavalry should be sent into Upper Silesia, alike to prevent a diversion of the enemy into Moravia, and to keep in check

the garrisons of Neisse and Kosel, another of from 12,000
to 15,000 men should take up a position on the Queis,
prepared to act according to circumstances, either to
strengthen the Silesian army, or to lend a hand to that in
Saxony. He also recommended that the regiments of
border troops and of hussars, which it had been proposed
to disband, should be at once increased to their full strength
and sent back into Silesia.

Loudon's plan was in principle accepted. The court of
Vienna made, however, the unfortunate mistake of in-
trusting the command-in-chief to Daun. Loudon was
however directed to take provisional command until Daun
should arrive.

The allied German armies were thus ordered : In Saxony
under the command of Field-Marshal Serbelloni and Prince
Stollberg were 45,000, composed mostly of the Reich's
army. In Silesia, altogether 81,000, of whom 11,000
constituted the garrison of Schweidnitz, and 70,000 lay
in the winter quarters in which they had been placed
by Loudon.

On the 23rd of March, Loudon assumed at Waldenburg
the command of this army. The position was different to
that of the previous autumn. The Russian corps under
Czernichef, 16,000 strong, had quitted its quarters in the
Glatz county and was on its way homewards, speedily
however, to be sent back to join Frederic. The latter had
at the moment 65,000 men under his orders. The junction
of Czernichef would increase them to 81,000. It was
Loudon's object to preserve Schweidnitz, and if necessary
to fight a battle for that purpose. He therefore brought
his army within striking distance of that place, in the lines
formed by the villages of Giersdorf, Seifendorf, and Sorgau.
The corps of Field-Marshal Beck occupied Hohenfriedberg,

that of Brentano was posted between Schweidnitz and the Zobtenberg.

In the middle of May, Daun came to assume command. The position taken by Loudon did not please this general, who at once concentrated his army within five miles of Schweidnitz, on the plain between Zobtenberg and the Weistritz. The position was strong for defence. Frederic on his side lay between Breslau and Brieg, waiting the return of Czernichef, who had received orders from the Czar to co-operate with the Prussians for the recovery of Schweidnitz.

The months of May and June passed uneventfully, both armies occupying the same positions, neither leader caring to attack, Frederic only endeavouring, not with any marked success, to alarm Daun about his communications.

On the 1st of July, Czernichef joined Frederic. The latter then broke up his camp and advanced the same day in the direction of Würben. On the 3rd, the movement, continuing towards Würben and Striegau, threatened to cut off Daun from Braunau and the Bohemian passes. Daun moved then on Kunzendorf, and whilst causing his right wing to intrench itself at Burkersdorf, Leutmannsdorf and Ludwigsdorf, placed Brentano on his left on the heights of Adelsbach. Here he deemed himself quite able to repulse any attack.

Frederic could not attack Schweidnitz whilst Daun held that strong position. He therefore made repeated efforts to force him to give up his hold on that important fortress, now threatening his flanks, now his communications. But Daun was wary: he kept always in mind the object to be fought for, and though forced occasionally to change his position, he for long maintained his touch with the fortress. When seriously threatened he changed his head quarters to Dittmansdorf, having his left at Friedland, his right at Langwaltersdorf. Frederic was engaged in endeavouring to turn the right of this position when, suddenly, Czernichef brought him secret information to the effect that Peter had been dethroned (9th of July), that Catherine II. reigned as Czarina in his stead, and that he himself and his army were recalled!

Frederic received this information the 17th of July. It was of a nature to baffle all the hopes he had begun to entertain, to cast him once again into a sea of uncertainty. The departure of the Russians would leave him weaker than the enemy from whom he had been planning to take Schweidnitz. He would find himself in the position of the previous year, the only difference being that his chief opponent would be the Fabius instead of the Marcellus of the Austrian army.

But it is in times of great difficulties that real genius asserts itself. Never was Frederic more brilliant, more daring, more successful than when he was placed in circumstances which would have overwhelmed an ordinary man. Scarcely had he recovered from the first surprise which the information of Czernichef had roused within him than he devised a plan which for daring and genius was not inferior to any one of the many which had illustrated his career. Pointing out to Czernichef that the secret was known to himself alone, that at least three days must elapse before he could receive his official instructions, he begged him to stay yet for these three days, and seem—only seem—to act with him as though their relations had undergone no change. Were Czernichef to agree, he would attack Daun's right wing at Burkersdorf, and cut him off from Schweidnitz.

There must have been a halo of attraction about Frederic

—a fascination almost irresistible. There can be no doubt that if, under similar circumstances, the Austrians had made a similar request to Czernichef, Czernichef would have roundly refused them. But he could not resist the king. Though that which he was asked to do was a clear dereliction of the duty he owed to his sovereign, he agreed to do it.

Without delay Frederic proceeded (20th of July) to carry out his plan. With the Russians in line threatening the Austrian left wing, he attacked their right in great force. Daun, ignorant of the St. Petersburg revolution and its consequences, dared not concentrate his whole force to repulse the attack on his right, and, after a stubborn resistance, gave up his hold on Burkersdorf. This was all Frederic wanted. During the night that followed Daun's retreat he rendered Burkersdorf proof against attack, and proceeded at once to besiege Schweidnitz.

It is difficult to understand the inactivity of Daun during the sixty-three days of that siege. The garrison of Schweidnitz was 9,000 strong; it was commanded by a most capable general, General Guasco, and the besieging army was certainly not superior in numbers to the Austrians. Yet during those sixty-three days Daun made but one serious attempt to molest the Prussians. This, delivered at Reichenbach on the Prince of Bevern (16th of August), was so near to success, that any other general but Daun would have repeated the attack. But the cautiousness of that general was fatal to the House of Austria; it caused the permanent loss of Silesia.

After a siege of sixty-three days, Guasco, finding his fortifications in ruins, and his supplies exhausted, was forced (11th of October) to capitulate. So thoroughly had that general done his duty, that, when, issuing from the place, he defiled at the head of his officers before Frederic, the king thus addressed him : " Sir, you have done all that was possible in the defence of Schweidnitz; you have set a glorious example, but you have cost me 8,000 men !" Well, indeed, might the Austrian commander be proud : he had forced Frederic to spend sixty-three days on a task which Loudon had accomplished in five hours !

With the fall of Schweidnitz the campaign in Silesia ended. The re-conquest of that fortress had given back to Frederic his hold over entire Silesia, the county of Glatz excepted ; and, unable to drive the Austrians from that county, he turned his steps towards Saxony, in the hope of gaining there something which, in the event of peace, he might offer in exchange for it. He succeeded entirely, for at the close of the campaign, of all Saxony, Dresden alone remained in the hands of the Austrians.

It was clear now to every one that the war was at an end. The military genius of Frederic had worn out his enemies. After seven years' fighting he held all Saxony except Dresden, all Silesia except Glatz. If he was exhausted, his enemies were exhausted also. Some of them, too, had already fallen off from the alliance against him. Russia had concluded a separate peace; France and England had come to an arrangement (3rd of November); Austria and Saxony alone remained. With these, negotiations were now entered into. At the hunting-box of Hubertsburg, in Saxony, Hofrath Collenbach on behalf of Austria, and Geheimrath Fritsch on the part of Saxony, met Legationsrath Herzberg representing Prussia. The conditions of peace were designed beforehand. In return for the county of Glatz—the Glatz which Loudon had conquered—the Prussians restored Saxony to its king. In a word, the Seven Years' War had confirmed to Frederic the acquisition of Silesia ; it set its seal on the principle of the right of the strong to despoil the weak—a principle which, it must be admitted, Prussia had before, and has since, always acted upon.

For it was when Maria Theresa was helpless, surrounded by enemies, coveting even her ancestral dominions, that Frederic, without the shadow of a right, had despoiled her. In the war, the conclusion of which I have just recorded, half a million of men had been sacrificed, towns and villages had been reduced to ruin that he might retain that spoil. He did retain it, and in retaining it consecrated the principle of the supreme right of brute force directed by genius.

For the success he attained was attributable mainly to his genius. True there were other causes at work to aid that genius. There was the deplorable condition of the French army; the half-heartedness of the Russian generals; the fact that the only enemy in real earnest was Austria. On the other hand Frederic enjoyed the enormous advantage, to a strong man, of being his own commander-in-chief. He had to look to no one for his orders, was responsible to no one, was able to attempt even the impossible. "Who dares to blame the king, who dares to call him to account," writes Pezzl in his Life of Loudon; "if he leads his infantry into a slaughter-house, as at Prague? if he attacks with a tired handful an army three times his strength, as at Leuthen? if he begins a costly and fruitless enterprise, as at Olmütz? if, that he might be decisively victorious he is decisively beaten, as at Kunersdorf? if he recklessly exposes his armies as at Maxen and Landshut? He is master. Victory or defeat affect him alone. Every one must be silent or blindly obey."

Not only were the Austrian generals opposed to him hampered by the necessity of having to consult the Council of War before undertaking a serious enterprise, but with one brilliant exception, they were men wanting either in talent or in nerve. To the first class belongs Prince Charles of Lorraine, to the second Count Daun. The extent to which this general carried caution made his appointment as commander-in-chief fatal to the ultimate success of Austria. The extremity to which he was influenced by this feeling prevented him even from following up a victory; it thus neutralised the advantages fortune had placed in his hands. The opportunities granted to him were all thrown away. He never fought Frederic, except once when under the influence of Loudon at Hochkirch, unless he were attacked; and he never followed up a victory. His timidity prevented the annihilation of Frederic at Liegnitz. Such a man is often valuable as a subordinate; he is valuable even to defend a weak state against a strong one, but to conquer—and the *raison d'être* of the Seven Years' War on the part of Austria was the re-conquest of Silesia—he must always fail. Had his position and that of Loudon been reversed, had he been a divisional commander and Loudon been commander-in-chief, it is not too much to affirm that the result of the war would have been very different.

If we examine the conduct of this general throughout the war we can find much to admire, much that serves as an example, but little to find fault with. The capture of the convoy at Domstädtl, within hearing distance of Frederic's army, the defeats of that monarch at Hochkirch and Kunersdorf, the victory of Landshut, the storming of Glatz and of Schweidnitz—the latter again the result of a superiority in manœuvring to his great rival —are feats which would place him in the very front rank of generals. It is true that neither at Hochkirch nor at Kunersdorf did he command in chief. But it was he who inspired and contributed to gain the first; it was he who won back the second after it had been lost by the Russians. Had he on either occasion commanded in chief the war would have been then and there ended. Alone of all the Austrian generals, Loudon had realised the fact that a victory not followed up is little more than a victory in name. Alone almost of all the Austrian generals he never was allowed the opportunity of putting his theories into practice. At Hochkirch he was restrained by Daun; after Kunersdorf he was almost forcibly kept back by Prince Soltikoff.

But his victories constitute but a small part of the great services rendered by Loudon to the House of Austria. A battle, a successful siege, are not the only proofs of the genius of a warrior. These depend very often upon circumstances beyond his immediate control. But that which can be emphatically asserted regarding this commander is that but for him the war would have been brought to a conclusion at a much earlier period. But for him the Russians would have been conquered at Kunersdorf; the king, flushed with victory, would have turned back on Daun, there would have been no capitulation of Maxen, and the peace would have been precipitated by three years.

Frederic, though always ungenerous and sarcastic in his writings, whether referring to his own generals or to those of his enemies, could not refrain on more than one occasion from expressing his admiration of Loudon's great abilities. On the field of Liegnitz—which, it will be remembered, Loudon was compelled to quit because Daun and Lacy had failed in their engagements to support him—Frederic, struck by the able and orderly manner of the Austrian retreat, exclaimed to those nearest him: "Look there!

Loudon sets us an example of the proper mode of retiring."
Again, at the close of that campaign, distinguished by the
manner in which Frederic had more than maintained his
position against the greatly superior forces of Daun, the
king expressed his gratitude to Maria Theresa that she had
not given the chief command to Loudon. It is a remarkable
fact, moreover, that when Loudon was acting as a divisional
or corps commander, the king was always careful to take
upon himself the command of that portion of his own army
opposed to him.

It was indeed a misfortune for Austria that she did not
intrust the command in chief of her armies to Loudon.
The cause is not, perhaps, very far to seek.   Loudon had
come to the Court of Vienna an adventurer.   At the outbreak of the Seven Years' War he was but a lieutenant-
colonel in command of border troops.   He had inherited
no great name, possessed no family interest, and, but
for the support of Kaunitz, would have been friendless.
Kaunitz could not advance him.   It was only after his
own merits had brought him into the very front rank
that Kaunitz could use his influence to protect him
against the jealousy which his quick and unexampled
advancement had obtained.   He was the only man in
the Austrian army, not a prince or one of the principal
nobility, who had obtained so rapid a promotion.   Still,
in the eyes of the Austrian court the fact that he was
an adventurer was never wholly forgotten.   And it had
been a maxim of that court, since the death of Wallenstein,
never to intrust uncontrolled military power to any single
man.   Even Eugene had been obliged to bend to the
authority of the Aulic Council.   The fact that Loudon was
almost disgraced because he had taken Schweidnitz without
having first asked the permission of that Council explains

many things. Even if he had been made commander-in-
chief he would never have been, like Frederic, unfettered.
And for a man of genius to succeed in war it is necessary
that he should be able to act promptly, on the spur of the
moment, without being forced to wait for consent to a movement, the success of which would depend upon immediate
and rapid execution. Had the opportunity been ever offered
to London, had he been invested with supreme and unfettered command against Frederic, it is not possible to
doubt that Austria would never have been compelled to
sign the renunciation of the stolen province of Silesia.

CHAPTER XIII.

THE Empress-queen was not ungrateful to the great soldier who had combated so valiantly on her behalf. Besides many orders, she had bestowed upon him the estate of Klein-Beczwar, in Bohemia, not far from the battle-field of Kollin.

On the conclusion of peace Loudon proceeded to Prague. The magistracy of that city, out of gratitude for the manner in which, during his period of command, he had preserved Bohemia against invasion, had presented him with a house. This house he occupied when duty called him to the capital of the kingdom.

The summer of the first year after the war he proceeded to Karlsbad to drink the waters. Here he made the acquaintance of the poet Gellert. A warm friendship was soon formed between the two men, and it is to the reminiscences of the poet that the world is indebted for a more intimate knowledge of the inner nature of the soldier than would otherwise have been obtainable. Every morning the two friends walked together to the wells, every day they strolled together and dined at the same table. Of their relations, and of the opinion he had formed of his companion, Gellert wrote the following interesting account :—

"One of my first and dearest acquaintances was General Loudon, a man of a peculiar character ; earnest, modest, somewhat sad, like myself. Speaking little, like myself. but speaking, when he did speak, well and to the point ; never indeed talking of his own exploits, and but little of war ; an attentive listener ; his whole behaviour evincing the same simplicity and rightmindedness which characterised his conversation. He is not tall, but well-built, thin, but less so than I am ; has light grey or rather blueish eyes, deep set in the head, and meditating, just like mine. It was only gradually and by degrees that he became intimate with me, perhaps my own desponding mood was the cause.

" 'Oh !' said he one day when he met me in the avenue, 'I would come to you very often, but—I don't quite know —I am afraid I should intrude upon you.'

"Another time he said—

" 'Tell me, Professor, how you have managed to write so many books, so much that is lively and jocose ? I can't understand it, when I see you in this mood.'

" 'I will tell you how,' I replied, 'but first tell me, General, how you managed to win the battle of Kunersdorf and to take Schweidnitz in a night ? I can't understand it when I see you so quiet.'

" Then, for the first time, I saw him laugh ; he never even smiled ordinarily. He had informed himself very exactly regarding my tastes. He first invited me to dine when he was quite alone. The dinner consisted principally of farinaceous food ; he let me drink my own wine, allowed me to go soon after the table had been cleared ; in a word, he let me do just as I liked. I never heard from his mouth aught but what was good, and I noticed that he was truly religious. I selected a small library for him, for he was ever regretting that he had had so few opportunities for reading. But, in point of fact, his quick intelligence and his earnest attention to everything he undertook supplied the want of scientific knowledge. He was, besides, very fond of reading.

"'I would give much to know,' said he to me one day, 'what you would like to have, that I might give it you.'

"'General,' I replied, 'even if you would give me the whole world, the gift under my present circumstances would be indifferent to me.'"

The above extract gives some insight into the quiet, modest, retiring nature of the man who, in a campaign, was the bold, active, far-seeing general with whom even Frederic dared take no liberty. The life which he lived after his return from his visit to Karlsbad was truly patriarchal. He purchased from Baron von Brandau the estate adjoining his own,—that of Gross-Beczwar,—devoted his time to improving it, added considerably to the house, and lived there, an earnest and working proprietor, in philosophical tranquillity. Twice during each year only did he visit Vienna to pay his respects to his sovereign, but his stay in the capital was but of short duration.

In 1765 Loudon visited Aix-la-Chapelle to take the waters there. He returned thence the same year on hearing a rumour of the death of the Emperor Francis, to whom he was sincerely attached. The rumour proved true, for the husband of Maria Theresa died at Innsbruck on the 18th of August. The following year Loudon was appointed inspector-general of infantry; but this office was abolished three years later.

In 1769 the Emperor Joseph II. paid a visit to Frederic

II. in his camp at Neisse. The emperor was accompanied by Prince Albert of Sachsen-Teschen, the Count of Dietrichstein, and Generals Loudon and Lacy. They returned from this interview, which was of a purely formal and introductory character, by way of Glatz, where the emperor spent the time in making Loudon explain to him the operations by which he had taken that fortress.

On the 13th of November of the same year, Loudon was appointed commanding-general in Moravia, and commandant at Brunn. Twelve days later he was nominated a privy councillor and a member of the Aulic Council.

In 1770 Frederic returned the emperor's visit, coming for that purpose to Neustadt in Moravia. A sham fight of two large divisions of the Austrian army, drawn together specially for the purpose, took place on the occasion. Loudon commanded one of these; the manœuvres on both sides were free. So skilful were those of Loudon that he speedily brought his adversary into a position whence it was impossible to extricate himself. Frederic expressed his delight in unmeasured terms of praise, and when, at the banquet after the mock fight, Loudon, with his accustomed modesty, was about to take a seat low down on the side of the table opposite to him, Frederic called him to his side, with the words already recorded:[1] "Come here, Herr von Loudon, I would rather see you by me than opposite to me." On his departure the king presented Loudon with two splendid chargers with their trappings.

One of the results of the interview between the emperor and Frederic was a clear understanding regarding the policy to be pursued with respect to Poland, a policy which resulted in the first partition of that country. After the three allied powers had occupied the provinces claimed by

[1] Page 15.

each, these were, in a national council held at Warsaw, (1772) formally transferred to them. The emperor did not delay to visit his new acquisition. Accompanied by the generals Loudon, Nostiz, and Pelligrini, he traversed, almost entirely on horseback, in all weathers, and often under great difficulties of road, the length and breadth of the province of Galicia. Sometimes they met with strange adventures. It happened one day that on arriving tired and hungry at a poor village on the frontier, the travellers found nothing to eat, and no one to cook anything they would care to eat. They came at once to a resolution worthy of soldiers. Each agreed to place upon the table, within a certain fixed time, a dish cooked by himself. They dispersed then over the village in search of such " raw material" of food as would require but little preparation. The appointed time had not expired when each brought in his dish and set it upon the table. It need scarcely be added that the meal was enjoyed more than many a costly dinner at Vienna.

It was during the year 1773, that the system, called from its author, Herr von Raab, the Raabische system, was introduced into Bohemia. It invited the landed proprietors of the kingdom to bestow their vast agricultural lands in lease or in fee-simple on their cultivators, instead of enforcing the system of villainage. The reform was greatly favoured by the emperor. To the large landowners it was, however, distasteful, and when in the spring of the following year Herr von Raab endeavoured to convert Loudon to his views, he failed. So great, however, was his popularity amongst his tenants, that when, three years later, the peasantry of Bohemia, incited by this reformer, rose generally and devastated the properties of the large land-owners, they spared those of Loudon. The effect upon him however was such as to disgust him with a residence in Bohemia.

He sold then his two estates in that kingdom, and with the proceeds and with those arising from the sale of two houses in Vienna which had been bestowed upon him by the Empress-queen, he purchased the estate of Hadersdorf about thirty miles from Vienna. The property lies in a pleasant country, surrounded by hills and forests, and intersected by brooks within easy distance of the left bank of the Danube. It possessed a castle or manorial house, some twenty farm houses, and a mill. Here, in 1777, Loudon settled down to farm his own lands. He spent his time amongst his people, building, planting, and improving, till suddenly the sound of war, called him, another Cincinnatus, from his agricultural pursuits.

Before that call reached him, it is worthy to be recorded that he received, 1775, an offer, which he refused, of a bâton of marshal from France, if he would exchange the service of Austria for her service; that, the same year, finding his efforts ineffectual to reduce the system of enormous correspondence about trifles which prevailed in the Austrian army, he resigned his command in Moravia; and that, in 1777, he was requested by the Empress-queen to instruct her son Maximilian in the rudiments of the art of war: for this purpose he had to make periodical visits to Vienna.

Simple as were his habits, rising as he did daily at 5 o'clock, and spending his time in gardening, in feeding his swans and his fish, Loudon was at the same time greatly given to hospitality. His wife, who shared his tastes and sympathised with all his feelings, was ever glad to welcome the officers who had learned in the hard school of war to love and to revere her husband. Amongst the visitors was his early patron and honoured friend, the Chancellor Kaunitz. The emperor, too, frequently paid him flying visits; and amongst those who most enjoyed his society were the emperor's brother, the Archduke Leopold, at a later period emperor himself, a man of taste and culture; the Archduke Ferdinand; and the Prince and Princess of Sachsen-Teschen.

The tastes and the nature of Loudon himself may be read in the lines of which the following are an exact translation, written with his own hand on a bower or hermitage he had built for himself in the centre of a thick fir forest on his property:

"Oh simple nature! Who thy friendship has
Covets no treasure, with a hut is pleased,
Loves a cool stream, and revels in the wood
Made by the nightingale its chief resort."

CHAPTER XIV

On the 30th of December, 1777, died the Elector of Bavaria, Maximilian Joseph, the last of the old Bavarian or Wilhelmish branch of the house of Wittelsbach. Whilst it was admitted that the representative of the younger or Rudolph branch of that house, Karl Theodore, Elector Palatine, had claims to the greater part of the inheritance of the old Bavarian branch, it could not be denied that the legal right of Austria to certain portions, especially to those known as Lower Bavaria, were superior. Amongst those who admitted that legal right was Karl Theodore himself. He signed therefore a convention with the emperor by which he bound himself to give effect to those claims.

But the great increase of strength and influence which this arrangement would give to Austria was not at all to the taste of Frederic II. This ambitious sovereign endeavoured then to hinder, first by diplomatic means, and when those failed, by actual war, an arrangement which would have given Austria complete command of the Danube, and have closely concentrated her German dominions. He, therefore, assembled two armies, of one of which he assumed command, the other he intrusted to Prince Henry, and, to finish the war at one stroke, resolved to march by way of Bohemia and Moravia, to Vienna.

But he found Austria ready to meet him. The emperor had a force of 200,000 men under arms guarding the frontiers of Bohemia. When the news reached him (4th of July) that the Prussians were actually in march and were approaching by way of Glatz, he took up a position covered on the one side by the Elbe from Hohenelbe to Königgrätz, on the other by the Iser from Semil to Jungbunzlau. This position was strongly fortified and defended by an army of 150,000 men. Here the emperor, supported by Lacy and Haddik, commanded in person. Loudon, meanwhile, just created a field-marshal, was commissioned, at the head of 50,000 men, to deal with Prince Henry, and to prevent his junction with the king. Premising that Frederic found the Austrian position too strong to be attacked with any chance of success, unless he should be joined by his brother, I propose to leave the main armies of the invaders and the invaded in the fixed position they occupied almost from the very outset, and to follow the movements of Loudon and Prince Henry.

Aware that Prussia was then acting in alliance with Saxony, and that Prince Henry was recruiting his army in Dresden, Loudon, whose orders were to act strictly on the defensive, took a position (4th of July, 1778) in the first place at Niemes, a small town between Tetschen and Jungbunzlau. Discovering a few days later that the Prussians were about to march on Aussig, about midway between Tetschen and Leitmeritz, where he had posted his cavalry, Loudon, having still a strong detachment at Niemes supported by another at Gabel, moved his head-quarters on the 9th to Pleisswedel—a position whence he could support, in case of need, any one of those three divisions. At the same time he detached six regiments of cavalry and the reserve artillery to Gasdorf, a village on the Elbe between Leitmeritz and Melnik. To Wettel, in the vicinity of this village—Gasdorf—he moved with his whole force on the 10th, and uncertain yet whether Prince Henry would advance by Aussig or by Teplitz, extended it during the following three days to its right, so as to occupy the passes of Gabel.

It was not till the end of July, however, that Prince Henry was able to take the offensive. He had under his orders, inclusive of 22,000 Saxons, an army exceeding 70,000 men. His first object was to join the king, so as to give Frederic the strength necessary to attack the Emperor Joseph's position ; failing in that, to march on Prague, and to make of that city a base for further operations. To attain the first object it behoved him to march on Turnau, on the Iser, which covered the Austrian position at Semil, and the occupation of which would cut off its communication with Hohenelbe. When he should thus have turned, so to speak, the left of the Austrian position, the prince could move round to the Elbe, take Arnau, and threatening the Austrian rear, whilst overlapping its front, could force it to abandon its strong position. In this view he would have to march through the Lausitz and the district of Bunzlau. Prince Henry adopted this plan, but to deceive Loudon he made as though he would march by way of Rumburg and Zittau, gave orders for the formation of a camp for 100,000 men at Bautzen, and directed movements of troops in the Erzgebirge.

But Loudon was not deceived. He remained in his advantageous position a calm spectator of the prince's doings, waiting till his movements should be unmistakably pronounced.

He had not long to wait. On the two last days of July the Prussian troops crossed the border, driving before them, often after a hard fight, the Austrian outposts. Carefully marking the direction the prince was taking, Loudon, divining his intentions, moved back his army to Hirschberg. Too weak to offer battle to the prince—for he had only 50,000 to oppose to his 70,000—compelled to direct particular attention to his right flank, and aware that a further retrograde movement would enable his adversary to carry out the march on Turnau unchecked, he determined to march northwards along the Iser, and drawing all the detached corps to himself, to occupy the key of the position, a position which, whilst it would bar the enemy from crossing, and would cover the emperor's position, was yet near enough to that position to receive from it assistance in case he should be attacked. It was a masterly plan, and the ability with which it was carried out equalled the skill of the designer.[1]

As the army of Prince Henry approached, the Austrian divisional commanders, Giulay and De Vins, who had been posted between Gabel and Zwickau, fell back, under the orders of Loudon, on the main army. Two days later Prince Henry took up a position between Zwickau and Krumbach. The same day the Austrian corps of Giulay and De Ligne crossed the Iser and encamped at Backofen, whilst Prince Liechtenstein, who till then had held Leitmeritz, moved on Gasdorf (on the Elbe). The day following Loudon established his head-quarters at Kosmanos, on the left bank of the Iser between Backofen and Jungbunzlau. He was joined there on the 5th by Liechtenstein with the bulk of his corps. This officer had left the remainder, con-

---

[1] If the reader will procure plate No. 22 of Stieler's Hand Atlas, he will be able to follow accurately the movements I am about to describe.

sisting of three battalions and eight squadrons, under General Sauer on the Elbe between Leitmeritz and Melnitz, with orders to observe the enemy, and should they show a disposition to cross that river, to fall back on Prague. The same day, likewise, Loudon pushed on De Ligne's corps to Münchengrätz. This position constituted then the right of his army, the centre being at Backofen, and his left at Kosmanos—all on the left bank of the Iser. On the 6th, Loudon concentrated his centre and right at Münchengrätz, leaving his left under Field-Marshal Lieutenant Riese at Kosmanos, with instructions to guard the river between Jungbunzlau and Backofen. At the same time he despatched Major-General Browne, with five battalions of grenadiers and a division of hussars, to Bredl, still further to his right, with instructions to watch thence the movements of the Prussians as they advanced by way of Wartenberg towards Böhmisch Aicha.

Meanwhile the emperor in his intrenched camp had noticed the disposition shown by Prince Henry's army to unite itself with that of the king. To strengthen Loudon's hands and to aid him to baffle Prince Henry, the emperor had on the 4th sent a strong detachment to Turnau and had posted another between that place and Münchengrätz. The concentration by Loudon of his centre and right at the latter place on the 6th completed the junction between his army and the emperor's, and made it impossible for Prince Henry to carry out the turning movement he had contemplated without a battle. Nor was it in Frederic's power to help him. Whilst Loudon had been manœuvring in the masterly manner I have described, the king had vainly used all the artifices of which he was so great a master to entice the emperor from his position. Deeming himself not strong enough to attack that position, he was forced then to await the junction which Loudon's skilful movement rendered impossible.

It had been Prince Henry's intention, in communication with the king, to cross the Iser at Kosmanos, München-grätz, and Turnau. But when he reached Niemes, and had examined thence the Austrian position, he recognised that, notwithstanding his great superiority in the three arms—eighty-one battalions and 115 squadrons against fifty-three battalions and eighty-five squadrons—it was not to be attacked with any chance of success. He then likewise had nothing for it but to wait impatiently in his camp until either Loudon should give him an opening, or the king should entice the emperor from his position ; or, last chance of all, until a demonstration which he had directed under General Möllendorf against Prague should produce some result.

He waited in vain. Loudon was not to be drawn. Rather, with that daring watchfulness which characterised him, he successfully counterworked every demonstration made by the prince. Tired at last of playing at soldiers, Frederic, on the 24th, concentrated his army at Hohenelbe and Langenau, and made as though he would attack the left of the emperor's position, whilst Prince Henry the same day pushed forward a portion of his army to Reich-enau. It was evident that a great attempt was being made to effect the desired junction. But though the distance between Reichenau and Hohenelbe was not great, two important rivers guarded by two separate armies traversed it, and it required only care on the part of the Austrian leaders to render it impossible. That care was not wanting.

On the 27th the Prussians made a great effort to force the road to Prague. On the morning of that day the Prussian general, Platen, marched with an overwhelming force of cavalry on Budin, attacked the Austrian advanced posts at Welwarn, and drove them back to Miskowitz. At the last-named place, however, the Austrians came on their supports, and these in their turn drove back the Prussians to Budin. Whilst this fight was going on, the Prussian generals, Möllendorf and Sobeck, marched to Protzen and Tschebus, threatening thence not only the left flank of the Austrian army on the Iser, but the Austrian magazines at Nimburg. To baffle this movement Loudon detached Prince Liechtenstein with seven battalions and twelve squadrons from Kosmanos to Benatek. This advantageous position allowed him alike a shorter communication with Nimburg and complete communication with Brandeis (on the left bank of the Elbe), the occupation of which by the enemy would have been disastrous, if not fatal, for it was by Brandeis that communications were maintained with Prague and with the corps of General Sauer. This masterly arrangement completely checked the enemy's movement.

A few days later an enemy, more powerful even than the Austrians, appeared amongst the Prussians. Forage and food supplies of all sorts began to fail them. The horses of the cavalry and artillery died by hundreds. The men crowded into the hospitals—to the number at one time of 12,000; desertions became plentiful; whilst, to add to the perplexities of the king, the autumnal rains set in with a violence and a continuance which threatened to destroy the mountain roads. Under these circumstances Frederic resolved to retire from a position which might any day become dangerous. Resolved, however, that the way to follow him should be barred to the Austrians, he issued orders that the entire country between his camp and the Silesian frontier, and as far on either side as his foragers could extend themselves, should be shorn quite clean, should be made—to use his own words—"into a kind of wilderness."

Prince Henry was likewise reduced to straits scarcely less trying than those from which Frederic suffered. He had already realised that he could do nothing against the skill and daring of Loudon ; that he could neither join his brother nor even maintain his winter quarters in Bohemia. His communications were threatened by the heavy snow which almost intermingled with the autumnal rains. He called in, then, his detachments, and after mercilessly ravaging the country, sent his sick, amounting to 6,000 men, his heavy baggage, his ovens, and his heavy artillery, to the rear ; then, repairing the existing bridge, and throwing another over the Elbe at Leitmeritz, he fell back the 4th of September in the direction of that place. But Loudon had kept his eye fixed steadily on all his movements. On the 5th he despatched a border battalion to drive the Prussian patrols from Hühnerwasser—midway between Niemes and Münchengrätz—and from the monastery of Pösigberg in its close vicinity. The attack on Hühnerwasser succeeded, that on Pönigsberg failed ; but the Prussians evacuated that place on the 9th, and their whole force marched that day from Niemes towards Leitmeritz. They crossed the Elbe at that place on the 13th and 14th.

The information that his enemy had effected this passage was received by Loudon with joy. Exclaiming, "At last I have the prince on the very battlefield on which, since the beginning of the campaign, I have been wishing to meet him," he sent orders to his several corps to concen trate at a named point, then selected from amongst his officers one whom he could entirely trust—Major de Traux, of the corps of engineers—he directed him to proceed with all haste to the emperor to request an immediate audience; to put, then, plainly before the emperor the actual state of affairs, and to engage on his behalf to gain a decisive victory over the prince if the king would only send him a reinforcement of twelve battalions. De Traux set off, reached the emperor's camp the same day, was admitted to an audience, and delivered his message. Unfortunately, Joseph II. knew nothing of war. Still under the impression that he was in danger of being attacked by Frederic, he exclaimed to De Traux in reply, "This request is a very curious one, especially as I was just about to send a courier to him to tell him to send me all the troops he could spare." "Your Majesty," replied De Traux, with the frankness of an honest soldier, "would commit a great strategic mistake if you were to weaken your other army to strengthen yourself at a point where no danger is to be apprehended. The King of Prussia is no longer animated by the spirit of enterprise which distinguished him during the Seven Years' War. Age has tempered his boldness, and never would he dare, in the face of your army, to clamber up the steep banks of the Elbe, to attack you in your advantageous position, and, in the evening of his days, to risk the laurels gained in eleven campaigns." Field-Marshal Lacy, who was present at the interview, supported the request of De Traux, and declared it would be unpardonable to allow so favourable a chance to escape. The emperor upon this gave way, and ordered the despatch of the twelve battalions asked for.

As soon as he learned that his request had been granted Loudon broke up from Benatek and Münchengrätz, crossed the Elbe at Brandeis, and the Moldau at Weltrus, and marched to Budin. He found the enemy's army disposed in the following manner: Möllendorf with the advance occupied the heights of Libochowitz, on the left bank of, and covered by, the Eger, whilst the bulk of the army lay encamped in the vicinity of Ziskowitz. Of the corps composing the Austrian army, those of Nugent and De Vins were posted at Leitmeritz and Tetschen, threatening the left flank of the enemy, those of Sauer and Otto at Laun and Saatz (right bank), and Kraaden (left bank of the Eger) threatening the enemy's right and line of retreat. Loudon thus occupied a position from which, on the first movement of the enemy—and that movement would in a few days be inevitable—he could attack him with advantage. The eyes of all were turned to watch with anxiety the manœuvres of the only two generals who, according to the admission of Frederic himself, had not made a mistake during the Seven Years' War.[1] But just as the hour for dealing a decisive blow was about to strike, Loudon was surprised by the arrival in his camp (23rd of September) of the Emperor Joseph. It seemed that the Empress Maria Theresa, whose passions, like those of Frederic, had become tempered by age, and who saw before her only the daring leader who, having robbed her of Silesia, had held that province in the face of all the armed force of the Continent, dreaded more than anything else a victory over the Prussians. Judging from the events of the Seven Years' War, she believed that a victory over his armies would inflame Frederic to such a degree as would render him more formidable than he had ever been. She had, therefore, ordered her son to forbid a battle, even though victory were certain. It was to soften the disappointment which he knew this order would inflict on his ablest general

---

[1] Talking one day to his generals over the events of the Seven Years' War, Frederic is reported to have said : " We all made serious mistakes except only my brother Henry and Loudon."

that Joseph now visited his camp. How bitter was the disappointment cannot be told in words. Chained by his orders not to fight a battle, Loudon was forced to witness the disastrous retreat of a demoralised army over bad roads and in inclement weather!

How demoralised the army of the king had become, how it suffered from the various causes I have mentioned, is proved by the fact that between the 1st and 30th of September Frederic's army alone lost 18,000 men, and 6,000 to 7,000 horses. The remainder of the latter were so reduced by want of food that the soldiers had to lead them. The roads were covered with the carcasses of draught horses, and the soldiers, starving and in rags, deserted whenever they could. Such was the end of the last campaign of the great conqueror of Silesia!

Prince Henry's plight was scarcely better. Yet, even in his critical position he displayed all the qualities of a great commander. His natural line of retreat lay by way of Gabel and Zittau. Fearing, however, lest a too prompt retrograde movement would endanger the safety of his heavy guns and baggage, and would tempt the enemy to penetrate into Saxony, which, by such a movement, would be left entirely exposed, the Prussian general resolved to penetrate into Bohemia, and to make a show of an intention to winter in that country. He accordingly crossed the Elbe at Leitmeritz, and made as though his design was to march on Prague. He continued this movement, followed on a parallel though distant line by Loudon—till he learned that his heavy *matériel* was safe; he then turned northwards, and, harassed all the way by the several corps of Loudon's army, began a retreat, which, for its disastrous character, could compare only with that of Frederic. By the end of September both hostile armies had evacuated Bohemia.

During the winter constant skirmishes took place—one
at Habelschwert, in the Glatz country, very much to the
advantage of the Austrians. Meanwhile Maria Theresa,
still haunted by the idea that she had still before her the
Frederic of her youth instead of a Frederic whose campaign
had been illustrated by a remarkable absence of daring,
was pressing on secret proposals for peace. Her efforts so
far succeeded, that on the 13th of May (1779) the conditions
of peace were signed at Tetschen. It was a peace,
however, in which Austria, so far successful in war,
renounced the greater part of the claims for which the war
had been undertaken. She was awarded only the Inn
circle, that is the country between the Danube, the Inn,
and the Salza, a territory of nearly 200 square miles, and
possessing then some 60,000 inhabitants. On the other
hand, Frederic had to pay the cost of his interference,
amounting to about 29,000,000 of thalers, or £4,350,000.
The war, moreover, did not increase his reputation as a
commander. Without fighting a serious action he had lost
more than 20,000 men !

CHAPTER XV

THE year following the peace of Tetschen, the 29th of November, 1780, died the Empress Maria Theresa in the sixty-fourth year of her age. This is not the place to write her epitaph. But it may be fairly asserted that the sovereign who, in her tender years, succeeded to an inheritance begirt by foes all intent on despoiling her, and who left that inheritance increased, rounded off, inhabited by a contented people, and who earned the respect alike of friends and foes, was no ordinary woman. A modern historian has said of her that "of all the crowned autocrats of the world, Maria Theresa is a pattern of domestic and princely virtues to which few have attained, and in which she has been surpassed by none." She was generous, high-minded, and resolute. In her bearing she was majestic, in her acts even heroic. In her early days she credited other crowned heads with the possession of the same virtues which adorned herself. When, before the first invasion of Silesia, some one warned her of the intentions of Frederic, she wrote to the king to denounce the man as a calumniator. Of a quick temperament, she ever spoke her ideas with vivacity and force. Yet she was the tenderest of wives, the most devoted of mothers ; by her virtues, an ornament alike of her sex and of her age. Rightly is her memory still cherished as that of the second founder of the greatness of Austria.

On his accession as sole ruler, Joseph II. devoted himself with all the earnestness of his simple, yet earnest and impassioned character, to his plans of universal reform. Of those plans this is not the place to write ; I will touch only very briefly upon that portion of his foreign policy which led to the war with Turkey and the re-employment of Loudon.

Joseph had never forgotten or forgiven the conduct of Frederic II. during the war of the Bavarian succession. He had resented and protested against the peace of Tetschen. Taking a calm survey of continental Europe he beheld only two great powers who would be inclined to aid him in preventing the further aggrandisement of his natural enemy. One of these, France, exhausted by her efforts in the war of American independence, seemed sliding down very rapidly into the trough of national bankruptcy. But the other, Russia, ruled by a woman of great natural ability, the Czarina Catherine II., was animated by a jealousy of Prussia and a dislike of Frederic, such as almost equalled his own. It became then the policy of Joseph to ally himself intimately with Russia. He had visited that country immediately after the conclusion of the peace of Tetschen, and had formed intimate relations with the Czarina. In 1784 these relations brought about a treaty by which each party guaranteed to the other the possession of his and her dominions, and concluded an alliance offensive and defensive. Whilst, in virtue of this alliance, Russia annexed the Crimea, Joseph, still intent upon remedying the conclusions of the peace of Tetschen, proposed in 1784 to Karl Theodore,

Elector of Bavaria, the exchange of the Netherlands for Bavaria. The life of Frederic II. was drawing to a close, and there seemed every probability that the exchange, if agreed to by Karl Theodore, might be successfully upheld by force of arms. Karl Theodore, who was childless, in January 1785 gave his assent to the proposal, but his nearest relative and heir, the Duke of Zweibrücken, protested eagerly against it, and implored the support of Prussia and the other independent German states to resist it. The result was the formation, mainly through the action of Frederic II., of a league called the " Fürstenbund " (3rd of July, 1785), to which Prussia, Saxony, and Hanover, in the first instance, and subsequently some smaller states, adhered, the avowed object of which was the preservation of the *status quo* in Germany. For the moment Joseph renounced his idea, and other causes prevented him from reviving it.

It was, however, partly with the idea of reviving it that he made a second journey to Russia in 1787. He met the Czarina at Kherson the 14th of May of that year, and made a triumphal journey with her to the Crimea. During this journey the Czarina succeeded in persuading Joseph to join with her in a campaign against the Turks. He returned to Vienna full of this project.

As soon as it was known in Austria that war against the Turks was to be carried out on a large scale, Loudon made a personal application to the Emperor for a command. Joseph's reply, considered by the light of subsequent events, deserves a record. "My dear Loudon," he said, tapping him familiarly on the shoulder, " you have already won your spurs ; you are now getting infirm ; enjoy the remainder of your days in peace."

But the incapacity of Joseph himself as a commander, and of those whom he employed, did not permit Loudon to enjoy the remainder of his days in peace. Taking with him Marshal Lacy as his mentor, the emperor entered the valley of the Save, whilst he despatched one corps under Prince Karl Liechtenstein into Croatia, and another under General Wartensleben into the Banat. At the same time a third corps under General Fabris was posted in Transylvania to maintain communications with a fourth corps, which, commanded by the Prince of Coburg, was to act with the Russians under Suwarrow in Moldavia.

But affairs did not march well. The emperor did indeed take the fortress of Schabacz on the Servian bank of the Save, but that was all. In the Banat, in Croatia and in Transylvania, the Austrian corps were defeated. Liechtenstein was beaten before Dubicza, and before the end of July the invaders were forced to retreat before the victorious Muslims. The only success of the campaign was achieved by the united forces of Suwarrow and Coburg, who overran nearly the whole of. Moldavia.

Disgusted at his failure and convinced at last that war was not his trade, the emperor sent in despair for Loudon, and made over to him the command of the troops in Croatia and Slavonia. Immediately the spirits of the army rose. Their confidence in their old general displayed itself by rejoicings in every camp. Once again a certainty of victory took the place of mistrust. A universal conviction spread that before many weeks the honour of the Austrian arms would be affirmed.

This changed feeling was founded on reason. On the 18th of August Loudon joined the army before Dubicza. He found that whilst he was journeying from Hadersdorf his old lieutenants De Vins and Brentano, anxious to retrieve their position before the arrival of the commander-in-chief, had avenged the defeat of Liechtenstein by storming the

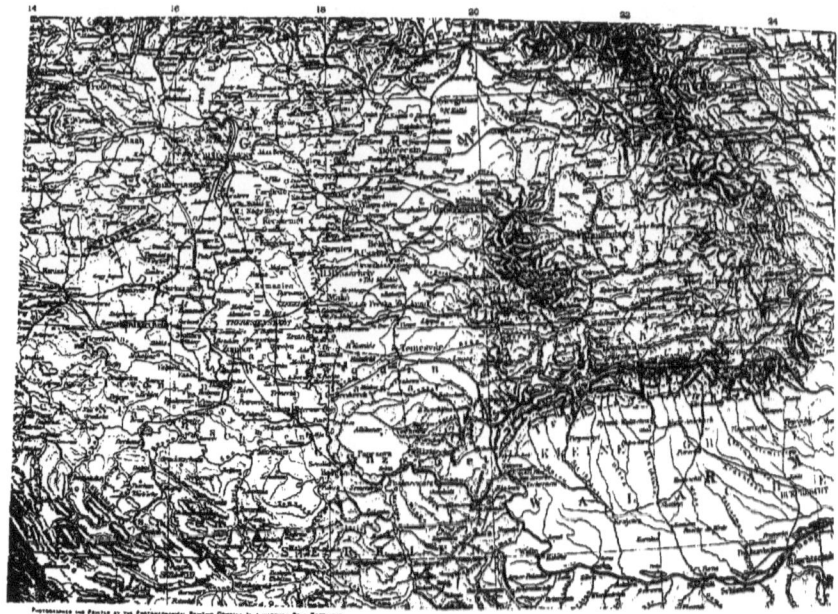

Map to illustrate Loudon's Campaign in the Borderlands of Austria.

Turkish camp before Dubicza and forcing the enemy to take refuge on a hill called Atschinoberg. There, in the few days that intervened before Loudon's arrival, the Turks had received reinforcements, led by the Pasha of Travnik, and had determined to attack the Austrians in their camp. At 3 o'clock on the morning of the 20th, the second day after Loudon had assumed command, they assailed with extraordinary fury the two wings of the Austrian army. But everywhere a prepared and steady resistance met them. Under the eye of their old general, who seemed to be ubiquitous, for he appeared always at the right place and at the critical moment, the Austrians fought with their former confidence, and repulsed the enemy at all points. The extraordinary part of the affair is that whilst the Turks lost about 700 men, not a single Austrian was killed; two men only were wounded. The Turks fled to the hill to watch thence the progress of the siege of Dubicza.

Space forbids me to enter into minute details regarding the attack made upon this and other places during the campaign. It will suffice to state that Loudon compelled first the retreat of the Turks from Atschinoberg, and immediately afterwards, on the 26th of August, the surrender of Dubicza, after a gallant defence by its garrison.

Loudon then turned his attention to the fortress of Novi. But it was necessary in the first instance to drive the enemy, commanded by the same Pasha of Travnik who had vainly assailed him on the 20th, from their intrenched camp at Jellovacz, a place at which the roads between Dubicza, Kostainicza, and the Unnathal united.

He commissioned, therefore, General Mitrowsky to cross the Save at Gradiska and storm the position. But the very movement was sufficient. The Turks burned their camp and retreated on a line which led them away from the road by which Loudon was advancing on Novi.

Before that place—which was a regularly fortified oblong quadrangle, the walls and bastions of which were built of hewn stone—Loudon opened trenches on the night of the 10th of September. Continuing according to the rules of art, the besiegers attacked and stormed the outer ditch on the night of the 17th, and proceeded to mine the counterscarp.

It was at this crisis that Loudon received intelligence that a strong corps was advancing to relieve the place. Still continuing the siege, he rode to the threatened point —the left wing of the covering army near Michinowatz— received the enemy's attack, and inflicted upon him a crushing defeat (20th September). Returning then to the fortress, he delivered his assault the following morning. This, in spite of all his efforts, was repulsed with loss— eighty killed and 210 wounded—and the siege once more reverted to its regular form.

Towards the end of September the autumnal rains set in : the rivers, Unna and Sanna, overflowed and threatened to sweep away the bridge of communication ; water filled the trenches, and it became impossible to work. On the 30th, however, the sky brightened, firing was resumed, the breaches were widened, and on the 3rd of October Loudon delivered a second assault.

This time he was successful. In spite of an obstinate defence, the Austrians carried the place. The loss, however, was again considerable, amounting to 220 killed and 353 wounded. That of the Turks throughout the siege did not exceed 400 killed, besides wounded.

Loudon had now gained the line of the lower Unna. It remained only to complete the campaign by the conquest of Berbir; but as the season rendered further campaigning difficult, if not impossible, he placed his army in winter quarters, joined the emperor at Semlin on the 8th of November to be present at a chapter of the order of Maria Theresa, of which he was a Grand Cross, returned then to Old Gradiska, made a minute inspection of the troops in their cantonments, then, transferring the command to De Vins, proceeded, the 9th of December, to Vienna.

The winter was spent in preparing for the coming campaign. The emperor, whose war this was, devoted himself to fill the magazines, to complete the ranks, to ensure plentiful supplies. He still cherished the idea of taking himself the command-in-chief. A severe illness, however, prevented the possibility of his carrying it out. He conferred the command of the army in the Banat, then, upon Marshal Haddik, that of Croatia-Slavonia upon Loudon; Coburg was still to act with the Russians in Moldavia.

Loudon reached his head-quarters at Old Gradiska on the 8th of May. Ten days later he visited all the outposts, and inspected first his army, which amounted to 34,500 foot, and 3,000 horse, and afterwards the enemy's line of defence. As commandant-in-chief of the artillery he had his old and trusted friend Rouvroy. Colonel Neu was chief of the general staff, and Colonel Arnal chief engineer.

His object was to besiege and capture Berbir, known also as Turkish Gradiska. For this purpose he selected a corps of 15,900 infantry and artillery, and 300 horse, and a considerable siege train. By the 23rd of June all the preparations for the passage of the Save had been completed. As that passage, from the position of Berbir relative to that occupied by Loudon's army would require the greatest prudence and circumspection, I propose, before referring to the manner of its execution, to give a succinct description of the threatened fortress.

Berbir, or Turkish Gradiska, stands on the south bank of the Save, exactly opposite to New, or Slavonian Gradiska. In fact the Save, which is here about 200 yards wide, marks the separation between the two places. Berbir is an irregular pentagon, surrounded by a wall of circumvallation twenty-four feet high. On its northern side, this wall, which is here covered by a ditch seventy-two feet broad, and twelve feet deep, is washed by the Save. The covered way, ten feet wide, palisaded, and provided with traverses and gabions, is further protected by a moat. Two gates, the one in the upper, the other in the lower face, open on the roads to Banyaluka and Dubicza. Nearest to the casemated face looking on Gradiska, was a cavalier forty-six feet high, whose guns were pointed on the Austrian position. On the side furthest from the river, and at a distance of about 1,500 paces from it, a very broad and thick wood, admirably adapted to cover troops, formed a semicircle.

It was to cross the river Save, defended by this fortress, and then to capture the fortress, that Loudon had assembled his troops at Old Gradiska. All preparations having been completed, Loudon, on the night of the 23rd, threw the bridge, for which he had collected materials, across the river a thousand yards above Gradiska. The first to cross it himself, he then on the spot traced out a bridgehead. A thick fog, which made darkness visible all around, and which cleared off only at 7 o'clock, enabled his workmen to complete and to arm this before the enemy had discovered them. An hour later the guns of Old Gradiska opened fire on the works. The fire continued all day.

The same night Loudon sent across the bridge 4,000 workmen, each provided with a palisade and implements, under the protection of four battalions of infantry and twelve guns. The lines which it was intended to occupy had been marked previously by the engineers, so that the labourers set to work at once, and continued throughout the night. The works on which they were engaged consisted of three redoubts, covered on the left by the Save, on the right by a rivulet named Verbaska, which empties itself into the Save about 400 yards south of Berbir. Besides these redoubts, they threw up earthworks along the meanderings of the rivulet, from the covered way of the east face of the redoubts to the Save.

Up to this time the Turks had seemed to view with indifference, if not with complacency, the action of the Austrian commander. But on the morning of the 24th they woke up and opened a heavy fire on the workmen. But these had progressed too far to be seriously disturbed, and they continued their labours throughout that day and the following night. On the 25th Loudon observed considerable movements of troops on the enemy's side, as though reinforcements were approaching from the direction of Banyaluka. Firmly convinced of the necessity of inclosing the fortress from that side also, he threw now a bridge across the Save at Unter-Varos above Berbir and led himself across it two battalions, ten companies and fourteen guns. Here likewise he threw up a bridge-head and three redoubts. These works were completed by the 27th. Approaching the following day by means of a parallel some 400 yards from the fortress and well covered from its fire by natural obstructions, he opened a heavy fire against the Banyaluka gate and the outer defences of the water bastion. By the evening he had practically demolished the gate, had broken down on both sides the walls with which it was connected, and had silenced the lower water bastion.

Whilst matters were so progressing on the eastern face, the Austrians were not less active on the western. Here they advanced along the Verbaska to within 200 yards of the covered way of the fortress, and establishing (3rd of June) two batteries, maintained thence a continuous fire. All this time a heavy fire had been kept up from Old Gradiska.

The fire from all points continued unabated till the 8th. At 8 o'clock on the morning of that day, and from that hour till 4 o'clock in the evening, Loudon noticed that a continuous communication was being exchanged between a body of Turks, some 5,000 strong who had collected in the thick wood behind the fortress and the garrison. The result of these communications appeared at 5 o'clock, when the garrison by twos and threes, with what baggage they could carry, and with all speed, made their way from the fortress towards the wood. Half an hour later and a dead silence reigned in the fortress. To ascertain exactly what had happened, two officers and four men who volunteered for the service made their way into the fortress. They found it entirely abandoned.[1] Loudon at once sent his cavalry in pursuit of the fugitives, and took possession of Berbir. Its capture had cost the army, during seventeen days of open trenches, thirty-eight killed, and 120 wounded. On the 12th Loudon himself conducted a reconnaissance as far as Banyaluka, but could find no traces of the enemy.

Whilst Loudon had been engaged in this operation, Austrian affairs had progressed favourably in Moldavia.

---

[1] It is said that they found an old Wallachian seated near the powder magazine. The Turks had commissioned him to blow up the magazine after their retreat; but he had been in no hurry to obey the order.

Suwarrow and Coburg had marched to the borders of Wallachia, there, at the end of the month, to achieve, at Foczan, a great victory over the Turks. But in the Banat the severe illness of Marshal Haddik had greatly impeded operations. After the capture of Berbir then, Haddik was relieved of his command, and Loudon was intrusted with it (28th of July). The great object of that army was to capture Belgrade. Loudon at once bent all his energies to accomplish this task.

On receiving this command Loudon proceeded (14th of August) to Semlin, visited his friend and predecessor, Haddik, at Fatak on the 16th, and reached the head-quarters of the army, which Clairfait, subsequently famous in the wars of the French Revolution, commanded. Immediately on his arrival he mounted his horse, visited all the outposts, and made a careful examination of the country immediately in front of him. The following day he held a long consultation with Clairfait at Mehadia, on the extreme left of the position, and settled with him the plan of operations. He then returned to Weisskirchen.

On the 28th of August, the Turks, aware now that Belgrade was in danger, made a demonstration against Mehadia. But Clairfait drove them with loss across the Wallachian border. On the 30th, Loudon set in motion the various corps and divisions of his army towards Banovze on the Danube, with the intention of concentrating between that place and Semlin. He hoped to be able to cross the Save on the 13th of September.

On the 9th, the advanced guard of the Austrian army reached Banovze, and on the night of the 10th, crossed the Save by a bridge of boats at Poliefze, and took possession of the heights of Ostrenitza. This guard was followed by the whole army. On the 15th, the army destined for the

siege stood on Servian ground. It consisted of ten battalions
of grenadiers, thirty-three of fusiliers, one of sharpshooters,
and thirty and a half divisions of cavalry. The siege train
was formed of a hundred and twenty 24-pounders, eight
18-pounders, fifty 12-pounders, and thirty 6-pounders.
Feldzeugmeister Count Kinsky, commanded the siege
under Loudon. South of Semlin Clairfait watched the
movements of the enemy outside Belgrade; whilst the
remainder of the army, which was much affected by the
unhealthy season—out of a grand total of 120,900 men it
had more than 33,000 on the sick list—occupied Semlin
under the Prince de Ligne.

From the 11th to the 15th, whilst his army was crossing
the Save, Loudon and his generals had carefully examined
the fortress. It may be interesting to note that amongst
those generals, were many who served subsequently in the
wars of the French Revolution, and who constitute, as it
were, a link between Frederic and Napoleon. Of these,
besides Clairfait already mentioned, were Alvinzy, the
beaten of 1797, Melas, the vanquished of Marengo, Hiller,
and Mack, the yielder of Ulm. The last named was
already beginning to earn the reputation which insured
him, afterwards, at a critical period of the nation's
destinies, the command of its main army.

Space compels me to limit the narrative of this important
siege to the barest outline. It must suffice to state that, in
1789 as at the time of Prince Eugene, Belgrade was formed
of the castle, the town, and the suburbs. The first, built
on a hill which had a steep declivity towards the town, and
a gentle descent towards the suburbs, was in the centre.
The town was built on the point where the Save joins the
Danube and was watered by both. The suburbs stretched
out in a sort of bow-form from the west bank of the Danube

to the east bank of the Save. Their three most important
points were the Raitzen suburb. to the south, the water-
suburb to the north, and the Palanka, which lying to the
south of the castle hill, turns and forms a horn-work in its
south-eastern angle. The garrison consisted of 9,000 men,
commanded by Osman Pasha, a brave and resolute soldier.

The fortress itself had been greatly strengthened since
the time of Eugene. It was well furnished with provisions,
and carried 456 guns of various calibres. To aid in its
defence, the Turks had brought twenty armed saiks[1] up
the Danube, but these were held in check by a superior
Austrian flotilla.

Loudon resolved to attack the place on the north and
west sides. He made his army occupy the lines formed by
Prince Eugene in 1717, whilst he widened and improved
them. At the same time he erected batteries and redoubts,
threw up intrenchments, and did all that a careful general
could do to inclose the place. As commandant of artillery
he had with him his old and trusted friend, Rouvroy.
Serving under him to win his spurs, was the emperor's
nephew, Francis, afterwards the first Emperor of Austria.

From the 16th to the 30th of September, Belgrade was
continuously assailed with showers of shot and shell. In
the interval various occurrences took place discouraging to
the defenders. A relieving force under Abdy Pasha had
halted at Esupria, alarmed by the attitude of the Austrian
free corps in their vicinity, whilst on the 22nd, Suwarrow
and Coburg inflicted a total defeat on the Grand Vizier,
90,000 strong, at Martinyestic in Wallachia.

On that very day there fell a heavy rain which somewhat

[1] A Saik is a Levantine merchant vessel with one mast, but that
very high.

delayed the siege operations. Matters however, had up to that time progressed so favourably that Loudon determined on the cessation of the rain to storm the suburbs. The downfall continued, however, without interruption, till the evening of the 27th. Loudon, assembling his generals, announced then his intention of storming on the 30th. "We must," he said to them, "succeed or die: I have promised the emperor to capture Belgrade, and I shall use every means in my power, all the energies I possess, to fulfil that promise. I am sure I can depend upon you, and that every man in the camp, feeling that he can in no case live for ever, will count his life well spent to gain the victory."

At 5 o'clock in the morning of the 30th, a heavy fire was opened against the enemy's works from the Austrian vessels in the Danube. An hour later the fire was taken up by the land batteries. It continued incessantly on the fort, on the suburbs, on the empty space between the Raitzen suburb, and the Turkish advanced posts, and on those posts till 9 o'clock. By that time the Turks had been driven into the suburbs. The order to storm was then given. The firing ceased, and suddenly the storming parties in four columns, each headed by a forlorn hope of volunteers, dashed to the front, broke through the palisades protecting the enemy's advanced portion, and charged into the suburbs. There a determined opposition met them. The Turks, fighting each house, defended themselves with extraordinary courage. Slowly, but surely, however. from house to house, from street to street, from garden to garden, they were forced back, till at last the survivors gave way and fled into the fort. They had lost upwards of 800 men, and twelve guns. By 1 o'clock the victory was complete: the

Austrians had taken the suburbs and its gates, had occupied the glacis, and intrenched themselves against the enemy's fire. Their loss was 110 killed, and 327 wounded.

During the night the Austrians worked at a parallel not far from the covered way. Upon this the Turks directed a heavy fire, and, at intervals, made four sorties. They were resolved to defend the fortress to the last, and their gallant commander, a worthy forerunner of his namesake eighty-nine years later, had still hopes to preserve it from the fate which had befallen the suburbs.

But Loudon, as resolute as his rival, employed, and employed well, every moment of time at his command. He laboured night and day at his batteries, and on the night of the 5th of October had the satisfaction of feeling that the end could not be very distant. On the morning of the 6th, then, he opened upon the doomed fortress a fire the like of which, for its concentrated fierceness, had never before been witnessed. Balls, grenades, and bombs were discharged by thousands into the place. Under its effects the walls crumbled, the hostile guns were silenced, conflagrations burst out in the city. At last Osman Pasha could hold out no longer. At 1 o'clock he sent a messenger to Loudon demanding a suspension of arms for fifteen days. "Not for fifteen hours," replied Loudon.

The fire continued then all that day, during the night, and till nine o'clock in the morning of the following day. Then did the pasha, abating from his pretensions, beg for a suspension of arms of only six hours. Regarding this request as the certain forerunner of a capitulation, Loudon granted it. The time passed—the Austrians manned their batteries—yet there was no sign of movement in the fortress. Suddenly, however, the gate of the fortress opened and three venerable Turks appeared, demanding to speak with the Austrian commander. They were Osman Pasha and two of his chief officers. They were conducted at once to the presence of Loudon, who received them courteously and arranged with them the terms of capitulation. These were, the immediate surrender of the fortress, permission to the garrison to retire with their personal and private effects to Orsova, and exchange of prisoners. Loudon further' gave to Osman Pasha a letter testifying that he had defended the place as long as it could be defended.

The capture of Belgrade excited the greatest enthusiasm in Vienna. The emperor, the court, and the populace united in doing honour to the illustrious man who had rivalled the great achievement of Eugene. " Would that he were here to see how much we honour and revere him," was the general cry. The emperor rewarded him by nominating him Generalissimo of all his armies. But Loudon, not content with his victory, was busily engaged in following it up. From Belgrade he proceeded to Semendria, also on the Danube, and forced it to surrender. He then marched with all speed to Orsova, and blockaded it. The blockade lasted all the winter, and terminated by the surrender of the fortress in April.

In other portions of the Turkish territories the Austrian arms had been not less triumphant. Coburg had occupied Bucharest, and had overrun eastern Wallachia ; Hohenlohe had occupied the so-called Little Wallachia—the country immediately south of Transylvania. In Servia, Liptay had advanced to Timok and had threatened Widdin. The free corps under Michaeljewich had reached Nissa.

But the capture of Belgrade and the other successes I have enumerated had roused the jealousy of the court of Berlin. Frederic indeed was dead, but his policy had survived him. The court of Berlin, whilst it had viewed with equanimity the action of Austria against the Porte, so long as Austria was being defeated, changed its tone the moment the genius of London had restored victory to her standards. Prussia then proceeded to suggest at Constantinople an offensive alliance which should force Austria to turn her attention to the defence of her German territories. The negotiations had proceeded so far, and had taken so serious a turn, that the emperor issued orders at the close of the year 1789, for the return of as many troops as could be spared from his eastern frontier. To command these troops the emperor nominated the conqueror of Belgrade.

But whilst they were yet marching, and before Loudon could quit the eastern frontier, Joseph II., who had been long ailing, died (28th of February, 1790). It is probable that his death favoured a peaceful solution of the question, for his brother and successor, Leopold II., whilst confirming the nomination of Loudon, and continuing the collection of an army on the Bohemian frontier, entered at once into negotiations for peace. An armistice was concluded for nine months at Guirgevo on the 19th of September, and a definitive peace was arranged at Svistov on the 4th of August following.

Four months before the armistice was concluded, Loudon had made a triumphal entry into the Austrian capital. He proceeded thence as quietly as possible to Hadersdorf, and after a stay there of a week, proceeded, the 11th of May, to inspect the troops posted in Moravia, Galicia, and

Bohemia. By this time these formed an army of 150,000 men, well provided in every way, and ready to meet with confidence the attack, which the Prussians who had drawn the Poles into their quarrel, were now threatening. Loudon set to work to complete the arrangements necessary for forestalling such an attack by an invasion of the enemy's country. He then returned, 28th of May, to Vienna.

CHAPTER XVI.

DEATH AND CHARACTER.

THE question of peace or war was still uncertain. After a stay, then, of three weeks in Vienna, Loudon again repaired, 18th of June, to Moravia, to inspect the troops. He reached Mährisch-Neustadt on the 21st, and rode thence every day to make a close examination of the cordons along the frontier. In this manner he passed seven hours every day on horseback. The exercise seemed to agree with him, and though he was then seventy-four years old, he still looked healthy and strong.

In his many actions Loudon had received but one wound, and that in his early youth, in Alsace. Though the wound had healed, its consequences had always made themselves felt : inducing severe attacks of hæmorrhoids, of colic, and of other similar ailments. But after annoying him for a day or two these attacks had always passed off.

On the 26th of June, Loudon, visiting the right of the Austrian position, had ridden to Grätz, about three miles south of Troppau. He then dined with Prince Lichnowsky. The food of which he partook at his dinner brought on an attack of indigestion, and he had a feverish night. He determined, nevertheless, the next morning to continue his inspection and to ride to Heidenpilz. He set out accordingly; but he had scarcely crossed the river Mohra, just outside the town, and ascended an elevation which had been intrenched, than his quarter-master-general, Mack, noticed that he kept his seat with difficulty. Mack sent at once for a carriage and had the general conveyed to Neutitschein (south of the Oder). Here he remained, suffering from agueish fever, under the care of his staff surgeon, Göppert, confined to the house, till the 5th of July.

On that day, he felt so much better, that, much against the wish of his doctor, he insisted upon taking a ride. He rode, not slowly, but at a trot, even at a gallop, and returned apparently refreshed. The next day, however, he felt very tired. But this did not prevent him from keeping an invitation he had to dine with Field-Marshal Botta. On this occasion he ate with a good appetite, and was more cheerful than ordinarily.

On the 7th he was better, complaining only of a pain in the loins, but he insisted, nevertheless, upon taking a ride He returned from this wearied and unwell. The following morning he was very ill. After an attempt to dress himself, he returned to bed. His body then began to swell, and he felt that his last hours were approaching. He sent then for a lawyer and dictated to him and signed his will. Other physicians were called in, but their efforts to stem the progress of the disease were unavailing.

On the 9th the swellings and the pains increased. The latter became so intense that they could scarcely be borne. "I know I am dying," he said to Göpperts, "and I am resigned; but assuage, dear doctor, if it be possible, the agony of this pain, for I cannot bear it." The same day he partook of the last sacraments.

Up to this time, in spite of his agony, he had dictated all

the despatches to the emperor, but on the 9th he made over this duty to Field-Marshal Colleredo. On this occasion he said to the field-marshal, "You will be kind enough to announce my death to the army. It is the army which I feel it so hard to quit—these men who have always fought so bravely. It has been my pride to fight by their side, my glory to be their leader. Thank all the generals, all the officers, and all the non-commissioned officers and all the soldiers for the love and devotion they have shown me. I commend to you likewise my wife. See that nothing be done to cause her the slightest vexation." He then bade farewell to the marshal. Observing his nephew, Alexander von Loudon, on his knees before the bed, weeping, the dying hero bade him rise up and exhorted him to live as a man and a Christian: "Love your God," he added, "and never injure your fellow men; reverence your sovereign, and be a true defender of your country. Providence raised me from the dust to a greatness which I never sought. I have always only tried to do my duty. In that let me serve as your example." Prince Philip of Liechtenstein, Botta, Mack, Hiller, Stipschitz, and other officers, speedily to become more or less famous, were in the room. He bade them all an affectionate farewell.

From this time his agony increased more and more. To alleviate it the doctors who had attempted one operation now tried another, but with slight success. Bleeding and other remedies were then tried. In vain, however; fresh accesses of fever ensued. On the evening of the 14th he sank into a slumber. His face was sunken, his pulse was intermittent, his limbs were cold, but his eyes, when at intervals he opened them, were still bright. At 7 o'clock he requested to be raised a little higher in his bed. The request was complied with, but almost immediately he glided down—and died.

In this manner—on a day when in a neighbouring country there was acting a scene which ushered in a revolution not yet extinguished [1]—passed away, in his seventy-fifth year, a man who, for half a century, had been the sword and the shield of the House of Hapsburg; whose genius and calmness in danger had won the admiration and respect of the great soldier-king of the age, whose whole life had been a display of those noble qualities which attract the affection and devotion of subordinates, the friendship and esteem of equals, the confidence of the highest. "It was not only that which he had done," writes Baron von Janko, in his admirable life of the great Austrian commander, " which had made him great: it was because all his thoughts were lofty ; because his character was such that to him the value of the thing done and the thing suffered received its true appreciation by being sifted through a mind from which self-love was always absent; because his character was such that every man, were he born in the purple or in the peasant's hut, was bound to honour it ; because, in a word, in the loftiest sense of the term, he was a man."

Loudon was buried at Hadersdorf, in a secluded spot at the west end of the park, where, the preceding year, he had planted some young trees he had brought with him from Servia, and which he had called the Turkish Garden. The marble mausoleum which surmounted the tomb—the stones for which he had brought from Belgrade—bore, in the first instance, this inscription :—

"NON GRATA PATRIA, NON IMPERATOR, SED CONJUX."

---

[1] The storming of the Bastille.

This, however, as it seemed to imply a reproach which was not intended, was replaced a little afterwards by the following : —

"GIDEONI. ERN. LAUDONO CONJUX, CONTRA VOTUM SUPERSTES, AC HÆREDES POS. 1790."

London adds another proof of the truth of the axiom, of which Hannibal, Cæsar, and Alexander are ancient, Condé, Turenne, Marlborough, Eugène, Frederic, and Napoleon are modern examples, that a great general is born, not made. He had had no scientific education, no special training. His cool and resolute nature, his clear brain, his power to think and act under tumult and difficulties, brought him very quickly to the front rank of his profession. The extraordinary gift of memory which enabled him always to recollect a man whom he had once seen, his power of bearing fatigue, the fact that he never for a moment forgot the end and aim of his calling, his tenacity of purpose, helped him greatly to attain that position. How, when captain and major on the Croatian frontier, he devoted his leisure to the study of maps and plans, has been related in its place. But he did more than study maps and plans. He never travelled without minutely examining the country he traversed. The idea that this or that place might on some future occasion become the seat of war never left him. The features of the various salient points of the Austrian dominions became then fixed in his memory, and enabled him, when the time of action arrived, to rely upon himself.

In other respects he possessed all the qualities of a great commander. To a quick conception, which enabled him to master very rapidly all the points of a position, and which yet never tended to rashness, he added a remarkable power of effective execution. His experience in advanced post fighting, his preference for attack, the pains he bestowed to see that the plan he had laid down beforehand was carried out in its entirety, the profound conviction that he had done nothing so long as anything remained to be done, contributed greatly to his success. With the men his popularity was unbounded. His power of bearing fatigue, his daring horsemanship, the perfection which he had attained as a shot, won their admiration. His voice in command, on the day of danger, produced always an electric effect. The soldiers felt that under "Father Loudon" they would be at least shown the way to victory, and this conviction rendered them almost certain of attaining it.

Opposed to the greatest captain of the period, a captain unfettered, whilst he was chained to the skirts, now of Daun, now of the Russian commander, and always restricted by the necessity of consulting Vienna, Loudon emerged from the contest with honour. Whenever they met, Loudon, except on one occasion, always had the advantage. It was Loudon who forced Frederic to raise the siege of Olmütz, who beat him at Kunersdorf, who, for a month, with an inferior force, barred to him the road into Silesia, who planned Hochkirch, who took Schweidnitz under his very nose. Even in the solitary exception, Liegnitz, in which the brilliant conception and quick movements of Loudon were made resultless by the dilatoriness of Daun and the want of enterprise of Lacy, he gave Frederic—as Frederic declared to his generals— a lesson in the art of drawing off an army. That which in the hands of any other Austrian general of the time would have been a decisive defeat, in his became only a repulse from which the adversary gained but small

advantage. Recollect, too, how all the time he was chained
—forced to arrange his action according to the views of
inferior men. Who can doubt that if his hands had been
as free as were the hands of his adversary, if they had
been as free as were the hands of Soltikoff or of Daun,
Frederic would have been crushed for ever at Kunersdorf;
or failing Kunersdorf, on his march thence into Saxony; or
failing that, at Hochkirch ? The infatuation of the court
of Vienna—an infatuation based on the recollection that
the first Austrian victory over Frederic had been gained by
Daun—retained throughout the war the chief command in
the hands of a man who did not possess the genius of attack.

Probably no one had studied the character of Frederic
more thoroughly than had Loudon. It was by the knowledge thus acquired that he was so often able to divine his
plans and to defeat them. To obtain his ends no labour
was too great, no inconvenience too unbearable, for the
great Austrian commander. His care for the soldier was
unremitting. He always felt that good food, rest, and
good shelter constituted elements towards success. He
never bothered his men about trifles. He insisted on all his
orders being obeyed ; saw that food, straw, and ammunition
were at hand, and inspired them by the feeling that they
were all parts of a great whole, all working with him for
a definite end, and sharing with him alike the dangers, the
privations, the glories of the war ! He was essentially a
just man. Whilst he maintained the strictest discipline, he
was full of acknowledgments for acts of desert. All therefore strove to please him. His modesty and self-abnegation
were remarkable. No great commander ever spoke or
wrote less of his own deeds than Loudon. His reports
are full of acknowledgments to others. He was always

R

anxious to push deserving men to the front. But he never
forgot a blunderer. And yet—and this is another point
in which Frederic possessed an advantage over him—
the court often compelled him to retain blunderers at
his right hand—Draskowich, for instance. Frederic, on
the contrary, never again employed men who had once
failed.

In person, Loudon, resembling in this respect almost
all the great generals of the world, was short, measuring
under five feet six. He was well-built, but was always
very thin, even to leanness. He had a high and well-
formed forehead, a good nose, and a well-shaped mouth
and chin. From under his eyebrows, which were thick
and massive, shone a pair of deep set, light grey eyes,
betokening earnestness, resolution, thought, and strength.
His ways were very gentle, except when he was in
action; then all the passion of his soul seemed to change
his nature.

He could not speak French well, and he had learned
German at mature age. He expressed himself, then,
especially in his earlier periods, with great brevity. His
terseness, indeed, sometimes fell short of courtly requirements. It is related of him that on the occasion of one of
his visits to Vienna, representing to the Empress-Queen
the wants of the army, he said : "Your Majesty must let
me have" this or that. "Well," replied Maria Theresa,
smiling, "If I must, I shall do it."

He died, in a good old age, full of honour. Perhaps, to
posterity, the most convincing testimony to his genius will
be that of his great rival. Often did Frederic display by
his acts, during the later years of the Seven Years' War,
his respect for Loudon. On three memorable occasions he

expressed it : once, at Liegnitz, when Loudon showed him how to retire in the presence of a superior enemy ; a second time at Mährisch-Neustadt, when he begged him in words which expressed his real feeling, to take a seat beside him ; a third time at the same place, when talking over the events of the war, then a thing of the past, with his generals, he exclaimed : "We all of us made mistakes, except my brother Henry and Loudon."